My Lucky Face

My Lucky Face

A NOVEL

May-lee Chai

SOHO

Library of Congress Cataloging-in-Publication Data

Chai, May-Lee.
   My lucky face: a novel / May-Lee Chai.
      p.   cm
   ISBN 1-58947-094-4
   I. Title.
PS3553.H2423M9   1997   97-6167
813'.54—dc21   CIP

Chai, May-lee
My lucky face : a novel

First Edition
10 9 8 7 6 5 4 3 2 1

This book is dedicated to my mother,
Carolyn Chai
(1934–1996)
who taught me never to fear change.

Acknowledgments

I would like to thank all my friends in Nanjing; Winberg Chai; Jane Dystel; Howard Goldblatt for wonderful comments, great classes, and much encouragement; Marilyn Krysl, teacher, mentor, friend; Linda Hogan; Emily Honig; Naomi Horii; Lani Kwon Meilgaard for faith, friendship, and a critical eye; Madeline Spring for introducing me to Huang Shuqin's film *Ren gui qing*; the Institute of East Asian Studies at the University of California at Berkeley; and especially Jeff and Virginia, for everything.

Table of Contents

1.	The Virtues of My Flying Pigeon	1
2.	The Wall	8
3.	Foreign Ways	27
4.	Bedtime Stories	38
5.	Auntie	46
6.	Mother	63
7.	In-Laws	72
8.	Father	76
9.	Go-Betweens	86
10.	The Funeral	98
11.	The Foreign Teacher	104
12.	People I Have Let Down	115
13.	The Fight	122

Contents

14.	Practicalities	135
15.	Woman of Steel	148
16.	Reality Like Cold Soup	155
17.	High Society	164
18.	Nai-nai and Ye-ye	179
19.	Family History	187
20.	Mrs. Mu's Mother-in-Law	191
21.	Helen of Shanghai	203
22.	The Middle Part	215
23.	Happy Family	225
24.	Happy Holidays	235
25.	Dreams	249
26.	The View from the Drum Tower	255

My Lucky Face

1.

The Virtues of My Flying Pigeon

I've often thought if not for my Flying Pigeon, I would surely have gone mad. Sure, it wasn't the most fashionable brand anymore, sturdy with thick steel pipes when light and sleek was in style, black instead of bright pink or red like the lucky money envelopes only children used to covet. These things mattered so much, it seemed—color, style, brands, auspicious names like Forever or Phoenix, even an Eagle or a cheap Swan were better than the Pigeon in some people's eyes. Small people.

But my bike was strong, durable. My stalwart ally, when the silence of my apartment became too much to bear, the walls too close, even for me, so strong usually.

We'd ridden enough miles to have crossed the country by now, if such a thing were possible by bicycle. Perhaps a foreigner will do it one of

these days. There was always one of them in the news accomplishing yet another strange first—first to skateboard on the Great Wall, first to kayak on the Yellow River, first to hang glide off Mount Tai. Why not ride across China on a bicycle? If you had the time.

I had plenty of good times with my Pigeon. I didn't mean to complain. During my engagement, as I rode side by side with Shao Hong at midnight, steering with one hand, holding his hand with the other, my black Pigeon truly flew through the night air. During my pregnancy, the two of us mastered the potholes together, slowly. We fixed a special child's seat on the crossbar, perfect for my son, and before he left for school, I used to take him on long rides through my city, pointing out the sights.

But lately, in the last few years of my marriage, it seemed I depended on my Pigeon more and more often to get me through the rough times, the sad and lonely times, when I took to riding at night, when I should have been at home. I'd roll through the cool streets, part of the stream of night riders. There were lovers, lonely students, workers racing each other home or perhaps to a job, foreigners, sometimes whole families on one bike—the father pumping away, wife on the back package rack, child on a seat rigged before the handlebars, and I felt very alone, calm. I could think.

I loved to watch the lights in the windows of the buildings I passed, imagining the families inside, the flickering flame-like colors of a television reflecting off the glass windowpanes, the yellow glow of a reading lamp, the blue light of a gas stove. It was a pity winter came so quickly. Winter, when it would be much too cold for my rides, the rains would come, sleet, and I would be trapped inside again. But I didn't waste the last of my autumn worrying like that. So long as I could still ride with only my wool sweater and a hat for warmth—and after a number of blocks, I needed to unbutton the sweater—I could escape.

Shops were beginning to stay open later, I noticed as the years passed. The free markets were lighted with strings of colored bulbs, the clothes hanging in the stalls looked as though they were covered in jewels. I saw large parties entering restaurants, weddings on every other block, it seemed. I liked the feeling that I was invisible, gliding silently on the dark streets, as I watched the lights around me.

I couldn't bear to be trapped inside our apartment. And yet if I had tried to explain to anyone a year ago, even six months ago, they would've called me crazy. With Bao-bao gone for the most part, and Shao Hong in his study, I had the dining room to myself. I could listen to the radio, I could read, I could correct my papers uninterrupted. Many teachers I knew would have traded their hectic, cramped lives for mine gladly. But I could have choked on the silence.

We didn't talk much, my husband and I. Hadn't for a long time. I used to tell myself, it's because Bao-bao's gone. We never had to be alone so much, just the two of us. Early on in our marriage, we spent all our time thinking about the baby, preparing for him, buying his bed, furniture for his room—it was so hard back then, shopping. We needed to make so many connections to buy the simplest things. An extra nice quilt, the crib. Money wasn't enough. Now, of course, all the stores had so many things to buy . . . if you had the money. My last major purchase, a new winter coat for Bao-bao, cost a third of my month's wages.

What did we used to talk about before Bao-bao was born? Well, we talked about the future, what the baby would be like, what he or she would need. I became pregnant six months after we were married. The first six months we just thought of places we could make love.

We were waiting for an apartment to ourselves. I lived with my room-mates at the dorm for unmarried teachers and he lived with his parents. We made love at his parents' apartment once. They'd gone for a walk

after dinner and we said we'd stay and do the dishes and as soon as they were out the door, Shao Hong held on to me and pulled me over to the couch and we kissed and then, it was frantic, really very funny, we didn't bother to undress all the way, just a few buttons. I remember he had one arm out of his shirt, it looked so naked, pale, the other completely clothed, and I tried to unbutton his cuff as he lifted up my blouse. We were so hot and cramped on their tiny sofa, Shao Hong kept sliding off. He had to prop himself up with one leg on the floor. I wanted to laugh. He put his palm gently against my mouth, "Sssh," he whispered, very serious, as if someone might hear. How sweet.

Then there were times we would seek out movie theaters, watch any awful kung fu or Hong Kong cop film just so that we could hold hands in the dark. I remember feeling the pressure of his knee against mine, so slight and yet soon that was all I could think about, the sharp point of his kneecap. I pressed against him a little more, a nudge, and his knee was firm against mine. I felt warm, and I turned towards him and I would have kissed him. I wanted to lean my entire body against him, but he held himself straight and squeezed my hand, pushing me away a little, subtly, and when I still leaned closer, he stared straight ahead at the screen and whispered, "Wait, not here. People can see." It's true, the theaters are never quite dark enough, although that doesn't stop young couples nowadays. They are quite bold, kissing in the back rows, holding hands on the sidewalks. I pass them on my bicycle. They're walking together at night, arm in arm, sometimes riding side by side on their bicycles, holding hands still. No one's ashamed now. It's funny to think how we all were back then, but part of me is pleased with this memory, when our love was a secret we hid, revealing it only to ourselves when it was so hot and pure we could not wait anymore.

Even the middle-school students are more open. Of course it's still

against the rules to have a boyfriend or girlfriend. Secretary Wang urged us to report any errant student. "Be vigilant," she said, in her shrill voice. (Like a yapping dog, Chen Hua said.) "Spiritual pollution from Western bourgeois influences is poisoning our students' minds." She meant they thought about sex and love, boys and girls discovering each other and their hormones. Of course, we teachers were always interested in our students' love lives; was it so terrible to gossip about them? They were adorable—the shy glances, the awkward conversations in the school yard while the rest of their classmates ran out the gate, not understanding, urging them to "Hurry up! Come on!"

Chen Hua and I liked to compare notes. Our classes overlapped for the second-year students, fifteen- and sixteen-year-olds. But we had to be careful when we talked in the cafeteria. Most of us didn't care about the Secretary's warnings, but Mr. Hong, the math teacher, watched and listened with the intensity of a cat stalking a mouse. A bitter man with a dry pinched face, he'd report his students. He might have already.

I had heard the funniest story recently. Someone reported a senior who had a girlfriend, one year behind him. They called in the boy's parents to criticize him, sat in the conference room on the first floor, formal stuffed chairs facing each other, tea cups that nobody drinks from.

"We'll have to expel your son if he doesn't correct his behavior," Secretary Wang admonished. She took herself very seriously. "He could be a bad influence on the entire school."

But far from being polite, the boy's father leapt out of his chair and pointed at the Party Secretary's nose. "How dare you say my son has a girlfriend! My son is a good boy! I won't let him come to your school anymore! You're a bad influence on him!"

And of course the Secretary was very angry and very alarmed and they yelled at each other for some time.

"Your son does have a girlfriend!"

"You can't prove it! You're making it up!"

Afterwards, everyone admitted that they'd never seen such a thing, a parent yelling like this. We have no authority, Ms. Yu said, shaking her head. It's hard being a teacher, parents don't respect us, the students don't respect us. You can make more money selling tea eggs on the street! she said.

But I couldn't help laughing when I heard the story at lunch when the older teachers gossip over mah-jongg. I could imagine the Secretary's face growing as red as her new French eyeglasses.

I heard that everything's all right now. The school sent the boy's father a gift, maybe some oranges and a sack of fine white rice. And the parents sent the Secretary a very nice picture of cranes flying over a mountain, framed with glass. She hung it in her office. I saw it one day as I was walking by, so I think this story must have been true. And anyway, the boy no longer talked to this particular girl, so it wasn't important anymore.

The foreign teacher was very upset when we told her during our first class with her in September. "We're supposed to *report* our students? That's terrible! This is *repressive!*" She paced back and forth in her office, her hair flying about her head, she waved her arms.

"We know in America all young people have boyfriends and girl-friends," said Ms. Yu. "And it is all right for them to have babies in school too, yes? But we can't afford this in China."

"What?" Cynthia put her hands on her hips. "Who told you that?"

"We read it in the paper."

"No, no, no. You don't understand. It's not all right to have babies in school, it's a problem."

"Yes, I think so, too," said Ms. Yu, pointedly.

"Teen pregnancy is a major social problem in the United States. Okay. But just because you're dating doesn't mean you're going to have children! I mean, it's more complicated than that." Cynthia was very frustrated, but restrained. She paced with her arms folded. "I mean, it's natural to want to have a boyfriend or a girlfriend in high school."

"Yes, even in China there are students who have babies," I said, trying to make peace.

"Sssh," said one of the older teachers.

"Yes, yes!" said Ms. Yu. "This is what I mean."

I sighed and looked up at Cynthia and we both laughed at the same time.

I knew she would understand more about China as time went on. Sometimes rules seemed very arbitrary, even "repressive," but not everyone obeyed them. The important thing was to learn how to live around them.

Sometimes on my bike rides I'd see one of my students or two. I only waved if they waved first, I didn't want to embarrass them. Love is a precarious thing.

2.

The Wall

Let me trace the roots for you of this disaster—no, of this decision, after so many decisions amid disasters. The beginning of my new self. It is late August. Still hot. I am at school.

The Party Secretary's eyes shine when she tells me I will be in charge of the foreign teacher, the young American she has found (who knows how) to come to our middle school and teach English for a year. I am lucky, she says; many, many teachers would *love* to have this honor. This opportunity for self-improvement. This great occasion for more education. To learn from the foreigner. Reeducate myself. Rise like a phoenix to meet the new dawn of the open-door policy, ride the fragrant wind of the learn-from-the-West-to-build-a-better-China spirit, and soar above the red horizon by using Western-techniques-with-Chinese-characteristics. The Secretary stops herself, realizing she is getting

carried away, and embarrassed, pushes her red plastic eyeglasses higher on her nose, then sips a little tea. The Secretary means well, it's just that all her oratory skills date from the Cultural Revolution.

I wait for her to recover. It is late afternoon and I am tired after a day of meetings, cleaning our offices, helping with the disaster of the lunch-room. A late summer storm has blown out the glass of a window in the teachers' cafeteria, and shards of glass, bits of brown leaves, trash, ciga-rette butts, and even an entire cartload of rotten persimmons has blown inside across the concrete floor, attracting large black flies that bite. My back aches.

It is warm in the Secretary's small office and far too dusty. She doesn't seem to mind, as she sits behind her desk, slurping her tea from a metal cup decorated with a picture of a fluffy white cat. But the School Head, Mr. Hu, is holding back a sneeze, pinching the top of his nose with two chalky fingers. Looking at him, I want to sneeze too. I realize the Secre-tary is looking at me again, a smile fixed on her wide flat face, waiting for my full attention.

"Besides, everyone says your English is the best—" She puts up a hand to stop me before I can protest. "We want to reward you for your hard work. For your dedication. For your progressive spirit—"

This time the School Head interrupts.

"You really suffered for the school that time in Beijing. Terrible, just terrible," he shakes his head, his chins folding into themselves like a fan. "We all felt so bad this incident had to happen to you." I know he would like to add "of all people," but he doesn't. I have to give him credit for that.

"We want to make it up to you, okay?" Mr. Hu smiles, nodding. Secre-tary Wang nods at him, then me, smiling.

I hate cadres. It's impossible to talk to them. It's impossible to refuse them as well.

Chen Hua will be furious when I tell her, I thought. I found her just as she finished her shift in the cafeteria. She was standing in the courtyard between our sickly French sycamore and an unidentifiable shrub. She leaned against the concrete Ping-Pong table, eating a juicy orange persimmon. She licked her fingers.

I waved to her. "Guess who just got assigned a second full-time job?"

"You're not pregnant, are you?" She dropped the persimmon pit and opened her mouth wide, ready to shriek with laughter.

"Funny funny." I sat beside her. "I'm in charge of the foreign teacher."

"What foreign teacher?"

"Our American English teacher. The one we cleaned out the old broken-furniture closet for. Her office. The one they're buying a new cassette player for."

"Oh." Chen Hua shrugged. "So what do you have to do? Be her translator?"

"Everything," I said. "Make sure the students obey her. Make sure she doesn't get sick. Show her around the city."

"You should be happy—this'll be great practice for when we quit teaching and get our tour-guide jobs." Chen Hua laughed happily and I saw that some of the persimmon's flesh was stuck between her front teeth.

This was our private joke. One of the older teachers had brought in an article about tour guides in South China making over a thousand dollars a month, taking free trips all over China, marrying the foreign tourists, emigrating—at the very least, getting paid hundreds of American dollars for sex. The article was titled, "Hidden AIDS Threat to China's Growth,"

a cautionary tale meant to keep the rest of us on the straight and narrow road to capitalism-with-Chinese-characteristics. But what we were interested in was the picture of one woman—never even went to college, only graduated from junior high!—wearing a fur coat and standing in front of a shiny black motorcycle. Lives in a high rise in Guangzhou. Didn't marry her Chinese boyfriend, doesn't intend to, and he doesn't care because he uses her foreign contacts as business connections to make millions. The picture caption read, "On the Road to Spiritual Pollution."

The older teachers were furious. "This is shameful!" "All of us Chinese will lose face because of these prostitute tour guides!" "This never happened when Chairman Mao was alive!" Chen Hua asked for the article and framed it. Hung it in the art teachers' office. "For inspiration," she joked. "For when Lin Jun and I quit teaching and go make some real money!"

Chen Hua was still laughing at me about my new duties with the foreigner, so I got up to go. She caught hold of my arm. "I'm sorry. Sorry. Just don't tell me that you won't have any time to be my friend anymore."

"No. I don't know why I'm so bothered. It's just their attitude. As if they're doing me a favor."

"That's always their attitude when they give us extra work."

We sat in a tired silence for a while, Chen Hua cross-legged like a tiny Buddha, me with my legs hanging over the edge of the table, stretching stretching my tense muscles. It seemed I was always in a bad mood.

"No, I'm not being fair," I said at last. "It is a good thing to have a foreign friend. It will improve my English."

"You're scaring me, Lin Jun."

"I'm serious. This is a good job. What's the point of being an English teacher if I never use my English? This is a good opportunity."

Chen Hua now hopped off the Ping-Pong table. "I'll remind you that you said that when you start complaining to me." She walked towards the school gate, small enough to be one of our students, but strutting with the confidence of a PLA soldier—no, a movie star. She stopped midway and waved good-bye, then cupped her hands to her mouth to shout, "And you *will* be sorry, Lin Jun!"

Pedaling home just in time to catch rush-hour traffic, I still felt unsettled, disturbed. Suddenly I didn't want to go home. I turned off Zhongshan Avenue and headed up a narrow alley. Bump bump bump, big mistake, I thought, but at least there's no traffic. There was no one else here except a few chickens tethered to a cart by a string around one leg. I used to raise chickens. I like chickens, I thought. A cat ran in front of my bicycle and I nearly hit it. I skidded over a pothole. I lurched towards the stone wall circling the crematorium. It was hot and dusty and the air was the color of old bandages. I didn't want to go home. I didn't want to be riding up this hill, my calves burning, I didn't want to be anywhere.

I climbed off my Pigeon and walked it up the hill. It was too hot still for this late in the year. It was too hot to have to be so busy. And what if my English wasn't good enough to talk to this foreigner? And I was supposed to be an English teacher! What would Shao Hong say? He would say I'd been foolish again, I'd let the school take advantage of me, give me extra work, no extra pay. Again. Maybe I wouldn't tell him.

I reached the top of the hill. There was a breeze here. A building was being torn down on the corner, half of the empty windows and vacant rooms exposed, half in a pile of broken rock, cement dust, dirt. Trash

from the workers' discarded lunches swirled up in the breeze like smoke. I couldn't see the crooked alley in front of me. From where I was perched, on the top of the hill, the road before me looked like a sheer drop, a cliff that fell straight into the tall gray stone wall that I knew was the back wall of Normal University, where I went to school a long, long time ago.

The sharp glass triangles cemented at the top of the wall, to keep out the unauthorized, caught the low slanting rays of the sun. The glass was beautiful, on fire, liquid gold. I jumped on my Pigeon and, without looking at the ground, raced towards the beautiful gold light. No need to pedal, I was coasting at top speed, my legs stretched out on both sides, free, the wind in my hair, drying my sweat, as I was falling falling falling.

Luckily, my Pigeon's brakes were still very good.

The alley behind my old school was shadowy and cool, lined with tall sycamores, the huge leaves, bigger than my hands, sighing in the breeze. I rode alongside the wall. Cool. Calmer. I could think.

I thought what was really upsetting me was not the idea of the extra work. It was their insensitivity. Their coy allusions. Their ill-hidden titillation. Oh, the hardships I had faced that I would now deserve the plum assignment, the foreign friend, the exotic distraction. Poor Lin Jun. After all that's happened. After the disaster in Beijing. After all that. We should be kind to her, poor thing. Show her we haven't forgotten. Give her the foreigner. And then maybe she'll be okay. Then maybe she'll tell us everything.

I didn't want to be filled with hate. I didn't want to be bitter. I'm only thirty-one, I thought . . . I'm too young to be bitter. But they thought I was weak and I did hate them for that. For a little while anyway. For the moment.

What happened at Beijing was simple. It wasn't even Beijing. It was a suburb. Badaling. At the Great Wall. I'd gone to a teachers' conference. I guessed the number the Party Secretary drew out of the Mao cap and I won the right to accompany Mrs. Mu on the trip to the teachers' conference. We went on the official tour to the Great Wall. While there, a Chinese couple committed suicide. Blew themselves up with a home-made bomb. (How does anyone even know how to make a homemade bomb?)

I find the bodies. I find the injured foreign tourist. I'm interrogated by the police. I'm interviewed by every damn newspaper in Nanjing when I get back. Everyone wants to know: what did they look like, what did you feel like, how damaged are you, how terrible, how terrible, how exciting. I don't ever want to be so bored that I'd ever ask anyone such questions.

The school was very kind to me, the Secretary filled with remorse. It was she who pulled the number out of the hat, the number I had guessed and written down on a slip of paper. It was she who was respon-sible, she said. (Responsible for what? I thought.) The reporters came to the middle school. The reporters interviewed the Party Secretary. She said I was very brave and that I was doing well, recovering nicely from the trauma. "Recovering"? That meant I was an emotional wreck, a dis-aster. One paper even had me sobbing hysterically on the train all the way back from Beijing, nineteen hours to Nanjing. The conductors had to comfort me. The paper quoted one of them, a Mr. Zhao Yu-jing, twenty-two years old, a conductor for five years, who said that I was very beautiful, even when I cried, and that he brought me tea seven times. I am the picture of *wenjing*, of the soft refined weak woman.

Chen Hua said if I hadn't been beautiful, no one would've cared. But it made a good story this way, a beautiful middle-school teacher—read: shy, lonely, repressed, oh, isn't it so romantic—who heroically fights to

save an injured foreign tourist from the tragic double suicide of dis-traught lovers. Chen Hua said she could hardly wait for the movie version. I told her to be quiet for once.

I hadn't even wanted to go to the Great Wall. I would've rather gone into Beijing, explored the capital, such a big exciting city, gone shopping. We were stuck out in this tiny teachers' college, an hour and a half by bus from downtown Chang'an Boulevard. The conference was dull. Meetings, meetings, meetings and then huge heavy banquets where nobody could eat anything, except the cadres who had ordered all that heavy oily food in the first place. Who eats roast duck in August?

They chartered a bus to take us to the Great Wall, China's pride, the symbol of our nation. I know all the myths. Ten thousand *li* long. To keep the barbarians out. The only man-made object that can be seen from space. (But it's not true. Those American astronauts saw the Amazon or the Nile, some river, from their rocket, not the Great Wall. I am a teacher. I hate these inaccuracies.) The bones of all the poor Chinese slaves, conscripted to spend their lives building the wall for that evil despot the Qin Emperor, are buried in the wall. The wall was washed with the tears of their mothers, their widows, their orphans, who journeyed to find their sons, husbands, fathers, only to find their bones in this prickly, jagged wall, draped over the northern hills like a sleeping dragon.

We arrived midmorning and it was so hot that two elderly teachers from Harbin, one man and one woman, immediately suffered heatstroke and had to be helped to a small snack bar, force-fed orange sodas and Coca-Cola, fanned until we were sure they would recover. Then we walked together, a band of wide-eyed teachers from the provinces, past row after row of stands selling cigarettes and obscene playing cards, sandy cookies with ants crawling in the plastic bags, Chairman Mao

buttons and English-language translations of the Little Red Book, movie-star magazines, plastic guns, lighters shaped like Panda bears, Japanese film, and ugly T-shirts emblazoned with an anonymous artist's blurry rendition of the Great Wall. The air was sticky, colored beige with dust, the wall was a monstrosity of sharp-edged stones, filled with bones. It looked like the spine of a dinosaur that had lain down to die thousands of years ago, its vertebrae now exposed to the sun, dried, bleached.

Climbing on the wall was a task. In some sections we walked bent over nearly horizontal to the ground. In others we walked down slopes so steep we had to hold on to the notched battlements so that we didn't slide down the bricks worn smooth and slick by ten million tourists' tennis shoes. I was exhausted. My calves ached. My knees ached. The air was still, no breeze, only heat, only dust.

Mrs. Mu insisted she had to walk to the guardhouse at the very end of the restored section of the wall on the left side of the entrance, rather than the more popular, longer section to the right, where the other teachers headed immediately. She said she didn't want to follow the crowd. She told me she had a private reason she wanted to see the wall without all the other tourists watching. I nodded. Of course, I'd go with her, I said. No problem.

The view was not spectacular on this side, just crabgrass, brownish weeds, a ragged shrub. We looked behind us at the spectacular other half of the wall, our colleagues like tiny ants crawling over a bone. We persisted.

"There is a legend about the wall," Mrs. Mu told me. "One end crumbled because a woman came there looking for her husband. He had been forced to leave their village to work on the wall. The emperor's guards had come in the middle of the night, dragged him out of their bed. They had only been married three days. The woman had to travel

for ten years, facing many hardships, to find passage to the north. And when she finally arrived at the wall, she discovered she was too late. Her husband was already dead and his body had been buried in the wall. She then began to wail and cry. She cried so much that the gods heard her and had pity on her, and struck the wall with a bolt of blue lightning. Only the guardhouse remained. The wall beyond lay in ruins."

I wondered why this story meant so much to Mrs. Mu. After a couple thousand years, most of the wall lay in ruins anyway.

"When my husband was sent to the countryside, I used to think of this story," she confessed, giggling a little. It was funny to see her act like this. She was a very old teacher, close to retirement age, over fifty, and her hair was now completely gray. She wore very thick black glasses, the kind that went out of fashion years and years ago. But when she giggled like that, she seemed like a little girl.

"I thought your husband was from the countryside. Isn't his family farmers?" Chen Hua had told me.

"That is my second husband," Mrs. Mu said.

I felt bad immediately, and very tired, too. Neither of us spoke for a long while until at last we reached the end of the wall.

"What a pretty little room," Mrs. Mu said.

The guardhouse was small, inhospitable. A square with four large windows in the stone. You could see for miles in all directions. Miles of nothing but shimmering dirt, a few dusty brown plants. No flowers. No trees. I wondered if it had always looked like this. I wondered how horrible it would look in the winter, to look out onto miles and miles of snow. I couldn't imagine how terrible it would have been for the Chinese soldiers who for hundreds of years had been stationed on the wall, young farm boys turned into soldiers in this wasteland.

Mrs. Mu was posing in one of the windows, her back against the side

of the guardhouse wall, one leg bent, her arms around her knee. "Too bad I forgot my camera. I'm so stupid." She clicked her tongue against the roof of her mouth in dismay.

"Don't worry," I said absently, staring out into the bright sunlight. "They'll take a group picture of us after lunch."

"At least it's cooler in here." Mrs. Mu fanned herself. Her cotton blouse was soaked with perspiration. But I felt too cold in the tiny stone room. I had to leave, but I couldn't bear going back with Mrs. Mu, chatting, pretending to be cheerful. I couldn't bear the idea of meeting with the rest of our teachers' group. The inevitable endless lunch with all the speeches and the toasting and the forced cheer. What was the matter with me?

"Is something the matter?" Mrs. Mu was standing next to me, peering into my face anxiously.

"Oh, no, no. I'm just too cold in here."

"Yes," she nodded. "You're right. It's not good to move too quickly from hot to cold." We stepped out of the guardhouse back into the bleaching sunlight.

She turned to go.

I looked past the end of the guardhouse, to the plain yellow earth below, the gritty soil. I wanted to walk, but not this aching climb over the bricks, fighting past every tourist stopped to take another picture. At least, this far out there were no other tourists. About ten minutes before, we had passed two young foreign women who had paused to take pictures. I wanted to leave before they arrived.

"Mrs. Mu, I'm sorry, but I don't think I'll go back yet. I'm going for a walk." Already it was as if my body were acting on its own, I was merely following it. My left leg draped over the edge of the wall. This end was not too high up. Maybe two meters from a pile of stones on the ground.

"What are you doing? Be careful!" Mrs. Mu rushed to my side to steady me.

"I'm going to walk on the hill," I said, swinging my right leg over. I balanced on the edge of the wall. It would not be a hard jump.

"You don't want to see more of the wall?" Mrs. Mu called as I jumped onto the earth.

I waved to her. "I'll meet you all for lunch. Don't worry," I called. I walked away, my back to the wall.

What was the matter with me? I had become such a moody woman. It was too hot for a walk really, but I had to be alone, and it is so hard to be alone. I walked without seeing, just to feel my legs move, one foot in front of the other. The ground was fairly level here. A few rabbit holes. Or snake holes. That made me pay attention more. There was the sound of a loud shot, like a gun in a movie or a car backfiring or a crash. But there had been loud explosions all morning. A construction boss blasting rock from a nearby quarry, one teacher had speculated. Or the Army practicing maneuvers nearby. That's what our guide had told us. The moment we got off our bus, a loud BOOM, then another. "Oh, it's just the PLA." She rolled her eyes. "They really are annoying. A friend of mine wanted to set up a café with music, a karaoke machine, live performers on weekends, but how can you compete with that kind of noise?" She tossed her head prettily. Chen Hua would have had something to say about her, I knew, but I appreciated her honesty. I don't know how many of us would have dared announce before a group of strangers that we found the PLA annoying.

Finally, I knew I had gone far enough. I just felt it. Like someone staring at my back. Two eyes on me. I turned around. I could see the wall over the edge of the horizon, I'd been walking downhill. I hurried and nearly tripped, turned my ankle. I walked more carefully, but my

ankle still hurt. I was being punished. Punished, I thought. For being selfish. For leaving my husband alone and my son while I went on a trip. I should have given up my lucky number. Let another teacher have the chance. An older teacher who might never again have the opportunity to see our capital. I was practically running now, despite my throbbing ankle. I felt eyes on me, men hiding in the brush, watching, everywhere. I ran to the top of the hill.

Smoke fluttered out of the window of the guardhouse like a giant flag of ink. How strange, I thought. Some joke? I thought. Some kids? But I knew it wasn't a joke. I didn't want to move. But I didn't want to stand alone on this hill a hundred yards from the wall, the only thing that connected me to my group, that would bring me back to the group, who were probably waiting for me. How long had I been gone? I didn't dare look at my watch. I looked at the smoke coming closer and closer to me until I could smell it. It smelled nothing like a fire.

I ran. My ankle felt like ice, like stone, like something tied on to my leg but not a part of my body. And then I was at the wall, and I knew something was terribly, terribly wrong. Where was everybody? How could I climb back up? What had I been thinking? I reached up and then jumped and threw my arms over the side and threw my leg over. I'd climbed over the gate of my university, my thick coat over the glass shards at the top, nine feet to the ground. This was nothing. Nothing. But I couldn't grasp the stone properly. It was slick. I slid over the side of the wall onto the bricks.

And then I heard everything. I don't know why I hadn't heard before. A woman screaming crying moaning, a sound like an animal being beaten, a horrible sound. I didn't want to move but I moved towards the sound into the smoke of the guardhouse. There were bodies lying on the floor. One body slumped over the edge of the window, as if the

person—a man? a woman? I couldn't tell—was looking out the window. And then I saw the body had no head. And I screamed and screamed and screamed. I couldn't move. Then one of the bodies on the floor moved and stood up and stood over me and grabbed me, pulled me, hard. Pulled me toward another body, a foreigner, a woman, a pretty face. And then I saw the top part of her head was split open, her red brains where her forehead should be. The body that was holding on to my arm let go, and I nearly fell over. This body knelt down beside the pretty woman's head, pressing the brains back into the head, holding them there. Then the body moved and I saw it had a face, a woman's, an ugly face with a huge mouth, like a hungry ghost, this huge open mouth the size of half the face, and the mouth was howling, and I ran. I backed out of the guardhouse and fell onto my rear end. Hard so that my spine hurt all the way up to the base of my head. And then I scratched at the smooth brick until I could push myself up again to my feet and I ran away.

Then I heard the woman's screams, clearly, in English, she shouted, "Help! Help me! Help help help!"

I ran sliding down the steep parts, my ankle in flames, but I didn't care. I saw a group of Chinese tourists, a family, the mother in her green policewoman's uniform, the father and son in matching T-shirts and shorts. I ran toward them screaming. The woman faced me, grabbing her child to her, the husband put his arm out, protecting them from me. "Help," I screamed. "Call the police!" The woman knelt to the side of the wall, her body protecting her son from me; the husband shoved me away roughly. I ran away from them.

The people in the distance grew larger. They were stopped, pointing

at me. Cameras were pointed at me. "Help!" I screamed. "An accident! Help!"

They said I told every group of tourists I met, and that many of them, dozens, rushed with their cameras to the guardhouse at the end of the wall, and that many of them took pictures of the foreign woman kneeling over her wounded sister, the decapitated body, the blood splashed against the stone and bricks. The smoke was gone by the time they arrived.

I remember shouting at every face I saw, and no one seemed to understand me. I screamed in English and Chinese. I begged for someone to call a doctor, find a doctor. When I finally reached the entrance to the wall, where the other teachers and our guide were waiting for me, they said I flew down the steps, my arms outstretched, and when they saw the blood on my hands, on my pants, on my shoes, they thought I was the one who had been injured. The Public Security Bureau was waiting for me. There'd been reports of a crazy woman on the wall, assaulting the tourists. I shouted at them to do something.

Forty-seven minutes passed before the army sent a team of six medics with an olive green tarpaulin stretcher to the end of the wall and brought the injured woman back. This time, a medic held his hand to her head. A woman, a tall dark-haired woman, was walking behind the stretcher. This woman was not injured. Her mouth was no longer gaping open in a howl. She was quiet. Another man was holding her arms to her sides, he must have been trying to help her walk but it looked almost as if she were his prisoner, someone to be subdued. They loaded the stretcher into a tiny bread loaf–shaped ambulance. I don't remember any sounds. No siren. No voices. Nothing.

I am sitting in a darkened room, dim sunlight filtering through the dust on the windows. The police are interrogating the woman whose

sister they have taken to a hospital in Beijing. Beijing is an hour away at least. Maybe the hospital is not in Beijing. Who told me Beijing? Someone has told me this, before I was brought into this tiny room, waiting, while they question the foreign woman. A cup of tea is at my elbow on a low wood table. I am seated in a straight-back chair with a tired vinyl seat that at one point must have been a cushion. The sunlight falls straight through the window into a dull pool of gray light on the wooden floor.

Someone says, "It was a bomb."

I look up and see another of the teachers, an older woman, from a big city. Shanghai? Tianjin? I don't remember. She is not talking to me. She is drinking a cup of tea out of a green ceramic mug and she is facing Mrs. Mu, who is looking at me, her eyes wide behind her thick glasses.

A door opens, and a man helps the woman shuffle out. She sits on a chair in front of the man's desk, or rather he puts her in front of the chair and she slumps into it. She buries her head in her arms. She is crying. I can tell by the way her shoulders shudder, but I don't hear anything. It is very quiet.

I look down at her white canvas tennis shoes and I see there are little flecks of red, little chunks, and I realize they are pieces of flesh.

When I can see again, I am lying on the floor, the smooth dusty wood floor, and I am staring up into Mrs. Mu's face. She is nodding and her mouth is opening and closing. Someone else is pushing on my neck. I try to squirm away, but then the hand grasps my neck even more firmly, it hurts, and I am lifted up, and someone is trying to drown me, hot liquid splashes against my chin, runs down my neck. I find my strength and push very hard at the shadow in front of me, and I am free, no pressure on my neck. Mrs. Mu is there, she puts a hand on my shoulder.

"You fainted," she says.

"Have some tea," a voice says, and the cup of liquid is pushed back towards my face.

I scoot away. I struggle to sit up. I am crouching on my knees, my hands flat on the smooth wood floor. Then I remember where I am, and I'm afraid. I look around, at the chairs looming above me, the huge desk, the huge dark windows, and I see that the foreign woman is gone now. I am relieved.

"She's okay now," the voice says. I see it is a man in a uniform. He is speaking to a very young man, a boy, whose uniform is too big for him. He is holding a cup of tea in his right hand.

Mrs. Mu stands next to me. I grab hold of her arm and I pull myself push myself to my feet.

The official police report said that at 12:23 P.M. August 12, a home-made bomb was detonated at the far end of the restored section of the Great Wall of Badaling. A Chinese man, married, aged forty-three, was killed instantly, as was a Chinese woman, divorced, aged thirty-seven, who was decapitated by the blast. Relatives of the couple came forward after the initial reports of the explosion in the newspapers and identified them. A twenty-three-year-old foreign woman, a tourist from New Zealand, died during surgery after suffering a massive wound to her head. Her sister, age twenty-six, was uninjured.

The official report says the man and the woman were lovers. They wanted to be married, but the man's wife refused to grant him a divorce. In their despair, they decided to commit suicide together on the Great Wall, the symbol of Chinese lovers forever separated.

I'd wake up some nights from a nightmare. I am at the wall. I don't remember the dream, the images, but I wake up cold, and I think of the

couple on the wall, the poor tourist, her sister. But it's not the horror of the blood, the ugliness, that I think of. I clench my fists, I kick, nearly waking my husband. I sit up, filled with anger. How can people be so selfish?

Who hasn't had a hard life? I ask you. Who? Should we all kill ourselves then?

But after two years, I didn't think about it anymore. Not like people thought I must have. I hated their pity. Their curiosity. Poor Lin Jun.

I was not so fragile.

When they introduced me to the foreign teacher, they mentioned first of all "Lin Jun has a boy's name!" The Party Secretary was satisfied with the introduction, even smug. She nodded with approval at the other teachers after someone translated what had been said.

"Oh?" The foreign teacher seemed uncertain.

I realized that I was meant to explain. "When I was a little girl, in the Cultural Revolution time, my parents were away, in the countryside?" I was unsure of my English, my thick accent, but the American nodded, in an exaggerated fashion meant to encourage. "I wanted a revolutionary name. So I chose Jun. Jun means soldier, did you know? But I didn't think this is only for boys!"

Secretary Wang was still nodding contentedly, glad to see her teacher could actually speak English, although she had no idea what I'd said.

"What did your parents think?" The American stared.

"They didn't know." I smiled, my mouth twitching at the corners as I realized I could say anything, anything at all, and who would know the difference. But I told the truth. I explained, "My Auntie did not like it at first, but she said it is better than my real name, Hua-yun. That means

clouds like flowers. Too dreamy." I shook my head. "'Soldier' is better, I think."

I smiled, the American smiled, the Secretary continued to nod. And I knew then, immediately, that I would like this American, and this new job of mine. Introducing myself to this foreigner who knew nothing about me, who would know only that I was "Soldier," not poor Lin Jun, the orphan, the traumatized survivor, sister of a common worker, poor, poor Lin Jun, who'd seen so much. Guess why she got to take care of the foreigner. Remember Beijing? Whisper, whisper. And I was not lucky Lin Jun, so beautiful, so lucky, lucky with a good-fortune face, a handsome intellectual husband, their only child a boy, a mother-in-law with good connections, a lucky, lucky woman. Look who's been given another privilege! *Aiya*, did you see the foreigner? She doesn't deserve any of this.

I knew what people said behind my back. What they'd always said.

I knew what Chen Hua thought—I was a pushover. But I could tell this foreign woman anything, reinvent myself, my life. Become something new. Better. Why suffer? Why wallow in your suffering? I thought. No pipe bombs for me, ever.

I preferred to live. By invention. Recreation. I could admit it finally although I don't think even I understood then how true this was.

3.

Foreign Ways

The night in September when the go-between business came up, I was especially moody. I glanced at my reflection in the kitchen window, a white face fluttering against the black air. Dark was coming earlier though winter was still months away. I saw my face drowning in the shimmering surface of the glass. My good-fortune face, Auntie Gao had told me long ago. With a face like this, a girl could go far. But looking at myself that night, I did not feel happy or cheered or especially lucky.

Steam from the rice cooker condensed against the cool glass and dissolved into a hundred drops of water. The song on the radio wailed, suddenly louder. An American song about painful love, the singer shouted and moaned, an ugly voice, so much better than the Chinese

songs they played from Hong Kong and Taiwan, always happy, always beautiful.

I wiped my hands on a dishrag and went into the living room to sit and read, waiting for my husband to come home. The room was nearly bare. After six years of marriage, we still had only the pieces that we bought during our engagement. The round wooden table, four straight-backed chairs, and the standing lamp. The television was broken, silent and dark next to the new radio, which did work, usually. We kept it on the top bookshelf by the window. The small plastic shelves held my "library," grammar books mostly; it was hard to find good novels in English.

I closed the thin blue curtains by the window opposite the table. The fabric was cold against my fingertips. I realized that it was time to put up the padded cotton shades, keep the cold night air at bay. Some other day, I thought. I was so tired right then, lazy too.

I took my seat at the table, my books at arm's reach, but I didn't open my English text or my students' exercise books for grading. I stared into the whorls and patterns of the dark wood, glossy from wear, and thought of nothing at all.

My husband returned at the usual time and in his usual silence.

I had a reason to move, at least, so I set the table. "We have a foreign teacher at our school. A woman." I added rice to his bowl.

"Your middle school's not as bad as I thought." Shao Hong laughed mirthlessly. He could be trying to make a joke. He could be angry. I didn't ask.

"How was your work?" I tried to put some more meat in his rice bowl, but he pushed my hand away.

"Huh," he said. "So does the foreigner have blond hair?"

"No, no. She's American but she has, I don't know how to describe it . . ." I pointed to the varnished tabletop. "Her hair's that color."

"Hmm," he said, his mouth full. "Maybe she's not a real American."

"Of course she's real. Our school had to verify everything." Then I saw that my husband was merely teasing. How dismaying that I could no longer tell his playful moods from his morose ones. I shook my teacup to settle the leaves to the bottom.

"So, my wife is making foreign friends. Maybe she's planning to find an American husband and leave the old one behind in China."

I snorted at his joke, I was going to play along. "Maybe you'd like to be a bachelor again?"

"Since you and the foreign teacher are so friendly, you can convince her to date my supervisor. The old man needs a wife. I hear foreign women will take any man they can get."

"So this is what you talk about at work?" I blew on my tea, but I sensed an opening. It'd been weeks since Shao Hong even mentioned his work. When we were first married, he talked about nothing but. I tried to connect the dots between our sentences. "He's almost fifty, right?"

Shao Hong pulled a paper from his bag and read as he ate.

"Maybe I do know someone for your supervisor," I said, smiling, a little challenging: he thinks he can dismiss me so easily. But he didn't look up. He was tired after work, not playful. I should have known better. I put my hand to his forehead. His skin was moist and cold.

We ate the rest of the meal in silence, then I gathered up the dishes. Shao Hong hid himself in his study, his typewriter filling the apartment with a steady tapping sound like rain. I washed the dishes. The rhythms of our days were so predictable, even the sounds we made were so familiar that I barely heard them anymore, more like echoes, static on the radio.

Was it any surprise that the idea of acting as a matchmaker should have intrigued me? Something new. Something useful. Maybe fun. Shao Hong might be sorry for being so flippant, I thought, for dismissing me. I could show him.

I was thinking of Chen Hua. She was talented, lively, yet she was already more than thirty and unmarried. She was not conventionally beautiful, but if you looked at her closely, really looking, not just measuring things off on a checklist, she was stunning. The whiteness of her skin, the flash of her eyes, the gracefulness of her gestures. I loved to watch her talk. It was hard to concentrate sometimes.

Chen Hua had been sent to study with the opera when she was very young. I always wanted to ask her about these days; they seemed exciting, glamorous. But we all knew better than to bring up the past at random.

Right then as I washed the dishes, I thought she'd make a wonderful mother. I wanted to see the child she would raise. I wanted someone to compare techniques with. Actually, I thought she'd make a strange mother, and I wanted the foil. I couldn't reassure myself in a vacuum.

(Already you can see that I was heading for trouble, that I was trying to change things, recast my friend, our roles, our lives. In a movie, strange music would have accompanied my dishwashing, a slow drum, an eerie flute solo. But I was oblivious, happy even.)

The Monday-morning meetings were the worst part of my job. They had always been long, but since the June fourth incident at Tiananmen, an extra half hour had been added. Secretary Wang was quoting from the paper that day I told Chen Hua about my plan. I was especially impatient for the meeting to end. That always made things worse.

"'The Number Three Middle School is a model for our citizens. The students heroically spent their Sunday afternoons, a time normally reserved for play and idle time with friends, cleaning the trash from the banks of the Sorrow Lake.'" The Secretary read to us as usual, her voice louder than necessary. Yap yap yap. "Why is our school not in the paper? Why are we not 'models for our citizens'? Why is there no mention of our new foreigner? It is the fault of our own laziness!" The Secretary tapped the table with her hand.

The conference room smelled of sweat and chalk. The math teacher in front of me yawned loudly and put his head on the table. I couldn't concentrate, even on my knitting, which I'd brought, as if I really thought I'd get any more done, be efficient. I've been in a slump so long, I dream, I stare without thinking.

I glanced around, looking for Chen Hua. Teachers and administrators sat numbly at the wooden tables. Some napped, some chatted, one man read the newspaper. It occurred to me that Chen Hua had skipped the Secretary's pep talk, although there would be repercussions. No one cared if we teachers paid attention during the political meetings, just so long as we were all physically present. The Secretary paid attention to the body count, not our attention level.

The history teachers at the table by the door rose to leave, their chairs scraping noisily against the concrete floor. I realized the Secretary had stopped talking. My ears had forgotten how to listen. I waded through the shuffling crowd, thinking I'd station myself by the door. Heels clicked on the floor, sandals slapped, someone shuffled by in old cotton slippers. I could smell garlic and jasmine on the clothes as bodies passed by. I stood on tiptoe to see above the heads surrounding me.

The scent of perfume announced Chen Hua's presence. I grabbed her tiny arm.

"Ah, Xiao Chen, I've been waiting for you," I whispered and sashayed her into the hall.

I pulled Chen Hua to the empty English teachers' office, quickly quickly before my resolve crumbled—I had no faith in myself, let's be honest. I sat her on the overstuffed sofa. Dust clouds rose around us. Such an office!

"Xiao Chen, have you eaten yet? Do you want a *baozi*? I'm never hungry in the morning these days. I think I eat too much before I go to bed—my husband says I'm getting fat." I babbled, trying to sound casual.

Chen Hua's wide eyes narrowed. "Mmm. Careful. You're beginning to sound like a tour guide."

"What?" I looked at her in bewilderment, then caught myself. Forced myself to smile lightheartedly. I couldn't be tricky. Sly. I was no good at this. "We haven't talked in a long while, have we?"

"What's the matter, Lin Jun? Is everything all right?"

"Oh, yes, yes. No, I'm sorry. I should be more direct." I panicked. It was a mistake to be so direct. I would insult Chen Hua. Who was I to suggest she needed a date? The implicit condescension! But it was also too late to stop now. "My husband's working very hard these days. A lot of overtime. He's really spending so much time with his boss—"

"Lin Jun!"

"All right. I'm sorry." I clasped my hands together. "My husband's boss . . . would like to meet you . . . I think." I bit my lips. So pathetic. Fortunately, Chen Hua was quick.

For a moment Chen Hua stared blankly at me. Her eyes were flecked with gold, but the pupils dilated until the irises were merely tea-colored rims. The effect was alarming. Then just when I thought I could bear it no longer, Chen Hua jumped to her feet, pacing the room like a tiger in

a cage. "How does he know me? Did you tell him about me? Really, Lin Jun, you are too much! You always act so shy. Who knew you were so sneaky!" Chen Hua paused, with one hand on her hip, and tapped her foot on the floor, punctuating each sentence. "Who is this 'boss'? How would I meet him, if I even wanted to?"

"Oh, it's very simple. He's a nice man, a senior editor—"

"A senior editor? And he wants to meet *me*? Really, Lin Jun, what's the matter with him? Is he a widower? Is he sick?"

"Of course not! I wouldn't—"

"Of course you wouldn't, I'm so sorry. I didn't mean to imply you'd introduce me to some sick old man. So, how does this work? Should I talk to other people first? What do I do? I didn't mean you're sneaky, Lin Jun. You're discreet, I trust you." Chen Hua stood completely still, her hands at her throat. "What shall I wear? I mean, if we meet. You'll arrange this, right? At your home? Or, no, someplace else. You're too pretty. I wouldn't want to be seen next to you—sorry—you know what I mean."

My stomach relaxed, I could breathe properly. I was not a complete failure. "Please, don't worry. I'll tell my husband."

"Good!" Chen Hua glanced at her wristwatch. "Oh, no, I'm late! I've got a class. Second-year, your brats." She nearly skipped out the door. "I'll leave everything to you, Lin Jun." She waved as she ran onto the balcony.

I watched my friend rush away, only her silhouette visible sliding through the thick coat of dust on the window.

I was late for my English class with the foreign teacher. I'd nearly forgotten. I ran up the flight of stairs, my feet slapping the concrete. An edge of the top step crumbled under my weight and I twisted my ankle slightly. "Stupid," I muttered to myself. Wincing, I tiptoed into the

foreigner's office where the class was held. I looked in the bank of windows, saw the circle of English teachers. Only the faithful made the effort now that the novelty had worn off. There was too much else to do besides improve one's English: we were good enough to teach our students *before* the foreigner, why did we need to attend another class now? was the argument. I hate this kind of complacency. It makes our country small-minded. Really, it's very old thinking, just like the Cultural Revolution.

The other teachers sat with heads bowed over their texts. The bushy-headed American sat in the middle, on the new coffee table. I tried to open the door slowly so that it would not squeak. It squeaked.

Cynthia looked up in alarm.

"Oh, I'm so sorry, Teacher Cynthia." In my excitement, I stumbled over the "th" and pronounced the name so that it rhymed with India. Mnemonic devices are only useful to a point, I've found. After that, they can betray you.

I couldn't concentrate. It was exciting and terrifying, the responsibility of my new undertaking. My husband would be pleased, of course, that is what counted most. I imagined him smiling at me. "Who'd have guessed?" he'd say. "So sneaky." His jet black eyes bright again, pleased. Maybe I could convince him to shave the thin moustache he'd been coaxing onto his face for weeks now. I could just bring it up, the way I used to, small points that I thought might make a difference in his presentation of himself. I used to lay out the shirts he could wear, with the proper jackets. It was hard on men, no one was used to the fashion changes, so quick now, but so important. I saw it in the streets as I rode to work, in the alleys with the free markets, clothing stalls and Western suits, labels on the sleeves, flapping in the breeze like flags. Some jeans sold for one hundred yuan, some for twenty. You needed to learn the

difference, so as not to be cheated, pay money for clothes that make you look naive. Shao Hong had good sense, his own kind of style—calm, he would never wear the latest suits, so expensive. But he liked nice fabric, colors hidden in the weave that you could only see from up close, and so soft. I had fingered the sleeve of one jacket—from Hong Kong, the man promised me—but we couldn't afford it anyway. Still, with Shao Hong thinking about a promotion, these details might prove important. A translator had to understand more than a foreign grammar. Shao Hong surely knew these things already, but I would have liked to talk to him about the details. It would be an opening at least. An acceptable display of interest in his work. Shao Hong had always told me to be vigilant in ways to improve "our situation," meaning his job. "Ambition isn't just for men, Lin Jun. I don't want a complacent wife," he had said so long ago. I'd been pleased. I promised him then that I would try my best to help.

The buzzer sounded. I blinked. "Good-bye," I waved to the other teachers as they filed out. My husband would be so happy tonight, I thought. I thought of a yellow blouse I had seen on my way to work that morning. A pretty color. With full sleeves and a scooped neckline. Appropriate for a celebration. Perhaps Shao Hong found me less attractive, perhaps that was why we talked so little. I could make him notice me. I could show him I was not so useless.

This was how my mind flew in open circles, one idea prompting another before I had time to finish the first. I couldn't concentrate properly, I wondered if I ever could. I didn't remember anymore.

Cynthia sat down beside me then, smiling. She drew her feet up onto the chair, hugging her knees. "What's up, Helen?" The foreign teacher called me by my English name. "Something exciting going on?"

I told her about my plans to be a go-between.

"Really!" Cynthia raised her thick eyebrows. "Are there still go-betweens in China?"

"Of course. But I'm not an official go-between. Just a fake one." I laughed at my own joke. I spread my fingers across my knees and wiggled each one, thinking of my own audacity. I told Cynthia how I had managed to set up the introductions.

Surprisingly, Cynthia did not look pleased. "Hmm," she said.

"I'm worried too that maybe I can't do a good job."

"Oh, I'm sure you'll do fine. It's just a little . . . sad."

I tried not to stare. I pressed my hands together to keep them still.

"It's sad that a professional woman, a talented artist and teacher, has to be introduced like a child to a member of the opposite sex before they can date." And the foreigner began to chew on her own lips, thinking.

I felt myself frown, then smiled politely. "Well," I said. "I think it's maybe more convenient this way in China. It's very hard to meet people outside your work unit. Really, there's not much time to meet people." I was not sure how to translate my exact meaning.

The foreign teacher opened her mouth, then closed it quickly without saying anything, fishlike.

I felt as I had as a child, when Auntie caught me napping instead of writing in my copybook. Whenever I was with Cynthia, I found I wanted to explain everything, so that she would not judge us so harshly, I wanted to defend China. But I didn't know what to say. Even the simplest things seemed complicated—being a good wife, raising my boy, helping my friend. How could I defend my country? There was so much that I hated about both of us, China and me, and yet I knew it wasn't really our fault. Maybe it's impossible to explain being Chinese to a

foreigner. The past was too complicated, and everything is based on this past.

All my hopes for my new pure self were fading, drying up, breaking into flecks of so much old paint. It didn't matter that the foreigner didn't know me, my background, my labels. She saw me new and fresh for the first time but what she saw she thought was defective. I could tell, looking at her looking at me.

4.

Bedtime Stories

I always liked to tell stories. I told stories to Bao-bao every night for four years until my mother-in-law used her connections and had him sent away to nursery school. I was unhappy about the conditions— we were so close to the school, why did he have to live there six days of the week? But this was the policy, it was a good school, the administrators didn't want to create hierarchies among the students—those whose parents live far away should not be punished. And some were children of intellectuals who were abroad. My mother-in-law worked hard to make the arrangements.

"Where is he going to go to school? Are you going to teach him at home like he's an idiot who has to be hidden away? Where is he going to stay while you two are at work? I can't look after him, you know Ye-ye's moods! It's so hard, sometimes Ye-ye's completely clear-headed, kind, I

can talk to him. Then he's angry for no reason, sulking or worse, throwing things. You don't know. You don't ever see him like that. You don't know." Nai-nai picked her teeth with a wooden toothpick. I had made a good meal, I could always tell when she picked her teeth, she was pleased.

Shao Hong ran his hand through his hair. "Why is our son excluded? We have a right to send him to the neighborhood's *youeryuan*!"

I couldn't find my voice, I hated this weakness in me, this catch in my throat. I couldn't believe they were taking my son away.

My mother-in-law glared. "Look, it's all Mao's fault, don't yell at me! 'Have as many children as you want! Big families are glorious! China's population is her fortune!' " Nai-nai spit the words out. "Ha, I was the progressive one—only one child! Even then when the government wanted everyone to breed like animals. And look where it's got us. Can't even fit all the kids in a neighborhood into school! Everything's through the back door now."

Shao Hong stood up, his hands clenched into fists, his veins throbbing across his forehead. "Someone bribed the school to take their brat, and now the nursery has no room for our son"—he paced, an angry tiger—"who is *legitimately* supposed to be enrolled! There's no law! Everyone's corrupt!" He forgot that Nai-nai had used her connections, her bribes, to get Bao-bao into the Number Three Kindergarten.

"It's all Mao's fault." Nai-nai shook her head.

I found myself crying. I tried to turn before they noticed.

"Crying won't do any good." Nai-nai was annoyed. She put her toothpick down and looked up at Shao Hong, appealing to his senses, as if to say, Can't you calm this woman down? Doesn't she understand anything?

But I couldn't stop crying. I got up, cleared the table, banged the

dishes against the trash to empty them. Chores did not help, mindless tasks, I was despairing and ridiculous and impractical. I cried so loudly, I knew they could hear me in the dining room through the kitchen wall.

It was a good school, the teachers were very kind, and the facilities were new. And it was so close that sometimes on my way to work, if I left early enough, I could ride around the block and catch a glimpse of the little children dancing in the courtyard for their morning exercises. Bao-bao seemed happy, he was smiling and he was never alone, encircled by a small group of friends. I was relieved, but he always cried Monday morning when I took him back to school, "Mama, why do I have to go? I want to stay with you. Don't make me go."

I'd say, "School is good for you." "China needs educated youths." "The teachers will miss you." "Everyone has to go to school." All these things. I hated myself for lecturing, but at least I didn't cry anymore.

"It's just like you and Uncle. Going away to the country," he said once, and I smiled immediately, pleased at his bravery.

"You're right! Just remember everything that happens during the week and *you* can tell me stories now. I want to know everything, everything." I kissed him on the forehead, but he squirmed away, already too big for my kisses.

Then after I took him to his school, watched him walk into the nursery, the teachers herding the others inside, the voices already surrounding him, laughter and shrieks and calls, I realized what he had said. "Just like you and Uncle"! What had I told him about those days when we lived in the country? During the Cultural Revolution, Mother had sent us to live outside Nanjing with a former classmate of hers, Auntie Gao, who had married a peasant. Mother and Father were sent far away, to be reeducated, and my brother and I had nowhere else to go.

Bao-bao's favorite stories involved the animals, of course. Auntie Gao's pigs (at least they were hers before the commune took over everything, although she secretly still considered them hers after that), the chickens, the arrogant roosters, the large gentle oxen. Bao-bao would love to see real farm animals. Someday, I told him, we'll visit a farm. There was a junior-high teacher—Mrs. Mu—who had married a peasant general during the Cultural Revolution. Her in-laws still lived in the countryside, just outside the city. She said we could come to visit sometime. Perhaps next Spring Festival, we'd start the new year with a trip to the countryside.

Everyone should have the opportunity to see how the peasants lived, I thought. It wasn't at all like the movies. More dirty, more congested, but also better—the smell, it wasn't like here in the city, all coal and exhaust and smoke. You could smell the earth, the night soil sometimes, but it was not so bad, not like pig shit. I wanted him to see the rice paddies reflecting the sky. Of course in the winter, there'd only be mud. Perhaps it would be better to try to go in the summer, when school was out, I thought, despite the heat. I vowed to talk to Mrs. Mu.

Many peasants were so very rich now, I wondered if I'd be surprised. The two-story houses for one family, the VCRs, the Japanese TVs, satellite dishes, all these things we couldn't afford. I read in the paper about one family that saved all their money and bought a car! There was a picture, black and white, so I couldn't tell what it was like really, but the text said it was red. Of course, Mrs. Mu said her husband's family was not really rich, not a "ten-thousand-yuan" family. Not yet anyway, she joked. She didn't like her relatives much. I could tell. It must have been hard for her, an intellectual with peasant in-laws. She didn't talk about it, but she held her face still when she mentioned them, her lips absolutely straight, tight against her teeth.

Still, it would be better for the peasants to be wealthy, not so thin and old by the time they were forty. Things hadn't changed that much. There would always be poverty in the countryside.

Anyway, as for Bao-bao's favorite story, it was about Yong-li's cock-fighting days. No matter how many times I told this story, he'd ask for it once more.

Uncle Bing ran the rooster fights even though it was against the law. "It's not gambling," he would complain in his gruff low voice, like a frog, if Auntie tried to scold him. "Who has any money? We're all equal, woman! The masses are united in the great proletarian leap forward!"

I imitated his voice as best I could, and I think I succeeded rather well. Bao-bao always giggled, and sometimes I would add a few lines to further the effect, although really Uncle Bing was a man of very few words.

Uncle resembled a rooster himself, he had small round eyes, bright and alert, never blinking. He had a long beaklike nose, a little red from his drinking. Some of the other men would tease him about it, calling him "yang gui," foreign devil, as they sat around us in the production meetings, waiting for the ration coupons to be distributed. He was a small man, tightly wound. He seemed very big when I first arrived, but really he was not so tall. By sixteen I was the same height.

He liked Yong-li from the start, pinched his round cheeks between his forefinger and thumb, grabbed him under the arms and swung Yong-li up on his shoulders. My brother was so small, a very thin thin boy at six, I worried about him. "Be careful, careful," I said that first day we met, watching my Di-di perched on this strange, silent man's shoulders.

Uncle Bing just laughed at me. Yong-li was quiet, eyes wide, scared but enjoying the view, too.

The men had cleared a circle of dirt behind a toolshed, outlined the arena with stones. They stood shouting as the two largest roosters

reared their heads up as high as they could, just like the lion dancers for Spring Festival, jumping high as the tamer approaches waving his paper fan. The feathers on the backs of their necks stood up like spikes. They held their wings out, trying to make themselves look bigger, and they eyed each other, first just staring, holding their heads sideways, each trying to size up his opponent, intimidate him. Then one hissed, throwing open his beak and sticking out his tongue.

They screamed next, their tongues extended, vibrating. It looked painful. Then the fight began: a thrust of the head, a sharp peck with the razor beaks, a swift kick with the fourth toe on the heel, clawing at the other bird. It was so fast, feathers flew, the birds screamed and screamed, it was not crowing. And then one bird drew blood—the bigger rooster, the faster rooster—leapt on the other's back, and rode it as if it were a hen, and the other rooster, humiliated, ran away as soon as it could. Or tried to.

Uncle Bing showed Yong-li how to stop the retreating bird. Yong-li ran around the perimeter, a giant cardboard square in hand or a basket or Uncle's jacket, blocking the retreating rooster's path.

"That's a winner you got there!" one of the men shouted, meaning Yong-li, not the rooster. Yong-li was quick.

Uncle Bing demonstrated to Yong-li how to hold the rooster, pinning its wings to its body so it wouldn't attack him. Then Yong-li could toss the bird back at the other rooster and the fight would begin again. Sometimes two men each held a bird and thrust them at each other, allowing them to peck at the other's face or throat. Then it became a contest between the two men as well, their skills; the roosters were their weapons.

It was a wasteful sport. The men lost cigarettes, carefully hoarded bottles of home-brewed *baijiu*, ration coupons. A cadre lost a Russian

fur hat that he claimed was given to him in the war. What was his name? I can see him with his thin moustache and shiny black bangs that fell across his face whenever he was excited, a black mole on his Adam's apple.

After he lost the hat, the rooster fights came to an end. They were decadent, he declared, birds were precious—we all ate so many chickens, there were only a few left, and the eggs did not seem to hatch one season. We were always hungry. The village couldn't spare the roosters. Cockfights were feudal, counterrevolutionary, anti-Mao. They were so many bad things, the men didn't dare stage them anymore. But one day I saw Yong-li and a group of boys gathered behind the toolshed.

It was winter, fresh snow still pure and white against the ground. I heard the shouts and ran from Auntie's house, where I'd been cleaning, or maybe washing things or studying Mao-thought, I can't remember. And the boys, gawky twelve-year-olds, all elbows and big feet, were shouting and laughing and then I heard one last cheer and the circle dispersed, quickly, each boy running in a different direction, a secret smile on his face, all headed purposefully away.

I ran toward the shed and I saw the dying rooster, lying bleeding in the snow, the red spilling away from it in bursts as it twitched. The victorious rooster, a large yellow bird the boys had nicknamed Lion, strutted back and forth, its chest puffed out, its head held high. It eyed me imperiously as I approached, my hands tucked in my armpits because it was cold.

Lion paced, then darted forward and pecked the fallen rooster again, once, twice. It cried, a sound like a baby screaming, then Lion jumped on his enemy and thrust himself against the rooster ferociously, tearing damp black feathers from its back. The weaker rooster cried louder, its whole body shaking, blood spraying into the air.

Yong-li ran forward and kicked Lion off.

Lion shook himself, preened his feathers with his beak, then ran a few yards away, hopped onto a fence post, and crowed. Puffs of steam clouded the air before him, like smoke from a dragon.

Yong-li peered down at the dying rooster. It now lay motionless, its one eye open and facing the sky. I didn't think Yong-li had seen me come, but then he called out to me.

"Look, Sis, it's a word." He pointed to the drops of blood clustered around the rooster's head. "It says 'heart.'" He laughed.

I wrinkled my nose at him and went back inside.

That was the last cockfight.

Sometimes I'd imitate the crow of a victorious rooster, then Bao-bao would join in until we both felt very silly and happy. We would laugh together until we couldn't laugh anymore.

Bao-bao always slept well on those nights. Sometimes when I got up later in the evening to check on him, I'd find him kicking in his sleep, smiling, though, watching rooster fights in his dreams.

5.

Auntie

Maybe it was strange, as my husband said, to tell your son stories about the Cultural Revolution, living in the countryside, but it wasn't *all* bad.

I remembered the weather, the great storms, lightning reaching out of the sky to touch the silver surface of a paddy, the time lightning struck a nine-hundred-year-old memorial stele and an old man leaning against it, resting after checking the crops when the storm came up, and how some of the women burned incense around the stele afterwards and placed bowls of pure white rice at its base even though the cadres told them not to engage in feudal customs. The spirit of the prince has been angered, they said.

We planted soybeans over the tomb of a minor prince of a short-lived dynasty that rose and fell sometime between the fall of the Tang and the

rise of the Song. Teacher Li explained in class that during the terrible feudal imperialist times the common people were like slaves to the whims of the oppressive lords who worked the peasants to the bone for their own pleasure, stealing the people's food, taxing them mercilessly, until the populace rose up in rebellion and overthrew their oppressors. Nanjing had served as the capital of nine such dynasties, for each time a dynasty was overthrown, the imperial court packed up their silks, their jade, their gold, brocades, scroll paintings, and texts and fled to Nanjing and lived here, oppressing the people until they died or the Northern invaders came and killed them all. Whoever was left buried these feudal princes in small tombs, now under our village's fields, and erected large stone statues on either side of a wide avenue that led to each tomb's entrance, which was sealed. The statues, in the forms of sacred animals—elephants, camels, winged lions, horned deer—or sometimes mandarins, lined the spirit path so that the spirit of the dead oppressive prince would not get lost. Histories were carved onto the stele so that everyone would know the virtues of the dead prince, his lineage, his names. Of course, what was written was all lies, he was a horrible person really. But the people were kind and the craftsmen skilled and that is why the stone statues had existed for so long. This is the way we learned history in those days.

We only had two figures. Teacher Li said there should be a whole row, but who knew what had happened to our village's. Torn down and broken up into bricks to build a new shed? Or a new dike to irrigate the fields? A lot of uses can come up for stone over nine hundred years.

My mother took me to see the sacred path just to the south of Nanjing's city gate, the only part left that the Japanese hadn't bombed. They had also missed the row of statues leading to the tomb of a minor Ming emperor. Mother took me there once—just me. I don't remember

where Yong-li was. Mother showed me the camels with long eyes, just like Chinese people's, and the elephants. She lifted me up on one so that I could sit on its smooth stone back. I wished elephants still lived in Nanjing so that I could ride a real one. I have no idea how old I was.

In our village, our statues were not quite as impressive. They were skinny and pock marked. The stele no one could read, it was written in classical Chinese. Even Teacher Li said he could not read the characters. I believed him. The other statue was a winged lion. Its body was a little long, catlike, and its wings looked like a chicken's, but this was our favorite. A flying cat, that was something.

Not long after Teacher Li told us the stories about the sacred path, Youth Supervisor Yue told us about the Red Guard teams in Nanjing who had gone to Qi Xia Mountain and beheaded all the arhats and Buddhas carved into the caves there. There were a thousand, he said, and they were all beheaded. He said the young students had also taken files and scratched out the characters on the stele on the mountain. They were thorough, going to all the feudal parks in Nanjing and removing the remnants of the oppressive imperialist and feudal societies. They were helping to build the new China. They were industrious.

We students decided we should knock over our stone lion and break it into bits and then the stone could be used to mend fences and dikes and maybe we could take a few stones home to mend holes in the walls that let the wind in. I can't remember who suggested this first, it seemed as though we all thought of it at once, the great collective will of the masses coming together. It was summer, too soon for the harvest, so a lot of the older boys were available to help us. I wasn't old enough to lead a brigade, I was only a Young Pioneer, but I vowed to do my best. I would haul stone, it was decided. That morning we all rose at dawn, I

tied on my red Young Pioneer kerchief, so proud, and we sang as we marched out into the soybeans, already fat and white on their stems.

It took all morning to knock over the one lion. We didn't know enough about physics to do it right. The boys just brought their fathers' tools—well, the commune's tools now—and hacked away. They chipped off the face, the eyes, rubbed the wings smooth of feathered details. It was hard going and we were all hot and irritable by noon. We tried to sing a few songs for inspiration: "Chairman Mao Is Our Shining Star," "The East Is Red," "I Love China." But it was very hot and we were hungry and we still weren't done yet.

Finally one of the boys decided they should attack the beast as if it were alive and so they struck it in the knees, from all sides at once. It worked. The knees chipped away and eventually the lion crashed head forward into the beans.

I heard the cheer. I'd given up long before and gone to sit in the shade of the stele. There were about four of us younger kids waiting there. I was about twelve then, Yong-li was too young to come with us at all. We were very conscious of hierarchies; age was important.

My group had gone over to the stele with the intention of carving away the characters off its surface. But we didn't have files, we'd brought shovels and trowels and I'd brought Auntie Gao's metal ladle. It bent in two on my first attempt to carve into the stone. My heart stopped beating for a full three seconds. It was horrifying. What would I tell her? I gave up then and sat in the shade. The others soon tired and we just sat, waiting for instructions from the older kids.

When we heard them shout, we all jumped up and ran over to the vanquished lion. We gathered in a circle, and the oldest boy said, "It's a victory of the people! Down with the feudal society!" And we all cheered. Someone said we should sing, but to be honest we were all too

tired and thirsty. Then the oldest girl said we should go back and tell Teacher Li of our deed and plan how to cut up the stone and carry it to the village—tomorrow. We all thought that sounded like a good idea.

Walking back from the fields, I remember it was still sunny, the sky clear, although it was windy. Far away along the horizon dark clouds suggested rain. We were too tired to chat amongst ourselves, we were quiet, so that I was conscious of the sound of the wind. Quite fierce for a sunny day. Someone—was it Gong Hua?—pointed behind us. "Look, a storm's coming!" The clouds were advancing rapidly, unfurling across the sky, black and green and gold, like a giant bruise. We could see the rain streaming to the earth. It was frightening. Would there be hail, a tornado? I'd learned to respect the weather in the countryside. We all broke into a panicked run. Before I reached Auntie's house, I felt the first drop, huge and cold like ice, splashing against my hand. Thunder boomed. I'd never seen a storm come so quickly. Later I would see many such storms, learn to recognize the signs, the pattern of hot days, the return of the wind, the copper-colored horizon.

Auntie and I watched from the open window, speculating whether the dark fingers extending from the clouds would actually touch the ground. Tornadoes were rare but one twister a few years back had taken the roofs of several homes, Auntie said, and a pregnant sow had been tossed into the air then dropped, killed.

Yong-li and Uncle Bing came running in, wet and smiling. I busied myself drying Yong-li off, washing his mud-splattered face. The thunder shook the house. Lightning bolts crisscrossed between the earth and the sky. As many as seven at a time. Then without warning, the rain eased, the thunder grew fainter and the storm had moved on.

We ran outside again, just to see the water gushing in between the paddies, roiling through the drainage ditches that ran alongside the

soybean fields. The drifts of hail were already beginning to melt. Yong-li ran and grabbed a fistful of the ice. He threw a bunch at me but missed. A few of his friends came running out and they too grabbed the ice, jumped over the banks. Just like winter. The peasants ran, cursing, into their fields to survey the damage.

"Hey!" Fat Ping shouted and jumped up and down. He pointed at twin rainbows, the first I'd ever seen. We traced their arcs through the air. "Come on!" He tore off towards the soybeans, splashing through the mud puddles. "Let's find the ends!"

Yong-li took off immediately after his friend and a half dozen or so of the other kids but I hung back. I knew Auntie would be angry if we got so filthy. There was work to do now that the storm had passed. But then I knew it was too late, we'd be in trouble anyway, so I ran after them, the mud sucking at my feet, the air cold as I gulped it down my throat.

I don't know who first saw the man resting by the stele, just sitting on his haunches, his back leaning against the stone. We waved to him to look at the double rainbow but he didn't answer. Someone shouted at him, "Comrade, don't be lazy! Get up!" But he didn't move. We had to laugh at him. But then suddenly all at once, we felt it, that something was wrong. I reached out and grabbed Yong-li's arm and pulled him closer. He held on to my hand tightly.

A couple of the older boys ran over to the stele. The man was dead. He was black, someone said. Charred like a piece of wood. Someone else said, no, his face was blue, and he looked like he was sleeping, except for the blue face. We all looked at each other terrified, I remember Fat Ping burst into tears. We knew we had caused this, by knocking over the lion, scraping away the stele's memorial. The dead prince and his ancestors wanted revenge. We didn't say anything, but we

thought the same thing: should we tell the grown-ups? I would've voted no. But it didn't matter. They found out anyway.

Fat Ping's mother hit him against the side of the head. *"Aiya!"* she cried. "My son is an idiot! Look what you've done! So much bad luck."

A group of men formed a circle around the dead man. I tugged Yong-li's hand and ran away, pulling him as fast as I could. The women were shouting to each other, their voices rising above the fields, cawing, like a flock of crows.

Auntie pulled us inside her house. She packed back and forth. "You're lucky you weren't killed in the storm, too. Don't listen to what they say. Don't listen."

We heard the women through the walls.

"Don't worry, don't worry," she said, pacing.

Yong-li was white as a ghost. He sat on the floor, hugging his knees, listening to every word Auntie said, his eyes wide. He nodded as she spoke. He looked the way I felt inside.

Uncle ran back inside a few minutes later. His whole body twitched. He stared at us.

"Don't worry," Auntie said loudly. "They were carrying out the Chairman's will."

At the dining hall that evening, Comrade Jiang gave a speech about science and superstition. We were all very hungry but he made everyone wait in line, our rice bowls in hand, while he spoke, the vats of rice and soupy cabbage growing cold and glutinous as we waited. He said, "Everyone knows lightning strikes the tallest object in a field." He implied that the old man must have been senile. "Comrade Lu should have gone inside when he saw the storm was coming." Then we all followed him in singing, "The East is red/The sun has risen/China has given

birth to Mao Zedong . . ." We were very hungry by then, but we couldn't eat until we had sung the verses three times.

Later there were study groups. There must have been. I don't remember now. It didn't matter anyway. For me, Auntie's word was all that counted.

People might say she was ignorant, superstitious, too emotional. All these bad qualities. But I wanted my son to respect her memory. She was mother and father to me, I could admit it now, no disrespect to anyone, it wasn't unfilial. I wanted to be honest. Honest. She was a complicated woman, she made my life very difficult, I feared her. I don't know if I could call it love exactly, but she helped me survive, to become the person I am today. And I wouldn't ever say that was a bad thing.

When I met Auntie for the first time, I was so disappointed. The buildup had been impossible to live up to. Mother had done her best to make Auntie seem perfect—"The prettiest girl in our school! All the boys wrote her love letters." "The fastest runner—even the boys couldn't catch her, yet she was so small!" She didn't want us to be scared. I can forgive Mother's exaggerations.

Because of Mother, I thought of Auntie in terms of the revolutionary heroines we studied every day in school: the Iron Brigade Girls, the women of Daxi, rosy cheeked, shiny black haired, young and cheerful, willing to sacrifice everything for the Motherland. Of course I was excited at the thought of actually meeting such a woman. I wasn't sure about living with her, though. I remember how my mother phrased it: "Auntie is a true revolutionary." She'd married a peasant, so no one struggled against her.

I knew my father's name had appeared on a Big Character Poster, kids

at school told me. He was counterrevolutionary. Intellectual. Bourgeois. After that, Mother let me stay home from school whenever I said I didn't feel well. She never asked me what was wrong. I always thought, Oh, I'm so lucky, she doesn't take me to the doctor. I felt guilty too: I'm lying to my mother, telling stories, and she, so trusting, believes me. What a bad girl.

Father? I don't remember him well. I remember him burning papers in a metal basin, I remember him yelling at us when we asked what he was doing. Mother took us to the rallies and we all shouted out against the counterrevolutionaries but I never thought of Father in that way. He was always distant, even before the trouble. My opinion of him never changed. Then he was gone, to be reeducated in the countryside. Yong-li cried because he sensed Mother was upset but I secretly felt happy. Now he wouldn't be here to yell at us all the time.

Mother was always cheerful, always smiling, when the aunties from the neighborhood block committee came to drink tea and talk about her work at the university. They smiled too but in a way that showed all their teeth, even the molars. When the aunties came, Mother told me to take Yong-li out to play. "Exercise is important to become strong citizens," she said. It seemed normal at the time.

And when she said we were going to live with Auntie Gao in the countryside, just me and Yong-li, I remember I thought why? why? why? I thought, You're going to be with Father and you're leaving us. You don't want us anymore. But then she told us the stories about Auntie Gao and I thought she was an amazing hero and I was lucky to be going to live with her. And everyone said we should learn from the peasants. I wanted to be good, above all else. For once. I imagined myself saving the village—beating flames with my jacket to spare the soybeans, planting rice until my fingers bled. We would have so

much food to eat that we would become a model village. Heroically I would walk in bare feet in the snow, firewood strapped to my back, so that the homes of the elderly would have heat. Just like the story-books. So I didn't cry when Mother said suddenly we would leave the next day.

The night before we left, I packed carefully, folding everything very neatly. Mother stood beside me for a long time not saying anything but Yong-li was peevish. She walked around the apartment with him; he clung to her neck, shouting, "I don't want to go!" I felt that he was very young and didn't understand anything.

When Mother brought us to the long-distance bus station early the next morning, Yong-li's face was red in splotches from his crying. Mother carried him as if he were still a baby, instead of a boy of six, holding his legs as he rode on her back, arms clasped around her neck. I was so jealous, so jealous, even now. I was only ten! I wasn't so big. Sometimes I would look at my students, so young, and I would remember how back then we all acted as if I were grown up. I followed a few paces behind, carrying our one suitcase. A sturdy brown bag, it had been Father's, but he'd only been allowed one piece of luggage when he left. So now it was mine. I thought it seemed a proper bag for a long journey, already worn and smelling slightly of oil. A manly smell. My arms ached, I could feel the muscles pulling at my shoulder blades, but I didn't complain. I pretended I was an Iron Brigade Girl, carrying a wounded comrade in from the field, she'd fallen ill, been attacked by bees, gored by an ox, all the things I imagined happened in the countryside. I was a real revolutionary, strong and brave.

The station was crowded; endless rows of blue-and-green-clad bodies took up every bench, every inch of the floor. A few peasant families

camped out on the stone floor of the waiting room, children sprawled out on patched quilts, large brown mothers nursing infants in front of everyone. Cigarette smoke made the air dark. A whistle sounded and a voice gargled over the P.A. I looked up to Mother for directions, but she merely squinted at the destination sign on the far wall, her mouth moving as she read. She began to move away, sucked into the mass of people, as if falling into a deep river. I fought at the legs and arms that came my way, struggling to keep up. And it wasn't fun anymore. We were being abandoned. I knew it then.

When we were finally allowed to board, Mother was crying. She handed Yong-li up the steps of the bus to the driver, then turned to me. She hugged me. Her breath was very warm on my neck; it was a chilly morning for July. "Remember to brush your teeth, no matter what anyone tells you. Sometimes country people have strange ideas." I pulled away, turned my face. I wanted Mother to know I was angry, and she let go.

The passengers waiting in line behind me pushed me forward, swept me inside the bus. I felt guilty and waved from the window, but Mother had already turned away, retreating into the cloth sea.

Yong-li slept the entire ride, not long, maybe an hour and a half, but the pressure of his head against my arm cut off the circulation. It hurt terribly. I wanted to cry but the pain helped me somehow. I didn't have to think. Everything was so strange. I should've been afraid, or lonely, or sad. But I only remember being annoyed at Yong-li. Such a baby.

The scenery passed by the window quickly but never changed. Green patches of soybeans and corn were divided by shimmering bands of water that reflected the sky just as if a mirror had been broken and scattered there on purpose. Mile after mile without buildings or towns or other buses anywhere. Hunched figures walked through the bands of

green, carrying large wooden dippers. They broke the surface of the mirrors then cast shards over the crops, over and over.

Auntie Gao was waiting at the bus stop when we arrived looking like city kids in our solid blue Mao suits, unpatched and unsoiled. Auntie rolled her eyes when she saw us. She was fatter than I had expected, twice Mother's size, with a flat face and small eyes that disappeared into the folds of her splotchy skin when she talked. I would not have recognized her as my revolutionary hero, but she came to us first, putting a rough heavy hand on each of our heads. Yong-li giggled.

"Follow me. Carry your things. You've got to be quick to survive in the country." I didn't know what she meant then. Auntie Gao walked very slowly, as if she were practicing *tai ji quan*. "Come on!" she commanded, her voice crackling like a fire. I obeyed.

I never forgot the first time she hit me.

It was over Mother's photograph, the only one. I wish, I wish I'd saved it.

We'd been in the village nearly four months before the letter—the first—with the photograph arrived. I know now it was a privilege to write to her children. She had to earn it. Poor Mother. All the hard work she must have done to write that one letter.

In the picture, Mother's hair was cut short, boylike. She looked very young. Sitting on an enormous tractor, she waved at the camera. Mother was a model worker. To be photographed was an honor, I knew that. "Women hold up half the sky," Mother wrote, quoting Chairman Mao. "I am driving a two-ton tractor! Women can do anything." The photo was black and white but I imagined that the tractor was a bright red, beautiful and shiny like the beads that Mother used to wear long ago, when that kind of thing was still allowed. My

mother, the hero. She'd come pick us up soon. Or send for us. I read the letter several times, expecting hints, but there was nothing. She quoted her work brigade leader, the number of work points she'd earned. I was angry about that, the lack of concern for her children. But I wasn't going to show anyone. I was going to be the daughter of a revolutionary hero, not an intellectual antirevolutionary bourgeois black element.

I showed the picture to Auntie Gao, who nodded and smiled, but not in the way I had expected. Auntie looked as though she had stubbed her toe. "Practice writing your characters," she said. She must have been horrified, I guess, seeing her classmate, the city girl, the university professor, dressed like a peasant. She must've known what suffering that signified, the work. I thought she was jealous.

"No!" I said, jumping out the door of Auntie's small wooden house. "I have to water the pigs!"

Auntie Gao waddled into the sunlight. She shook her dishcloth at me. "Your parents want you to study."

"No!" I said, running across the rutted dirt yard. I ran towards the well. "I'm a revolutionary hero! I do the work of the common people! Only bourgeois running dogs study books!"

The pigs were waiting for me. They were black with white bellies and ears that nearly touched the ground. Fluid ran down their chins from their nostrils. I splashed water into their troughs. The pigs oinked. I laughed back. I was a common girl! A screw in the socialist machinery!

When I returned from the pigpen, Auntie Gao was waiting. She grabbed me by the arm and threw me against the wooden table that took up most of the kitchen. A string of cabbage hanging on the wall fell to the dirt floor. I remember watching them fall. No one had ever hit me before. Father had threatened to spank me once when I wouldn't leave

his desk alone. I had hidden my cutouts from magazines and comics in his drawers, played with his ink stones—a sheltered child.

Auntie hit me again, this time with the broom. I remember crying. Why? Why when I was such a good girl?

"You stupid girl! What's more useless than a girl who isn't obedient!"

Auntie Gao picked me up by the arm and sat me down on the low bench beside the table. "Read your lessons."

"Di-di doesn't have to study." I wanted Yong-li to get in trouble too. I wasn't so innocent. I feel guilty about this, even now.

Auntie slapped me on the side of the head. My ear burned. I held my head with my hands, trying to focus my eyes. Auntie took my hands and wrapped my fingers around one of the worn copybooks the village school used. Everything was clear, sharp, I remember as if it were happening now. "Read this to me!" Auntie hissed, her face close to mine. I hiccupped. "Read!"

The characters circled the page. I had the first line memorized, it was simple, I had learned these lessons years before, but I pretended to read. Auntie's breath like a dragon's was hot against my neck. I hated her, I hated Mother, I hated Yong-li.

He came home riding on Uncle Bing's shoulders, smelling like the oxen he was learning to drive, chattering like a monkey. Auntie Gao handed their rice bowls to me to wash after every meal. I had to wash my clothes and his. If he did something wrong in school, if he broke something, threw rocks at the chickens, I was blamed. And he never spoke up. That afternoon, he must've seen that I was crying, but he allowed Uncle Bing to tickle him and ignored me.

Children are cruel.

* * *

But I'm not being fair. Auntie had my well-being in mind. She meant well. I know it, I know it.

Like when my period began. I was frightened. I showed her my soiled underwear, I thought I was dying. It wasn't as I'd imagined it'd be, the blood falling in clear drops, orderly. My blood was dark and chunky, my guts hurt. Auntie grabbed me by the hair. "Never let anyone see," Auntie warned me. She showed me how to wash, how to fold cloth into a pad. Hide everything.

The peasants were so ignorant. It's ridiculous that we were ever supposed to learn from them. Women were possessed by evil spirits, women were unlucky. If something went wrong—a sow rolled over on her litter, the soybeans were being eaten by grasshoppers—it was because of some woman! It was best not to let anyone know your time, lest you be blamed for something. All red was good red except a woman's own blood.

But there were other reasons to hide my period.

I stared at the boys who worked in the fields. They grew taller every month. I blushed (another bad red) when they called to me.

"Never talk to the boys," Auntie Gao warned, "or you'll never leave this place. You'll never see your parents again."

I was considered pretty. The boys in class would giggle, nudging each other. Even the teacher made comments. "The pretty soldier," he'd say. I hated it and the other girls hated me. They said I didn't have to work as hard, they said I didn't need to study, I'd get good marks anyway. They said I'd marry a handsome man, a city man. They knew I'd leave the countryside and they wouldn't. I worked harder than any of them. It didn't matter.

Auntie meant well. She frightened me, but she wanted to protect me. I honestly believe this.

*   *   *

Once, lying on my cotton bedroll, I had cramps so bad that I couldn't sleep. My feet were frozen, no circulation. It was cold: the coal stove was in the center of the room beside Auntie and Uncle's bed and the heat did not reach my corner even though we were separated only by a pale gray cotton curtain. I shivered. I listened to the wind race outside, slamming against the house. I wished it would blow the walls down, on top of everyone.

"Eat the pain," Auntie's voice buzzed through the curtain.

I sat straight up, my heart thumping. I had not heard her approach. Auntie drew the curtain aside and moonlight sliced across my midriff. I thought she was angry. I shook. She sensed the weakness of my city-girl body. I braced myself for her pinching fingers, her hand against my neck. The dark grew closer. I was dizzy.

But Auntie only knelt beside me, her thigh pressing into my side. She smelled of sweet cigar smoke. "I can read faces," she whispered, in a voice I had not heard before. Auntie's fat thick fingers held my chin, pushed my face one way then the other. "You are a lucky, lucky girl. You have a good-fortune face, like your mother." Auntie smiled. Her face cracked, the lines spreading to the edges of her jaw. "*Your* husband will be a better man, a city man, and your life will be soft like goose feathers." Auntie paused to pick her ear.

"There is a weak spot, here." She tapped a mole on my right temple. "And there is green in your eyes." She smacked her jaws. I saw that several of her teeth were missing. "Hmm. I don't remember what this means. Why don't I remember anymore?" Her voice dropped off, incoherent. Auntie was crying. "I read your mother's face, all the girls, all the pretty

girls, we were young, so young. I could read everything. Now I'm too old." She blew her nose onto the floor. Cleared her throat and spit.

"You're lucky," she continued. "You won't have to marry a stupid peasant who can't give you any children. Such a pretty girl." Auntie let go of my face. "Tonight you'll dream of your husband." Then she raised herself, pushing with one hand on the floor, the other against her fat knee, panting. She walked back to her bed slowly. I pulled the curtain closed, hugged my knees to my chest, burying my head between my arms. I couldn't sleep the rest of the night.

6.

Mother

My brother, Yong-li, said he didn't remember Mother at all. But I remembered how he cried when he learned she was dead, he howled, his face turned bright scarlet. He was too old to cry like that, I remember Uncle Bing saying, very alarmed. Auntie turned to me. "Make him stop. What kind of sister are you? Set an example!"

I told him Mother was a martyr for the people. The commune would erect a statue in her honor. Just like in the People's Park, remember?

He pushed me away. He wiped his nose on his arm, and I reached out to make him stop and he shouted, "No!" Then he ran out the front door. I squinted into the sunlight. He shouted as he ran, "You don't care! You hate Mother! You only love *her*!"

He meant Auntie, I knew. I stood beside Auntie and I wanted to fold up inside myself, hang myself from the crossbeam of the front door, feel

the weight in my feet pulling against my neck. I would be dead, they would be cursed, and sorry then.

Mother was part of a brigade building sandbag ramparts against the raging Yangtze, swollen from the endless rains that spring. She drowned.

Auntie ripped strips of white muslin for us to wear around our heads in mourning. She pushed the ghostly cloth into my hands solemnly.

"For you and your brother. Sew the ends so they don't fray away into nothing. No point in wasting good cloth," she said. Auntie left to finish pickling the spring radishes with the other women.

I stared at the cloth, so angry.

I found Yong-li behind the pigpen, pelting the piglets with dirt clods and rocks. They squealed and ran in circles, trying to escape the barrage. They sounded like babies crying.

"Oh, stop," I said, covering my ears.

He kicked a chicken as it ran by crazily, scared by all the noise. It was a laying hen, one of the best, and it landed heavily on its side, lay flat and still. It stood up and staggered and fell down again. I thought an egg must have broken inside it. It was terrified, its head jerked forward and back, looking in all directions, trying to understand. He ran over and kicked it once more and this time it clucked once, a choking sound, and died. We never told anyone how it died. I'm not sure who found it. It was a terrible waste to kill a laying hen, food was so scarce, our stomachs growled all the time. I was afraid that someone had seen and would report him, but no one ever did.

The commune gathered together in our dining hall that night while Party Secretary Ning praised Mother. The mosquitoes were huge, insolent, from all that rain. We swatted them with both hands as the Secretary's voice droned in our ears.

"She died serving the people! This is a glorious death. We should not mourn but rejoice. We should all follow Comrade Yao's example. Giving freely of our life so that the masses may prosper." The Secretary, an old man, spoke slowly, carefully, so that we could clap or cheer or shout slogans—"Long live Chairman Mao!" "The class war is never over!" "Revolution first"—in between his pronouncements. It was hot, our bodies pressed together on the small wooden stools, squatting, standing as the Secretary talked on and on, his voice breaking with the strain of his shouts as he made an example out of Mother's death.

I looked over at Yong-li to make sure that he was still awake. A giant mosquito was poised on his forehead. I slapped it, and the blood spilled onto his clean muslin headband, making a red stain like a third eye.

"What'd'ya do that for?" He pinched my arm, but I didn't flinch. I laughed.

Some of the farmers looked at me, a little surprised, but turned away quickly. I would have made a face at them. I was the martyr's daughter. What could they do to me, but talk and talk and sigh and call me a poor child, so unfortunate, and avoid us, as if we would bring them bad luck. Which was fine with me. I didn't want to talk to them.

I didn't cry then, and when I did later, it was for the wrong reasons. I must've been bitter, I must've resented living with Auntie, her life and Mother's death. I was young, but young children were so powerful then. Our words could hurt so easily. People rationalize about the Cultural Revolution now, that the children didn't know what they were saying, they were being used, power struggles between political factions, brigade leaders, party section heads. We were used and we enjoyed it. I have to admit this. It's terrible, but it would be worse to lie.

My time for revenge came because of school.

School was one dark room with a few other sons and daughters of rightists and reactionaries as well as the village children. Teacher Li was a former Nanjing University student sent to the countryside but too useless for any work besides teaching. He wrote characters on the pitted blackboard. Entire words disappeared in its uneven surface. Occasionally the other students asked me for help, they struggled even to copy the words from the board. I did feel pride, it's true. I knew I was clever.

I wrote an essay after Mother died. "The great soldier and peasant Lei Feng says all life can have its value, even if brief, like mother's. 'If you are a drop of water, don't you moisten an inch of earth? If you are a ray of sunlight, don't you lighten a bit of darkness? If you are a stalk of grain, don't you nourish useful life?' Lei Feng died when he was only in his twenties! He was a good man, teaching a comrade to drive when the telephone pole fell on his head and killed him. We do not know why these things happen, but we must not be sad. Lei Feng died serving the people. My mother died in the flood this spring, also serving the people! Is this not a glorious death?" I crossed out "death" and wrote in the characters for "life."

"When my brother and I put on white to show our mourning, I also was proud to be the daughter of a woman who really understood the spirit of Lei Feng."

Teacher Li was very pleased. He laughed and put his hand on the top of my head, a little heavy. "You are a very good writer." He did not say I was a good revolutionary or a good Young Pioneer or a forward-thinking antibourgeois common person. But that was okay.

Teacher Li gave my essay to the Party Secretary, or at least he must have given it to the Education Chair, who gave it to the Youth Director, who gave it to the Deputy Assistant Commune Head in charge of work-point distribution, who was good friends with Party Secretary Ning, who

was very pleased when someone, perhaps Teacher Li, read it to him, as he himself was illiterate. At the Thursday-night meeting Farmer Cao reported on a new method of planting soybeans that he had found would make it possible to use previously fallow lands, and the old woman Wen who had only one tooth, yellow and turned, complained that she was not so young anymore and shouldn't be expected to carry such heavy buckets of slop to the pigs and couldn't some of the young people, some of those useless city kids, do it for her, after such a long hard life it only seemed fair, wasn't she part of the people that they all were supposed to serve? Then Deputy Secretary Jiang announced that a work team would be formed to dig a new latrine as the current one for the cadres had flooded during the last rain and everyone knew its foundation was mud so that the walls sloped until last week it fell in upon itself in one big splash and so who would volunteer for this great proletarian act of service for the people? Then Party Secretary Ning stood up, brushing peanut shells off his lap, and announced that the revolutionary student Lin Jun would read her inspiring essay, "The Spirit of Lei Feng Lives on Always."

My heart beat so rapidly, I couldn't be sure I was breathing anymore. I stood very still and tried not to look at the faces turned towards me and instead read loudly and clearly the way the Red Guards had when they read, leading the rallies through the streets, music and drums, all the pretty girls with red ribbons around their necks, sometimes a sash, before Yong-li and I had to leave the city. The country kids had never seen anything like that. I had told them about the Red Guards and the music and all the beautiful teenagers, leaving out the later bits when the bad ones, that's how Mother had described them, started raiding the apartments around our family's and made so much noise late at night with their shouts and, once, gunshots. It had all been very exciting.

I read, everyone clapped and smiled, and Party Secretary Ning put his large round hand on my head. "Good girl," he said, patting.

I felt very important, and I liked this feeling. Later I overheard several of the women telling Auntie how clever I was and she shook her head, "Oh, her? Not at all. It's Lei Feng's words that are good." I hated her then.

A few days later—a week?—I was washing the laundry in the cold stream, high that year, too. Slipping on the muddy bank, I dug my cloth shoes in between two granite boulders and scrubbed until my hands hurt from the cold. Then I stopped and put my hands under my armpits, head down, waiting a minute for my circulation to return. Out of the corner of my eye, I saw a large woman, as old as Auntie, her big feet spread apart, a firm stance.

"Ah, Lin Jun, there you are."

"Comrade?"

The woman's smile was too wide, enough to hurt her face. She hesitated, I waited patiently while the woman struggled for the words. "I have to ask you a question." The woman paused again. Her eyes were very small and dark, like a pig's. I laughed, surprising myself.

"What's so funny? Don't you respect your representative of the Women's Federation?"

"Yes," I said, even though I thought, I'm not a "woman."

"I'm not joking around. This is very serious. Yes. Do you remember your essay you read to us?"

I readjusted the cap that I wore to protect my complexion. The bill cut the woman in half in my line of sight.

"Why did you 'put on white to show our mourning'? Didn't you know this is a feudal tradition? This is the new liberated society!" The woman's face was red and still. Then her tone changed. "You're just a child, really,

you are a progressive youth, our future." She smiled, baring her teeth again. "Someone must have told you to do this wrong thing. This is how I see it. This is what I was thinking, 'She must have been led astray.' "

I looked at this woman directly, not at all shy. I didn't hesitate. "My Auntie told us to do it."

The woman nodded. "I knew you were a good girl." The woman turned and climbed up the bank easily, soon disappearing over the rim where the sky met the earth, a black head floating above the tall bromegrass.

I don't remember what I was thinking, my heart was beating so fast. I knew the woman wanted me to say that. I knew that it would cause Auntie problems. And I felt excited, glad about that, revenge.

The next week, during the production-point meeting, the work brigade criticized Auntie for her feudal ways. How dare she promote superstition, corrupt the youth, didn't she know hundreds of millions of people were struggling right now all across China, sacrificing their life blood to fight the feudal past and she taught the old ways to the young! Auntie sat with her large, round face pointed at her lap, her wide legs held together, feet flat on the floor. The head of the Women's Federation stood up, waving her fist in the air and stomping her large foot. "We should struggle against the reactionary Gao Liang!" And the other peasants cheered. Auntie should criticize herself; the village cadres would read her self-criticism the next week and decide if she should be punished.

I watched from the back with the other girls, shouting and singing with the crowd. It felt good to be in the right for once, not to have someone telling me how I ought to be all the time. I thought if only the room weren't so hot, airless, and everyone smelling of sweat. I had to put my head between my knees. But I wasn't feeling guilty, just dizzy.

That night Auntie sat at the rough wooden table, writing her self-criticism neatly in a small blue notebook. I could not remember ever having seen Auntie sit at the table before. Auntie rubbed her face with her palms. "*Aiya*, Xiao Lin, how do you write the character for 'struggle'? I can't remember. Does it have the 'hand' radical or not?"

"No." I was darning my socks.

"Just like Lei Feng, so helpful," Auntie said sweetly, her voice smooth and soft.

I didn't dare look at her.

A moment passed and then Auntie asked again, "I'm so old, I forget too much. How do you write 'sacrifice'? After the 'heart,' what is there? Hm?"

Something in Auntie's voice made me afraid. I stared at my shoes and noticed that they were covered in yellow mud, from the stream. I'd forgotten to wash them. I scraped the toe against the floor, watched the scab of caked earth flake off.

"You can use my dictionary," I finally offered. I got up and dug the worn volume out of my pile of books by my bedroll. The cover was torn, I noticed, alarmed. I had no way of getting another one, I wanted mine to last forever. "Here." I stood at the far side of the table and held the book out to Auntie hunched over the table as if growing there.

Auntie looked up, then her hand shot out and grabbed me by the wrist, pulled me forward across the table. My chin hit the wood, hard. Auntie hit me across the ear with the dictionary, then slapped the back of my head with the palm of her hand. I struggled to get up, as Auntie held my face, my lucky good-fortune face, down against the table, her weight against my neck. Neither of us cried out.

I thrashed my legs, arched my back, and swung with my arms, but Auntie was stronger, heavier. I felt my nose hit the wood, again, again. I

could barely see. I reached up and tried to pull Auntie's hands out of my hair, but Auntie released me first. I scrambled off the table, and then Auntie kicked the table over, against my leg, and I fell to the ground. I remember Auntie's face, so red, fierce, contorted into a mass of wrinkles. I wanted to scream but couldn't. I wanted to jump up and run away but I couldn't move at all.

Auntie grabbed a rice bowl in one hand and drew her arm back. "How dare *you*!" But before she could throw it, the door opened and Uncle Bing and Yong-li came in, back from the men's study group.

"What're you doing?" Uncle Bing's voice sounded like a dog's bark— loud, sharp, the syllables unformed. "Don't be crazy!"

Auntie threw the bowl against the far wall. It shattered and she burst into tears. She cried loudly. It embarrassed me to hear her, the ugly childish sounds like hiccups and farts.

Yong-li helped me to my feet; my knees were still weak. He held on to my hand, and I realized he was terrified. He was shaking, and leaned against me. His small fingers were cold with his fear. I squeezed them with both hands. Somehow comforting him, I lost my own fear.

Uncle Bing righted the table, grunting once. He picked up the notebook, the torn dictionary, the pencil, ignoring his wailing wife. Then he turned around and hit her full in the face with his open hand.

I remember telling Yong-li, "Don't worry, don't worry." He sniffed, and didn't say anything.

I wished then that I'd killed a chicken, too. Instead.

7.

In-Laws

We took Bao-bao twice a month to visit my in-laws on the weekend when he was home from school. It was a ritual like the Monday-morning meetings, like the new anticorruption programs initiated every few months by the government, like thinking up a new way to drill my students on irregular English verbs. Potentially a good idea, but I was never sure it actually accomplished anything.

Our visit in early October for Mid-Autumn Festival was typical. Like all our visits for the past five years, Shao Hong was irritable, I was harried, and Bao-bao was doing his best to postpone the whole adventure.

"Hurry," Shao Hong called, pacing in the living room. "We're always late."

Bao-bao squirmed. "I don't want to go," he said, sitting down so that I couldn't pull his pants up.

"Nai-nai and Ye-ye love you very much. They want to see their grandson." I straddled him, pinning his shoulders between my knees so that he couldn't get away.

"I don't want to!"

"Sometimes you have to do things you don't want to." I was losing my patience. My hairband tumbled to the floor.

"Why?" The boy was not going to help at all, I could see.

"Because." I snapped his pants shut and pulled his shirt over his hard round belly. "Because this is a way to show you love someone."

"But I don't love Ye-ye and Nai-nai."

"Sshh! Don't say that. Of course you do." I picked up my hairband in one hand and hefted Bao-bao up on my hip. He really was too big now to pick up like that. He grew so fast. I set him down in the hall and took his hand.

"Hmph," Shao Hong said. He ushered us out the door.

Nai-nai did not answer until the fourth knock, as usual.

"Xiao Hu!" she cried, calling Shao Hong "Little Tiger" as if he were still a child. Nai-nai grabbed her son around the neck and kissed his cheek. I followed them inside, pulling our son with one hand, a box of moon-cakes in the other.

"Oh, look at Bao-bao," Nai-nai pinched his cheeks. I watched my son's face turn red. "You're too thin! Your mother doesn't feed you enough. Oooh." She looked up at me suddenly. "He's not sick, is he? We don't want to catch a cold."

"Good morning, Ye-ye," I called to my father-in-law, who sat in his armchair by the window. He did not acknowledge me. I couldn't tell if he was just moody or deaf or had fallen into another spell of despair.

"Oh, you're so late, Xiao Hu. Lunch is getting cold. I never know when

to start cooking. Sometimes you come early. Sometimes late. I never know." Nai-nai shuttled between the kitchen and the dining-room table, carrying bowls of stir-fry.

"Give it a rest, Ma," Shao Hong muttered under his breath.

"What?" Nai-nai sang, arranging the bowls on the table.

"Let me help." I escaped into the kitchen, pretending to look for a potholder.

I hated witnessing their fights. The weight of the past was so strong in my in-laws' home, it frightened me. But I knew this was not how Nai-nai thought. She saw her way as best: enduring, eating bitterness, and then bragging about it. Her misery circled the room in echoes. "I could've divorced Shao Hong's father, who would have blamed me? He was a counterrevolutionary, I was an idealist. I organized the first Mao study group in the neighborhood. I saved Shao Hong from the Red Guards. Didn't I tell you before?"

I'd heard these stories so many times. What they meant was, I was soft, I was spoiled, I would never measure up to her.

"Xiao Hu, you look so pale. You're working too hard. I always tell you just to relax sometimes. You were always like this, even as a child. So active." I heard Nai-nai laugh.

Ye-ye shuffled out of the room. He cleared his throat loudly in the bathroom then spat. He spat again.

I glanced out at my husband from behind the kitchen door. During the Cultural Revolution, he had been forced to denounce his father. No one would tell me the details. It was a slight against me, in a way, not telling me when it was so important still. After all these years. Another way to say I was just a daughter-in-law. I didn't fight about it, make demands. There was no point. I'd always tried to make things smooth

for Bao-bao. I wanted him to have grandparents, I didn't want to add to the tensions. And frankly, I thought, it was probably best not to know.

Shao Hong stared at the table, his cheeks bulging as he ate.

"Some people like to live in the past," Nai-nai said loudly, calling to her husband. How many times had they played this game?

Nai-nai shouted at the bathroom door, "You were the only one who suffered? Xiao Hu did what he had to do. What do little boys know? You think any of us had any choices? Poor Lin Jun's parents were sent down to the countryside. Where are they now? Huh? Your son could be an orphan now!" Nai-nai shouted, waving her chopsticks in the air, conducting an invisible chorus. "Talk to your father," Nai-nai whispered to her son. "He loves you. Go talk to him."

Shao Hong slurped his tea. "What's the use, Ma?"

I leaned against the refrigerator, the faint vibrations tingling against my thigh. I knew I should go out to them, eat, smile, eat. But they didn't seem to miss me. Even Bao-bao was eating the burnt pork strips that Nai-nai called food without me. Finally, I pulled back my shoulders and returned to the living room, took my place at the table.

My father-in-law refused to come out of the bathroom, however.

"He likes to think in there sometimes," Nai-nai explained with a shrug.

He knew how to deal with these family dinners, I thought.

8.

Father

"What a movie your life would make," Chen Hua liked to say. She meant this as a compliment. An exciting movie. A good movie. I'd shake my head. I didn't want to see my life over and over, everything repeated before my eyes. Once was enough.

I saw this movie once where a woman and her father are reunited many years after the Cultural Revolution. No, it wasn't traumatic for me, as you might expect. Not at all. It was entertaining. The woman was a famous opera star and the father a poor farmer, maybe he raised animals, it was never quite clear, just scenes of this old man with a white scraggly beard surrounded by sheep or goats or something bleating like that, which he beat back every few paces with a wooden staff. His entire world was dusty, poor, but he gladly spent all his life savings to pay for a banquet to welcome his daughter back to his village. They got drunk

together, the father and daughter, amidst a lot of candles, glowing around them on every table; the scene was caught in amber, so beautiful. And the actors were good—they both cried, not when they first saw each other, but much, much later after they were drunk and had been laughing together. I thought this was a wonderful movie.

I went to see it with Chen Hua. She was particularly taken with the scenes of the opera, the woman's performances and training. It reminded her of her youth when she studied with a provincial troupe. She kept nudging me to say, "Oh, it was just like that," or "They've got it all wrong." Especially when the woman didn't have an affair with her handsome troupe director and instead married some drunken card shark. But she liked the movie too, especially the scene at the end with the father. Everyone wishes this kind of scene could be true, I thought.

When Yong-li and I were finally reunited with Father, I was very nervous. I expected some kind of enormous rush of feeling to overtake me, us. It would be very embarrassing, with a lot of crying. I wanted to show how strong I was. I was sixteen, and I thought I was very much an adult.

Father's residence permit had been restored shortly after Mother's death. I don't know exactly when. It took some time for us to receive word in the countryside. But if it had been any longer, a few years, who knows? My brother and I might never have been allowed back into Nanjing. But we were still young, sixteen and twelve, still children in someone's eyes, and we were allowed to rejoin our father, our city residence permits restored. I've heard stories of families separated forever, Beijing intellectuals' children left in the desert out west for a decade, more, afraid to get married because then they'd never be allowed back into the city with a wife or husband and children, so they waited, lonely all those years. We were very lucky. At the time, I didn't know better, I

thought, Of course we're going back to Father, and I felt no relief or gratitude, just this apprehension. What should I say to him?

I imagined many, many scenarios. Tears rolling slowly, dramatically down my cheeks as we embraced. Violent cries as we mourned Mother together. The three of us hugging. I thought about yelling at him, "Why didn't you write to us? Where are all the letters you promised?" Sometimes he yelled back, an arrogant, angry man, and hit me across the mouth and I had to restrain Yong-li from kicking him. "No, Di-di," I'd say, holding him back, "after all, he *is* our father." And I'd suffer bravely, valiantly, in the face of this old man's scorn. Or sometimes, he didn't yell back, but he broke down and cried, admitting that he wrote us hundreds and hundreds of letters; every day, every year he wrote but he was afraid to send them to us, he was a black element, a stinking bourgeois counterrevolutionary intellectual. He did not want the stigma to travel, so he could only send one or two letters, cleansed of emotion, careful, hoping that we would read in the extended curve of a line, the flourish in a dot, the love he felt for us.

When we did return to Nanjing, Father met us at the bus station. We did not recognize him. His skin was burned brown, like dried figs, his hair was gray and wispy. He was not the loud young man I remembered, surrounded by books, ink on his fingers, shouting at us, "Be quiet so that I can think!"

The last time I had seen him, I was ten, Yong-li six. He recognized us, hugged us without looking in our faces and led us to his apartment. It was dark and bare. He had a small transistor radio on the kitchen table and a bird cage by the window. The bird chirped when we came in the door.

Yong-li looked at me. "This is Father?" He couldn't remember him at all.

"Of course," I snapped, irritated. "What a stupid question!"

Yong-li didn't say anything more. He stood by the bird cage and whistled at the strange greenish gray parakeet.

Soon there was a knock on the door and an older woman, obviously a neighbor, let herself in. She and Father exchanged glances. "So this must be Hua-yun and Yong-hua," she said.

I laughed loudly as did Yong-li, but neither of us corrected her.

Father said, "Don't be rude. This is Auntie Lu."

"I'm Lin Jun," I said.

"I'm Yong-li," my brother said, watching the bird.

"Oh, how nice," said Auntie Lu.

Auntie Lu made dinner for us and I could tell she was in love with my father the way the two of them looked at each other without saying anything and the way we seemed to intrude upon their space.

"Don't spit the tea leaves on the floor," she said, handing Father a steaming glass cup.

He reached for it without looking up from the table, knew exactly where she held it, just above his left ear. "Don't burn yourself," he said, "the thermos has a leak." He slurped his tea, inhaling air to cool his tongue, and spit the tea leaves back into his cup. They never said any more than this kind of thing.

It was winter, so cold. I expected the city to be warmer than the countryside but the tall stone apartment buildings were far colder even than the air outside. It snowed once, but the snow seemed to fall in gray wet piles. It was not beautiful and sparkling like the first morning after a snowfall in our village. Our village. I only thought in those terms once I'd left the village, never while I was there.

I never had time to get to know Auntie Lu. I concentrated on my

schoolwork. So much to learn after my years in the country school with our ratty copybooks, the peasants' children, so slow to learn. The Nile is the longest river in the world, 6,650 kilometers. The Yangtze, 6,300 kilometers long, is the third longest river in the world. China is the most populous nation on earth, nine hundred million people. The capital of New Jersey in the United States of America is Trenton. The great statesman and father of Bolshevism, Vladimir Ilyich Lenin, died in 1924, at the age of fifty-four. He loved to eat common brown bread just like the Russian proletariat. Chairman Mao said to learn from the peasants, to serve the people. He said, "Whenever there is struggle, there is sacrifice, and death is a common occurrence." China has had a continuous written language for 5,475 years. The names of the major dynasties are Xia, Shang, Zhou, Han, Tang, Song, Yuan, Ming, and Qing. Of the Six dynasties between the fall of the Western Han and the reunification under the Sui, the Eastern Jin, Liu-Song, Southern Qi, Liang, and Chen chose Nanjing as their capital. Lie, lying, laid, laid, but lay, laying, laid, lain.

So much to memorize for the senior-high entrance exams. I forgot what was truly important to know. And yes, it's true, I avoided her, pretended I couldn't hear as she hummed in the kitchen, sometimes revolutionary songs—"I Love China," "The East Is Red"—but sometimes older songs too—"Only You," "Mei-li, I Love You," and other songs that I had never heard of and can't remember now.

Auntie Lu came to make dinner and stayed late, flickering in and out of rooms as the electricity flitted on and off, the flames from our candles surging brighter as she passed. She was never still, and her voice and Father's were the same—faint, hard to discern, nondescript.

What did she look like? Her face was round and soft; her teeth, bad, brown, and stinky. She had small eyes, it was hard to tell behind her

glasses, but I remember thinking they were not as beautiful as Mother's had been: round, round eyes like grapes. Yong-li called Auntie Lu "Pig-woman," putting his index finger to the tip of his nose, pushing it up, squinting his eyes. Sometimes he made the face even when she was in the room. It didn't matter. Auntie stared at the walls and not at what moved in front of them. This was life with Father, surrounded by shadows and echoes, old people staring at ghosts I couldn't see. Only my books seemed real. Figures, dates, foreign verbs, no people, no feelings. My choice. Now I would like to know what kind of woman my father had fallen in love with. Just out of curiosity. But at that time, when I was sixteen, I thought I had better things to do.

When Auntie Lu's husband returned from the countryside, she stopped visiting, so I never got to know her.

Father committed suicide in the summer. It was so hot, I think the weather was to blame. People like to have romantic notions and say it was love—if they had known about Auntie Lu, I'm sure this is what they would have said. In the movie version, this is definitely how it would be told: he would see Auntie's husband and then with tears in his eyes, he would throw himself off a bridge. No, in the movie, Auntie Lu would be the one to kill herself, women always die in films. But really, I think he just couldn't take that sticky heat. Three hundred people died that summer from the heat—old people, babies, children. Nanjing is one of China's "Four Ovens." But it wasn't like an oven, it was like a rice cooker, and we were all the grains of rice.

Yong-li stayed outside all day, sitting in the shade of the sycamores with his friends, trying to break the windows out of buildings across the street with slingshots. He couldn't study, but I was driven. I studied though the pencil slid from my sweaty fingers.

Father took poison. I don't know what kind. The Public Security Bureau never told me. It's not suitable knowledge for a young girl. I woke up and the house was still that Sunday morning. No classes, but I rose early anyway. Normally I went straight to the table I used as a desk and opened my books, but this morning I was hungry. I heated some rice porridge, wondered if it was too selfish to fix an egg for myself. Yong-li was not home yet. He stayed with friends, roamed the alleys, a tough thirteen-year-old, going to show the city boys what he'd learned about fighting in the countryside.

The light was filmy that morning, the sun straining through a layer of dusty clouds. Father's bird still slept with its head under a wing when I padded to the kitchen in bare feet.

I thought I'd see if Father wanted an egg, too. I didn't really care what he wanted, so long as I could justify my own appetite. But as soon as I touched his door, I knew something was wrong. The smell like a dirty baby. I knocked. The door opened easily at my touch.

I must have screamed but I don't remember. Something woke the bird up. All at once it squawked and shrieked as if a cat were chasing it, a terrible sound, painful. It fluttered its clipped wings and fell to the bottom of its cage, shaking there. I wanted it to stop. I threw a book at it as I ran through the living room. I couldn't open the front door. I scratched at the wood, the latch was stuck. I heard the bird squawking. Then I was in the hall.

They say I ran to every door, banging with my fists, kicking, one, then the next, then another down the hall, still dark, hot already, no air. People were unbearably slow. I shouted and knocked. They moved so slowly, our neighbors. Like people underwater, drowning, they drifted out of their apartments, collecting in the hall.

"What's the matter with you?" A man with hair that stood straight up on his head shouted at me.

They were so languid. I pointed to our door. They moved like water buffalo, like they had to pull a plow through three feet of mud, twelve hours, they conserved their strength. I ran up and down the hall, brushing past their extended hands, they tried to catch me but they were floating and I, I ran, my feet on the ground, slapping against the cold floor.

Father was dead. His blankets were filled with shit, his belly distended like a ball. I'd seen dead animals before, pigs slaughtered, chickens decapitated, oxen bled to death with a jab in their jugulars. Even people. Old people. Still, my heart hurt, it leapt, when I saw him. Finally the neighbors sent someone to get the police. I didn't look again, except when they carried him out on a canvas stretcher, a sheet covering his face, the smell following, clinging. But the first glimpse I had stays in my mind, so horrible.

I stayed at the old couple's apartment next door to ours. The wife gave me a glass of hot water, the edge was chipped, I felt the sharp glass against my lip. A committee formed to clean the apartment, I heard the metal buckets drag against the floor, the sound of the women's voices, complaining. The slosh of dirty water spilling.

"*Aiya*, such bad luck," the old woman said. I could not see where she was. I stared at the gray curtains hanging in the far window. Her voice was somewhere behind me, dry like dead leaves crunching in her mouth.

"Don't say anything," her husband's voice whispered back. "The neighborhood committee's here."

They were afraid. I knew they had to be kind to me then and I felt a little calmer. I sat at their kitchen table, an old wooden bench really,

rubbed my finger along the edge, catching splinters, until they told me it was okay for me to go back again.

The neighbors stood in front of the building, gossiping on the sidewalk, shaking their heads. I watched them from the window when Yong-li came running in, his face red as an opera mask. "What happened?"

"Father's dead." I explained how I had found him.

He blinked at me. Pushed his lips together into a sneer. He was silent for a long time. I looked out the window again, but the sidewalks had cleared except for an old woman pushing a thin bamboo broom, swirling the dust and trash into a pile.

"What'd he look like?" Yong-li asked.

"I don't know. I don't remember. I didn't see anything."

"What's the matter with you? You didn't see? What were you doing? Stupid. Idiot. Stupid girl." He kicked the wall, over and over; I thought he would break his foot. He punched our door, broke the wood. Then he ran out. He kicked every door down the hall.

I heard his feet stomping down the stairs.

"Where are you going?" I shouted, not caring who heard. But he didn't answer me.

Yong-li came back late at night. I was glad, I didn't want to be alone and I had refused to stay at the neighbors'. I heard him drop his shoes as he crept inside the door.

I called out to him. I meant to sound strong, rebuking, but my voice caught in my throat, tore.

"Sorry," he said. "It's me."

He never asked me anything more about Father's death. But the

neighbors probably told him things, I heard them shouting together later.

I hated Father then. So selfish! I was studying all the time, working so hard, just so that I could tell him, "So there! I'm not so worthless. You should be proud." I wanted him to stop pining for some other man's wife. I wanted him to be a real father, our father.

Yong-li did poorly on his entrance exams into middle school, but he didn't care. "I want to be a worker," he said. That's what everyone was supposed to say in those days, but he meant it.

I always felt a little guilty, I was the clever one, the girl. Some of the neighbors said as much when they came to visit, after the cremation. I set out plates of watermelon seeds, peanuts, cups of hot green tea. The air was filled with the sounds of cracking seeds, like bones snapping between their teeth. "Isn't it funny?" they said. "The *girl* likes to study."

Yong-li slouched in the corner, teasing the bird so that it squawked unpleasantly and spit shells onto the floor, then he got bored. He left, striding past our neighbors, who smiled at him politely, in mock sympathy, curious at how we would turn out now that we were so cursed, orphans of black elements.

9.

Go-Betweens

I hadn't been thinking of marriage until Auntie Gao brought it up—I had just graduated from high school. She was always very practical. Her survival skills were quite strong.

"You should thank me," Auntie Gao said, direct, no hiding her feelings, when she arrived to take over the household, to look after Di-di while I was at college.

"I know," I said, bringing her tea.

Auntie settled onto the smooth wooden chair that had been Father's favorite. She ran her hands over the tabletop. "Bygones are bygones. Your father's work unit has apologized for making those crazy accusations against him. Like everyone else. Your family's name has been restored. A suicide won't change that now."

"Can I get you something to eat?" I set out the packages of sour plums and watermelon seeds.

Auntie spit the shells onto the concrete floor of Father's apartment and sucked on the pits. "Now we need to find you a husband." Just like that.

I was silent as I brought out the broom. At the time, I thought she was a superstitious old peasant woman who didn't understand anything about my life, life in the city. But she was wise, and she worked very hard all those years, making connections, listening for opportunities. I thought she had forgotten about the husband problem. Then after I graduated with my degree in English and was assigned to my school, she found Shao Hong.

"He is very handsome and his family is good." Auntie tapped her brown fingers against the top of my desk in my dormitory. "His family are intellectuals." Auntie rifled through the papers on the desk. "Perfect for you." She waited. "Well? Speak up. What's the matter with you?"

"I'm very grateful," I said. What else could I say?

"Yes?"

"I'd like to meet him."

"Of course! What kind of feudal matchmaker do you think I am?" Auntie moved on to the desks of my roommates, picked up the photographs of smiling girls. "Hmph. You have the best face."

Fortunately, I fell in love with Shao Hong. I admit it. I loved him.

Auntie had done well. He was handsome, with a long nose and bright eyes that stared at me all the time. He was a writer, like Father. He was brave and brash when he talked, like Mother. He said he would write books, someday he would be famous, like Lu Xun. I said I would help him. We registered at the Public Security Bureau and his work unit found us an apartment within six months of our marriage. I gave birth to

Bao-bao the next year. We chose the characters for his full name together—Liang-shan, "Bright Learning." We both agreed it was perfect, we did not argue at all. Then Auntie came and called him Bao-bao, "Treasure," from the start and it seemed a good name for such a small boy. We could save Liang-shan for later, a name to grow into. Shao Hong didn't like to call him Bao-bao at first, too babyish, but he gave in. Children should be coddled a bit when they are young. They had to grow up soon enough.

The only time I'd ever seen my in-laws happy was at Bao-bao's first-month party.

Ye-ye and Nai-nai beamed. They patted their grandson's cheeks. "He looks just like his father!" they declared.

Shao Hong moved among the guests, shouting loudly, his face red after drinking so much of the *maotai* his supervisors had given their "most promising assistant editor." I read to Bao-bao out loud as I carried him into the back room, the Baby's Room, where it was quieter, so that I could nurse him. Maybe some people thought it was strange, the way I read to him, talked to him as if he could understand everything I said, even when he was just a baby, one month old. But he'd look at me, very solemn, and I knew he understood. People underestimate children. It's terrible.

I was nursing him when there was a knock on the door. "So here you are!" Auntie entered without waiting for my reply.

Auntie moved slowly and leaned against the baby's Western-style bed, bought through special connections at a Friendship Store for foreigners. This was before foreigners were allowed to travel and shop throughout China, the television flashing pictures of them every day. Who could have imagined how things would change? But at that time, foreigners

could shop only at the Friendship Stores, full of special things that no Chinese could find anywhere else. I loved that bed, a lovely wooden cradle, painted bright red. It rocked evenly. So quiet.

Auntie leaned close to my breast and smiled at the baby. He did not see her; his eyes were screwed shut in concentration.

"Bao-bao!" Auntie screeched in my ear. She pulled my hair slightly, as if she didn't already have my attention. Her breath smelled of ginger. "You see, I was right."

Looking up at Auntie, I could only smile and nod. I was so happy, I couldn't speak. I was a lucky woman. She was right.

My own attempts at playing the "go-between" were less than successful. It was arrogant of me to interfere in someone else's business. Who knew what I was thinking? I was naive. What else can I call it?

I told my husband about Chen Hua, he told his boss. I thought of a way for them to meet, and then I forgot about it.

I was not completely stupid, as my husband liked to say. I had my reasons. Bao-bao's cold would not go away, he cried unhappily all that Sunday. I tried to comfort him, put salve under his raw nose, but he struggled in my arms and then whined for me to pick him up as soon as I set him down.

"What a son!" Shao Hong said angrily, before he disappeared out the front door. But once he was gone, Bao-bao was calmer and napped for several hours. When he awoke, his face was moist. He ate everything I made, including the fried *doufu*. He was a beautiful child. Watching him eat, I thought how blessed I was, how little I had to complain about.

I didn't think about the business with Chen Hua until mid-October, until I saw her saunter into the Monday meeting, so late. I almost didn't recognize her. She hardly looked like a teacher, more like a Hong Kong

movie star out of the magazines my students liked to sneak into class. Chen Hua wore black heels with a thin strap across her ankles, a shiny short skirt and a pink sweater with a soft bow at the throat. White powder covered her face and red circles defined her cheeks. She had even permed her hair: it floated around her head, cloudlike.

I could barely restrain myself from shouting across the room. Finally, as we all filed out, I pulled her aside. "So?"

"So what?" Chen Hua teased.

"How did it go?!"

Chen Hua's forehead was now the color of her rouged cheeks. She sucked her lips into her mouth. "Okay, I think. Your husband's supervisor, Old Zhang, doesn't talk much but it didn't matter. We went to the foreign film at the Victory Theater—a friend of his plus his wife and one of my roommates. It was a very good idea. Too bad you and your husband couldn't go. But we could only get so many tickets. My good fortune, your misfortune." Chen Hua laughed at her own joke. She continued without waiting for me to reply. "Actually, the movie wasn't very good. Even though it was American. *He* laughed all the time, though, so I guess someone was having a good time. I'm glad he likes foreign films."

"That's a good sign," I agreed when she paused for breath. "What does he look like?"

Chen Hua laughed. She covered her mouth with one hand and ran the other against a crease in her skirt. "Oh, he's all right. Not too tall, not too short. He has a bald spot on the top of his head. I saw it when he sat down in the theater. But it doesn't matter. If I liked hairy men, I'd look for a foreigner."

I laughed, too, although I did feel somewhat guilty afterwards; maybe I had been disloyal to Cynthia.

*   *   *

That night I didn't go for my bicycle ride, I sat at the kitchen table, waiting. Dinner had been ready for nearly an hour and still Shao Hong had not returned. Was there something wrong with one of his translations so that he had to stay this late to correct it? Perhaps the senior editors had changed the acceptable way of translating the foreign terms. The changing political winds blew hardest on translators. He liked to say this. I thought of worse things—accidents, women. Then accidents again.

Then I thought that he might be talking with his supervisor about Chen Hua! I felt less nervous. I thought of the way Shao Hong had smiled when we were first married, with his eyes bright and shiny, black like the night sky, full of promise. I wanted to see that smile again.

A thud like a falling book made me jump. I heard Shao Hong beating the mud from his shoes in the hall. I pushed my English notes aside and hurried to the door. "So what did your supervisor say?" I startled him by opening the door before he had found his key.

He scowled. "Don't shout. I can't even get in the door and you're shouting already."

"Sorry. But what did your supervisor think about Xiao Chen?"

"Don't you think I have more important things to worry about than your friend's love life?"

My face tingled. I realized I'd made a mistake springing on him. He was always so tired after work, and hungry. I was forgetful in my excitement. "Dinner's ready. Let's eat first."

"Shit."

"What's the matter?"

He turned to me, staring as if I were the one who was unreasonable. "She's too short."

"What did *he* say?"

He threw his coat over the back of my chair. He ran his hand through his windblown hair. It stood at attention at the touch of his fingers. "That's what he said. 'Too short.' What do you think? How could you find someone so ugly?"

"Chen Hua is not—"

"She's a dwarf. A Japanese midget." He laughed bitterly. "You made me look like a fool. I thought you'd have more sense."

"I'm sorry, but you didn't tell me what he was looking for."

"Don't act so stupid. You could have found someone who looked normal. Like you, at least." He stepped around me and made his way into the kitchen, to scrounge out whatever I had cooked for the evening. I watched his shadow fall against our apartment door. He stood as he ate out of his rice bowl, pushing food into his mouth.

It was the "at least" that hurt most of all. I am a vain woman. More than I like to admit. I wanted to cry over this insult. I was beautiful, everyone knew it, they told me my beauty was my good fortune, women were jealous, men stared. I was judged by my face—often harshly, often wrongly, but judged all the same. How could my husband not see? This is what I thought, standing next to the table, staring at my scattered lesson plans. I held on to the edge as he brushed past me, to his study. I heard the sound of paper rustling, and I suddenly thought of Auntie burning my mother's letters, such a long time ago. My stomach dropped to my knees. My husband yawned loudly, a honk that echoed through the apartment, and then his typewriter tapped and thumped violently. The kitchen window rattled from the wind that slipped through cracks in the frame. I was growing old, dusty, old.

I went to tell Cynthia finally. I wanted perspective, reassurance, to be told that I hadn't ruined everything. Normally I would have gone to see

Chen Hua, but under the circumstances, that was not possible obviously. I had been avoiding her, in fact. I know, I know, I'm not proud of this. But it's true, why lie now?

It was unusually bright inside Cynthia's office, the windows caught the afternoon sun. It was odd to be in such a sunny room and talk of such dismal affairs. Cynthia listened silently as I told her about the fiasco. The American did not interrupt even to shake her head.

I had to prompt her, nervously and with a smile, the way I'd coax a child. "What do you think? I don't know what to do now."

"Men are pigs," Cynthia said.

I didn't understand her at first; it took me several seconds to translate the non sequitur.

"How dare he? God, I can't believe this!" Cynthia shook her hair away from her face. "You were doing him a favor! How ungrateful!"

"Oh, no, no, it's my fault." I laughed nervously. Bursts of passion make me think of failed revolutions. I wanted advice, how to make such a disaster better. I didn't want to make things worse. "I am very lucky. He's a good man. I should know better really. His supervisor is so old already and has no wife. I should know he's a difficult man. Now I have embarrassed everyone."

" 'Too short'!" The foreigner teacher waved both her hands at once. The wind blew my hair into my eyes.

"But really, many men like women who are beautiful. I thought maybe because the supervisor is an intellectual he would like my friend. But men like pretty girls. I know this. They must have pretty faces, good handwriting, good editing. Good to look at and good for career. Nowadays, men like modern women. One point three meters. No shorter." Hearing myself speak, I realized how foolish I had been. What world did I think I was living in? I had set everyone up for such a fall.

"Hmph. But Chinese women are all short—" Cynthia caught herself.

Silence opened between us like a hole. I hurried to fill the gap. "Maybe I am very foolish. I don't know what to say now. Should I apologize? Write a note—or just say nothing, and it will be less embarrassing?"

"You should tell your husband and his boss to get real!" Cynthia's face drew tight, closed. "We shouldn't enable men to objectify women."

I sighed. I excused myself. "I must prepare for my next class."

It was nearly empty back in the English section's office—only a few older teachers sat in the back, chewing on watermelon seeds. They spit the shells loudly into a metal basin.

It was dark, like dusk. The morning light had already retreated from the windows. They were dull, nearly opaque with dust and grime from the street below. I stood by my desk, staring at my calendar, its bright characters. The thought for the day: "To be useful is my only wish"— Comrade Lei Feng.

The date was off. I had forgotten to flip the pages for several days. I ripped the sheets from the block and tossed the old days into the garbage pail.

Who knew what I'd been expecting from Cynthia? As if a foreigner's sympathy could solve my problems. I needed to accept responsibility for my own actions, my own stupid ideas. It's not so easy to be a go-between. Auntie had worked diligently. She hadn't introduced us until she was sure it would work out well. What was I trying to do? I was lazy and selfish, trying to fix everything so easy fast quick.

That night, I stayed at home and corrected papers. I didn't allow myself to enjoy a ride around the city. Shao Hong did not come home for dinner. Sometimes his supervisors made all the assistant editors and translators work late then go together to a restaurant where the senior

editors bragged and told stories and everyone else had to listen and laugh and tell them how clever they were. I told myself this was why Shao Hong was late, the poor man, such a bothersome job, always having to try to win his supervisors' favor. Always having to smile at idiots. That's why he was late. Of course.

I waited until ten before putting the dishes away and wrapping up his dinner. I opened the refrigerator door without bothering to turn on the kitchen lights. The glow from the small box spilled onto the dark floor, setting my feet afire. There was little room for the leftovers inside. Bao-bao would be home tomorrow from school. I had filled the fridge with his favorite foods—Lion's head meatballs, sticky rice *zongzi*, and orange Fanta soda pop. It was not spoiling him to make him feel wanted. After all, he was only home one day out of seven; it was hard for such a young boy, not yet six. I shifted glass bowls, and the round soda bottles rolled towards the door. I pushed the dishes back into place then dumped Shao Hong's dinner into the trash. There just wasn't any room.

I went to bed alone. I lay on my side, curled tight, cold. My shoulders ached. I couldn't think about school, I couldn't imagine what to say to Chen Hua, my stomach hurt. I kicked the blankets, drummed my ankles against the mattress. I sat up and punched my pillow with my fists. I wanted to cry so I thrashed more violently, kicking, punching, covering my head with my blankets so that I could not breathe, anything to keep from crying. And then, twisted in my blankets, sweating, I wished Shao Hong were there, I imagined him there, and he was not angry, not at me, and I grabbed hold of him, tight, pressing into his smooth, hard chest. I felt his arms around me, his fingers sliding against my back, resting on my waist, sliding between my legs. I wanted him there, willed him there, and I touched my face to his neck, tasting his skin, feeling the pulse in his neck against my cheek. And he wanted me, too. He grew

hard, I felt him against the soft part of my thigh, and I arched my back as he pushed into me.

But of course, Shao Hong was out who knew where, and I lay back in the tangled mess of the sheets alone.

I stood up, the wood floorboards freezing under my bare feet, and straightened up the covers. Then I climbed back into bed.

I didn't remember falling asleep but when I woke up, I could not remember where I was. I sat up, squinting into the dark. I heard footsteps outside the bedroom and I couldn't breathe for a second, just long enough to make me gasp. The footsteps turned to shuffles then a man cleared his throat loudly in the bathroom.

I lay back, able to breathe normally again. For a moment I had forgotten about my husband entirely, I might have been a girl again, listening to Auntie pace late at night, talking to herself.

Pulling the blankets around me again, I wondered what time it was, how long I had been sleeping, but I was too lazy to reach out into the cold air and turn on the lamp by the bed to read my watch. The toilet flushed with a roar and the walls gargled as the water rushed through the pipes.

It was funny I hadn't worried about Shao Hong. He'd never stayed out so late before, something might have happened to him on his way home from work, an accident. But the possibility had not occurred to me until that moment. I stared into the dark, able to distinguish depths of shadow now, the edges of my dresser, the outline of the door.

The door opened and he shuffled inside the bedroom, his plastic slippers made a faint clicking against the floor.

"What happened? Have you eaten?" I tried to sound casual, husky, as if I had just awakened from a nap. I hoped only I heard the edge to my voice.

"Mmm," he said. He undressed. I could smell smoke on his clothes.
"What was that?"

"The boss made us go out together again." I watched his shadow slip his sweater over his head. Then he stopped and kicked the dresser. "I hate them all."

I jumped out of bed and ran over to him. I nearly tripped over a shoe. I stood beside him and put my hand on his bare shoulder. "I'm sorry," I said.

"It's not your fault."

"I know. I mean, I wish I could help."

"Yeah." He turned away from me and put on his pajama top, buttoning it slowly. "I've got to sleep." He shuffled over to the bed and lay down.

I stood by the dresser, I couldn't see his dark form on the bed, I heard his tight, even breaths.

How we came to be this way, I didn't know.

10.

The Funeral

When Auntie died, I did not attend the funeral that Yong-li had arranged.

We met at his factory to discuss the details, sitting on a stone bench in the courtyard outside the cafeteria. I barely heard what he said as I watched my brother move. He had let his hair grow long in the back and a thin mustache struggled to reach the ends of his upper lip.

"Don't worry, Sis. I've got everything under control." Yong-li leaned back on cold stone, his elbows pointing away from his body in opposite directions. He looked thin.

"Shao Hong thinks he might be able to find a new work unit for you, something less strenuous." I searched in my purse for the name I had meant to give him.

"What are you talking about? I like my work." He tossed his long hair.

"But you don't have to work here. You're very smart. You really ought to enroll in one of the night schools, they have very good classes. I know a teacher—"

"Would you stop trying to run my life?" He lit up a cigarette and blew smoke through his nose. "Auntie's dead, you don't have to take over for her now. Just rest."

I closed my purse with a snap. "I'm just trying to help. You don't have to be rude. And when did you start smoking?"

He laughed. "So you'll come for the procession?"

"Oh, no, let's not do anything so public. It's . . . so . . . ."

"Yes, yes, yes. Too late. I've already hired the nuns."

"The nuns!" I exclaimed. Several workers filing out of the cafeteria stopped to look at me. I looked away.

"They're professional mourners. They'll march their bald heads through all the main alleys for an hour behind Auntie's ashes. We can all wail." He demonstrated, howling like a sick dog.

"Sssh!" I glanced around. "You're enjoying this," I accused him, quite shocked. "This is disrespectful."

Yong-li's face fell. He stubbed out his cigarette on the table, then rose. "I've got to get back to work."

"No, I'm sorry. You've done such a good job. I'm sorry," I called after his retreating figure.

He turned around, smiling, and waved. "I know!" he shouted and ran back inside.

On the day of the funeral procession, I awoke with a terrible headache. My brain hurt from ear to ear, something throbbed at each temple. I was too nauseous to eat breakfast and I could barely focus my eyes. I dressed in a white blouse and a pair of dark pants, but then could not decide upon the shoes. My pumps were the dressiest but I did not

want to walk in them for who-knew-how-long over the uneven stones of the alleys. I could wear my more comfortable flat felt shoes with the rubber soles, but they were red. They might not be appropriate. It was too ridiculous. I sat on the side of my bed, in my bare feet, until the hour of the procession came and went.

I paced through the empty apartment. Shao Hong had taken Bao-bao out for the day so that I would be free for the funeral. Undoubtedly he had gone to his parents'. My bare feet did not make a sound as I walked. The floor was cold but I did not want to put on my socks and slippers. I could not decide if I was being disrespectful to Auntie. I could not decide if I even felt sad.

I had cried when Auntie died, it had scared me, the numbness I felt. I missed Auntie, of course I did. I would miss her. But when I thought of Auntie, I thought of an old woman with her front teeth missing, pock-marks across her forehead and cheeks, and a thick brown neck. Auntie had never seemed young, yet one day she had been as young and healthy as Mother, as I.

It was chilly in the apartment, the sun had nearly disappeared behind the apartment building just west of ours. I leaned against the wall of the living room, hugging my ribs, and waited for my husband and son to return.

The last time I saw Auntie Gao, it was Mid-Autumn Festival. It had been unseasonably warm that October, the leaves had not yet fallen from the sycamores, the sun was warm, hot even, against my skin as I rode my bicycle to school. Then suddenly the week of the holiday, a cold wind blew from the north and all the leaves shriveled on their stems then fell, shattering into pieces on the sidewalks. The dead brown shards collected in the gutters. It would be a long winter, everyone said.

I was up an hour before dawn, cleaning. I scrubbed the floors, pushing the soapy mop into the corners, pulling out the furniture; I found dust balls the size of small oranges, a book I had lost months ago, an old pacifier. It was horrifying, how I had let my home go. Auntie would see everything, she who had worked so hard for me to have a home, who had hoped for me. I broke out into a sweat, my head felt hot, then I shivered uncontrollably. I should have started cleaning earlier, I should have bought better food, Auntie would say something awful, she would look at me and she would grab my chin with her thick dry fingers and look into the irises of my eyes and foresee sloth and disaster, she would know my husband and I had not made love in years, that my son cried too much, that I was the problem. I did not want to hear it anymore. Perhaps this sounds irrational, but it is how I felt.

But of course Auntie was coming and there was nothing I could do to keep her away. Panicking would solve nothing. I came home from school after my last class and immediately began chopping vegetables, wrapping wontons in preparation.

When Auntie arrived, bearing three boxes of mooncakes, tied with a bright pink plastic ribbon, I did not recognize the old woman trembling at my door.

"Yes?" I stood with the door propped open with my foot, wiping my hands on my apron.

"Lin Jun!" Auntie tried to push her way in the door; she stumbled on the floor mat. I caught her by the arm; she was light for such a wide woman.

"Oh, Auntie. You're early."

"The bus was early." Auntie sat down in Shao Hong's chair, panting. "I could hardly find you. The city has changed so much." She whistled slightly as she spoke; none of her front teeth remained.

Had it really been four years since Auntie had returned to the country-side to live with her husband? The time had passed quickly for me, mere instants. I remembered nursing the baby, as if it had been only months ago. I could see Bao-bao waddling across the floor, learning to speak, pulling at my pants leg. Four years. It is frightening to be so unobser-vant, letting time sneak away.

"You should have waited. I was going to pick you up." I put the moon-cakes on the living-room table. "I'll get you some tea."

Auntie took out a cigar and lit up, smoke billowing from her nostrils. "Where is your son?" Auntie shouted.

"Here, hold this." I placed the teacup in Auntie's hand, wrapping the rough thick fingers around the handle. "He's at school. He lives there now."

"Ho! You're a real modern woman." Auntie spilled some tea on the floor. I bent to wipe up the pool. I noticed that the cuffs of Auntie's pants were dirty, stained, and she had not bothered to mend a small moth hole behind her knee. Auntie smelled as though she had not bathed in a while.

I made a bowl of soft noodles for Auntie while we waited for Shao Hong to return from work.

Auntie slurped the broth noisily, sucking air in loudly until she belched. "This is really not too bad," she sighed, in a flat, old person's voice. Her hand shook, she could barely hold on to her chopsticks. She gripped them like a child, near the tips. "I wouldn't mind living in the city again." She sighed.

I pretended I could not hear. "I thought I'd make a hot pot for tonight. Does that sound good? Would you like to watch TV? Here, I'll turn it on for you. Shao Hong will be happy to see you again." I chat-tered on as I worked in the kitchen, my cleaver pounding loudly against

the cutting board, the sizzle of the wok drowning out any sounds from the living room.

By evening Auntie was very tired and weak. I had to walk her to the bathroom, hold the old woman's arm as she squatted over the toilet.

I tucked Auntie into bed on the sofa in the living room. "Do you want me to leave a small light on for you?"

"Yes, that would be nice." Auntie peered up from the blankets pulled around her chin. Her face was all loose flesh; the features ran into each other. I patted her head. The few hairs that remained were a soft gray, like down.

"Good night," I said. It seemed unimaginable that I had ever feared this woman, that Auntie could ever have caused any harm. I no longer knew if my memories could be trusted.

I lay on my side, my back to my husband, listening to his even breathing and the faint honk of Auntie's snores and I could not sleep. The dark seemed to close in around me. I pressed my fingers to my ears to block the sound, and only then could I relax enough to fall asleep.

Not long after Auntie's visit, Uncle Bing called me at work, shouting into the receiver. He was crying, nearly incoherent. "My wife is gone," he said.

"Oh," I said, stupidly. "I'm so sorry."

But part of me felt suddenly free. And this feeling both puzzled and frightened me.

I hoped this didn't mean I was a bad person.

11.

The Foreign Teacher

One afternoon in late October, I was grading grammar exercises, tortured sentences in the present perfect, when I looked up in surprise to find Cynthia knocking on my office window. Cynthia waved. I waved back. Cynthia shook her head and bounded in the door. "Come on," she whispered loudly, gesturing for me to get up.

I glanced around me, but the other teachers continued to throw their mah-jongg tiles enthusiastically, paying me no mind. I folded up my grade book and followed Cynthia outside.

It was cool on the open corridor that ran outside all the second-floor offices. The wind was blowing from the northeast, sharp and damp. I should have grabbed my hat.

"Look!" Cynthia crouched by the balustrade and peered between two rails.

I stood behind the American. It occurred to me that sometimes Cynthia acted like a child, or like a man. I squatted uneasily and tried to see what Cynthia was pointing at.

The senior-high students were practicing their exercise routines below in the school yard for the upcoming assembly. Their homeroom teachers stood before them, valiantly demonstrating, while the students stood in uneven rows, gyrating at the waist. They were having some difficulty keeping time to the music, which blared unevenly from speakers attached to the tall light posts. A few arms swung up as others swung to the sides. The older boys, who hung near the back of each column, did not participate at all. One boy with long scraggly sideburns smoked. I clicked my tongue and shook my head.

"The young people are very lively," I said, unsure of the proper tone to adopt. I could not understand exactly which part Cynthia was enjoying.

"Look at Secretary Wang."

I followed Cynthia's finger. Indeed, the Party Secretary herself was leading a column of seniors. She was rather large and unwieldly. She flapped her arms and bent at the knees. I could not make out the instructions she shouted. Then—how terrible for the Secretary—she squatted halfway to the asphalt, lost her balance, and tipped over onto her rear end. Several boys rushed forward to help her. The other students ceased their exercises and talked while they waited for the Secretary to brush herself off.

Cynthia laughed loudly.

"They're practicing for the Christmas pageant," I said.

"A little early, isn't it? It's only October."

"It's a surprise. In your honor. Everyone will perform something. They

want to be very good. At least, their teachers want them to be very good."

"Poor kids." Cynthia shook her head. She sat directly on the concrete, watching, then turned to face me abruptly. "That means I'll have to perform too, right?"

"Well, you can just sing a little song or maybe dance."

"God!" Cynthia tossed her thick curly hair over her face, then pushed her hands through her hair.

"Don't worry. I'll help you."

"You can sing for me. How 'bout that?"

"No, no, no." I couldn't help but smile. "But maybe we can think of something else for you. You can recite a poem?"

"Mmm." Cynthia breathed out loud and rested her head against the rails. "China is weird," she said.

"You don't have school assemblies in America?"

"We don't have all these performance-oriented things. I guess it's because we have better TV!" Cynthia laughed loudly, exposing all her teeth.

Sometimes the American seemed very strange. It must've been hard for her here. "Don't worry." I put a hand on her sleeve. I wanted to tell her that no one expected much from her, her presence as a foreigner at the school's assembly was entertaining enough, but I couldn't think of a polite way to explain.

Cynthia turned back to the students, dancing on the asphalt courtyard below us. "You can come over and eat at my *shitang* sometime. We can talk it over. *Liao liao tian, chi hao cai.* That would be fun."

"Your Chinese is very good."

"Oh, yeah. Right. It's just great." Cynthia stared down at the worn knees of her blue jeans. She looked very young.

* * *

In the end, Cynthia decided she didn't like the food at her cafeteria very much and took me to a small restaurant near her dormitory. The prices were very high. I felt mortified but Cynthia insisted that she always came here. I hoped she knew what she was doing.

The restaurant was like nothing I had seen before. It was not run by the government, no one wore white cooks' aprons or hats. There were waiters and waitresses, in tight foreign clothing. The women wore a lot of makeup. The men wore gold chains around their necks. American disco music pulsed from hidden speakers, strands of flashing colored lights circled the room, smoke and laughter filled the air. I readjusted the bow of my blouse nervously.

There were many foreigners, white people I assumed must be Americans, several black African students, but there were a few tables of Chinese men as well. Empty *baijiu* bottles littered the floor around them and still they dared each other to down another shot. Of all the loud people inside, they were the loudest of all. It was an embarrassment.

Cynthia seemed not to notice. She commandeered a small table for us. "Do you want to order?" She handed me the menu, which was written in large simple characters. Someone had also translated the menu into a direct if uninspired English. The prices were shocking.

"Oh, it's okay." I smiled nervously. "Whatever you want."

"Well, I usually get the eggs and green peppers—" Cynthia's voice was drowned out by a cheer coming from the corner table of Chinese. "Jesus!" Cynthia twisted around on her stool to stare at the men. "Why is it," she asked, "I always see tables of drunk Chinese men in restaurants and never any women? Don't women go out to eat ever?"

"These are not good men," I said, staring at the rough crowd. One of the men winked at me. I frowned at him then I gasped. At the same

time, the young man in the far corner bugged his eyes then tried to duck behind a menu. It was my brother. I didn't know what to do.

"Oh, excuse me a moment," I heard my voice, small and thin. I clutched my purse to my side and walked over to the rowdy group.

"Ho, what have we here?" One of the men grabbed at my leg.

"Hey, you asshole, that's my sister!" Yong-li stood up and shoved the table towards his friend.

The other men burst into laughter.

"Yong-li! What are you doing here?! I'm ashamed of you."

"Shit." His face was a bright scarlet from the liquor he'd drunk. He could barely focus his eyes in my direction.

I looked at his companions—all of them had long greasy hair and fancy American blue jeans, one man wore sunglasses. He raised a glass to me and tipped its contents down his throat.

"You should set an example in front of all the foreign friends." I glanced around uneasily. "What will they think?"

"Fuck," said one of the men, eliciting peals of laughter from the others.

"Hey! Shut up!" Yong-li stood up and pushed the man off his stool. I saw that he too was dressed in expensive foreign clothes; his shirttails hung nearly to his knees, a gold watchband glittered around his wrist. "Shut up, everybody," Yong-li repeated.

For a moment the men were silent, then my brother sneezed loudly and they all whooped again.

I walked over to Yong-li and pulled on his arm, leading him away from the table.

"Let go," he mumbled.

I led him to the far wall, near the door. "How can you embarrass me like this?"

"You shouldn't always be so afraid of what people think. Who cares? We're paying enough to be here. More than you." He stood uneasily, then tried to cross one leg over the other and nearly fell.

I was shocked by his rebuff. "You're the one who's afraid. Fancy friends, fancy clothes, don't want anyone to know you're just a . . ." I stopped myself.

Yong-li's eyes widened as if he'd been hit. I was immediately sorry. He turned away from me and hurried back to his table. The flashing lights made him seem even more unsteady, flickering almost. I followed him.

"C'mon, let's go. There's better dumps than this place." He finished the last of his drink. Someone threw a wad of cash on the table and his companions stumbled to their feet.

"Sorry," said one of the men, clutching my arm. "We are . . . ve-ry . . . so-so-sor . . ." He was unable to finish his sentence. I pulled myself free and returned to Cynthia's table. A bottle of beer and two glasses were waiting.

Cynthia looked at me curiously.

"Oh, don't worry." I tried to sound very casual. "It is just my brother and his friends. Men like to be lively." I shrugged.

"Hmm," said Cynthia, raising an eyebrow. "You were pretty impressive." Cynthia poured us both a glass. "A toast."

I was startled for a moment, still angry. Then I realized Cynthia meant for me to drink. I took the glass and sipped the beer slowly. It was warm and salty, not unpleasant tasting really. The last time I had drunk beer, it had been my wedding day.

Cynthia ordered far too much, more than four dishes. The restaurant's food wasn't that good, despite the prices, not at all like home cooking. Everything was too salty. We drank two bottles of beer and still I felt thirsty.

"Your face is red," said Cynthia, smiling, her lips greasy.

I put my hands to my cheeks. They were warm.

Cynthia laughed. "My old boyfriend had the same problem. What's the enzyme Chinese people don't have? I can't remember. He told me once. It helps process alcohol . . ."

I didn't know what she was talking about. I thought for a moment. "You had a Chinese boyfriend?"

"Well, no. I mean he was Chinese American." Cynthia shook her head, so that all her hair flew back and forth. "God, that was a long time ago."

"But you are very young. It could not be that long."

"Well . . ." Cynthia shrugged.

"I think Americans are very interesting," I said.

Cynthia laughed loudly. "Well, I think Chinese are interesting."

"That is why one is your boyfriend?"

Cynthia laughed harder. "No."

I leaned against the table. I felt very warm and sleepy. The restaurant was actually a very nice place after all. I watched the lights flash across the ceiling. "Is this restaurant like America?"

"What?" Cynthia looked around her with amusement. "Not at all. This is very Chinese."

"Oh really? But this seems very strange to me." We both laughed.

"Shall I order some more beer? Yeah, I will." Cynthia waved at the barmaid.

"Have you traveled to many countries?" I asked.

"No, not really." Cynthia held her hair off her neck with one hand and fanned herself with the menu. She took up a lot of space when she moved. She leaned her back against the wall and stretched her legs straight out in front of her. "I traveled a bit in Europe, did the train thing,

you know—France, Germany, where else did we go? Prague, I think. That was last summer before I came to China."

"Oh," I said, so jealous I didn't know what else to say for a minute. I played with the ashtray on the table, a metal flower cut from a beer can, the petals curled back from the ash stains, concentrated on it, not daring to look up. "Was it very exciting?"

"Well, it's not like China." Cynthia tapped her empty glass on the tabletop. "I like China better. Life is simpler here. It seems more honest."

"But China is very poor," I said. I twirled the ashtray in a circle. "We are a backward country."

"How do you know?" Cynthia sat up abruptly. "I mean, I hear that all the time. But what does anyone have to compare it to?"

"We see many American movies and television shows. America is very wealthy. Everyone has a car and a house."

"I don't have a car at home."

"But your parents?"

"Well, yeah, but . . ." The new bottle of beer came and Cynthia opened it by striking the cap against the edge of the table. The cap flew off. She poured us both full glasses. The foam spilled onto the tabletop. I took out a piece of paper from my purse and tried to sop up the liquid before it ran over the edge.

"Whoops," said Cynthia.

"Don't you miss your home? Your parents?" I asked. I put the wet wad of paper in the ashtray.

"No, not really. It was time I got away from home. I suppose that sounds strange to a Chinese, huh?" Cynthia sipped her beer.

"Well, maybe not so strange." I smiled. "When I was a young girl, I had

to live away from my parents. I lived in the countryside. It was the Cultural Revolution time?"

"Oh, yeah. I know about that." Cynthia nodded.

"Yes. Well, I think it was good for me. You are right. Sometimes young people should be independent. They need to have responsibility. I think I became very strong because of it. I know I could endure many hardships." I realized that I was speaking like the placards written for tourists at the museums, the martyrs' parks, but Cynthia seemed not to notice.

"Yeah, exactly!" Cynthia sat up excitedly, her eyes wide and bright. "That's what I think too. You need to get away from your parents after a while. Or else you'll never know what kind of person you are."

I struggled for a minute, searching for my own words. "Maybe I still don't know, but at least I can decide for myself what kind of person I want to be. Some people never learn this. They just follow other people's standards." My voice was louder than I had intended. It had been a long time since I'd made such a serious, confident declaration. It reminded me of something, but I couldn't remember exactly what.

Cynthia nodded and knocked her glass against mine so that it made a sharp sound like ice cracking.

I rubbed my finger around the rim of my beer glass. The edge was chipped. I put my finger on the crack, but it didn't hurt. "Still, you must be lonely, so far away from home."

"Sometimes," Cynthia admitted.

"Do you have many Chinese friends?"

"I'm trying to make Chinese friends. It's too easy to stay within the foreign community, you know. I want to branch out, or else I'll never learn anything the whole time I'm here."

"Do you find Chinese ways strange?" I looked at her closely.

Cynthia scrunched her nose up and twisted her lips. "Sometimes."

She smiled. "I'm not sure why exactly. At first, it's just the language, I think, I couldn't understand the accents—it's not like school."

I had to laugh.

"And the way people move, squatting, and always bumping into each other on the sidewalk, the buses. Chinese people touch each other more. Women and women. Men and men. When you would come up to me and touch my arm, that surprised me at first."

"We're always bumping each other but we aren't like Americans. We touch the outside but never show our inside." I put my hand to my heart, my temple, a little clumsily. "Women and men. Old and young."

"No, no, not at all." Cynthia seemed apologetic. "I mean, at first I had this plan, about learning. I don't know why I chose China, except maybe because I knew nothing about China. It was a challenge, you know. I thought, okay, I can study really hard and learn the language, study the history, then if I visited the country, I would understand *China*. All of it." Cynthia pulled her hair away from her face, holding it above her head with one hand, as if it were a handle with which to wield her head. "But it's not possible. Then I thought, I'll try to make one good friend, you know. And then maybe I can understand that one person. But . . ." Cynthia straightened up and smiled sheepishly, a little maudlin. "Well, tonight you showed I can't even do that."

I leaned my head against the wall, quite moved. "Well, I am glad you consider me your friend." I smiled and lifted my glass to Cynthia. We drank the last of our beer.

It was very late when I got home. I'd left a note for Shao Hong but it was still taped to the closet door. His shoes were not by the front door although the light in the living room was on. I checked the refrigerator

and found that he had eaten the dinner I had prepared for him. I felt a little better.

I took off my coat. The first time I tried to hang it on the nail on the closet door, I missed and it fell to the floor in a heap. I bent over to pick it up and nearly fell over myself. I realized I must have been a little drunk.

When I went to wash my face, I saw in the bathroom mirror that my cheeks were indeed a deep pink. I looked like something from a children's cartoon. I had to laugh. And then I couldn't stop until my eyes burned. Huge tears slid from the corners like shards of glass, they tore at my face. Still I could not stop laughing. I don't know how long this lasted.

When I could breathe properly again, I decided to go straight to bed. I would correct papers in the morning. Later. I was sleepy.

I awoke to find my husband pressing himself against me, his hand locked around my arm. It was too dark to see anything. He grunted softly as he thrust against me but he remained soft, as usual. My head felt light as my body rocked gently back and forth. He gave up finally and rolled over onto his back. I continued to breathe evenly, pretending I was asleep, I didn't want him to feel humiliated. We lay that way for some time.

12.

People I Have Let Down

I didn't know what to tell Chen Hua about the whole go-between fiasco. I was trying to think of a way to put it, or maybe I was hoping she'd lose interest. I don't know now what I was thinking. I wasn't thinking. I had put off telling Chen Hua anything for so long that I forgot to say anything at all.

It was a Wednesday morning, the last week of October, first week of November. I didn't have class, my second-year students were taking a long math exam. I walked into my office and nearly jumped when I saw Chen Hua seated at my desk. I didn't want to be so obvious. "Oh!" I tried to think of something better to say, something I could offer her to eat, but when I opened my mouth, nothing else came out.

"I haven't seen you for a while. I thought I could find you in your office. You're so busy these days." Chen Hua flipped through my desk

calendar, wrinkling her nose at the entries. She sat sideways on my chair. She wore a tight black skirt and a white silk blouse, unbuttoned at the neck. Something pushed at her breasts to reveal cleavage. I had always imagined Japanese women to dress like this. Stylish and to please men. I was so disappointed.

Chen Hua looked up from the calendar and stared directly at me. "By the way, have you talked to your husband yet about his boss?"

"Oh," I said, that awful word again. "Well, he's been so busy lately."

Chen Hua's face remained perfectly still. "I see."

"I'm sorry. I've been helping the foreign teacher lately, I haven't been thinking." I put my hands on Chen Hua's shoulders.

Chen Hua shrugged them off. "No, on the contrary, I shouldn't bother you." She stood up. She walked unhurriedly to the door then paused. "Really, Xiao Lin, I don't care. I've decided . . . it's unimportant." Her voice was deep and firm. She smiled, her lips drawing back from her teeth, turned her back and departed.

My own face grew hot. But I felt suddenly cold. I hurried over to the hot-water thermos to see if there was enough water left at the end of the morning to make a cup of tea. I shook the red metal thermos. It was nearly empty. I contented myself by holding it between my hands.

All at once, I laughed. I nearly dropped the thermos and had to hug it close to my chest. At least my dread was gone.

Shortly after that, my brother disappeared.

The last time I saw my brother, I was waiting for Yong-li outside his factory's dormitory. The grounds were littered with trash, empty cigarette packs, bottles, tin cans. Really, men can live like dogs when left to their own devices. I glanced at my watch. It was cold, the sunlight was

nearly gone, and I had work to do. A figure came running out of the shadows and tapped me on the shoulder.

"Hey, Sis."

"Don't do that! Yong-li, you nearly scared me to death."

He laughed. "Come on." He led me to the covered parking lot for the bicycles.

"What are we doing?" The wind blew my hair into my eyes. I squinted.

"Shh. I have some good news for you. I'm going to Moscow." He took a heavy drag off his cigarette, causing the end to glow bright orange. Smoke curled from his nostrils.

I waited for him to make sense.

"Well," he prompted me.

"Well, what? What are you talking about? Moscow!" I readjusted the strap of my purse on my shoulder. It wanted to slide down my arm.

"Would you keep your voice down?" He glanced over his shoulders.

I laughed at him. "You're acting ridiculous."

He tossed the butt of his cigarette to the ground then took out another from a shiny American pack in the pocket of his jeans jacket. He held the cigarette between his long fingers, delicately, like a gangster in a Hong Kong movie. I tried to knock it from his hand. "Hey, watch it," he said.

"Watch yourself." I laughed again but he looked away, shielding the cigarette from the wind as he lit the end.

"I'm really going, Lin Jun," he said.

I looked at my younger brother, silent.

"I have a great opportunity." His voice regained its bounce. "I've made a lot of friends this past year."

"Yeah, I've seen your friends." I wrapped my arms around my body.

"Do you always have to be so negative? You know, not everyone has it

as easy as you. You go to college, they find you a job, someone else finds you a husband. You don't understand my life." He blew smoke out his nostrils.

I hugged my purse to my body; at least it was something I could hang on to. "That's not true. I've always had to work very hard."

"I'd work hard if it'd get me anywhere."

"You can't go to Moscow," I said, so reasonable, so practical. "Do you have a passport? You don't have a family. They won't let you go. Who's going to sponsor you?"

"Who am I going to tell I'm leaving?" He paused to finish his cigarette. He exhaled the smoke slowly, teasing me. "I've made some friends. They can get me to Russia, no problem." He dropped his voice. "I'm going to stow away on a cargo shipment. The Russians can't get enough Chinese things. And if a few Chinese come along in the bargain . . ."

My brother had lost his mind. I was sure of it. Why hadn't I recognized the signs earlier? "It's not safe." I hated the squeakiness of my voice.

He shrugged. "People do it all the time."

"You'll get caught. You'll go to jail." I thought I might cry.

He mimicked me, "Oooh, ooh, I'm afraid, I can't do it."

"Stop it! Don't be so selfish. Think how I'll feel if something happens to you—"

"You'll live."

"If they catch you, it'll look very bad for Shao Hong."

"Fuck him." Yong-li cast his cigarette on the ground and stamped it out with the toe of his shoe.

I turned away from my brother.

"Sorry." He reached for my arm. I pulled it free. "Look, Lin Jun, if I get out, it'll be very good for all of you. I'm not going to *stay* in Russia. I'm going to America—"

"It's not so easy there," I said, the wind pulling my hair and stinging my eyes. I lowered my head.

"How do you know?" he asked, squinting, playing the tough man. "Look, I won't forget you once I make my fortune. I'll sponsor you myself. New York. San Francisco. Chinatown." His voice was only partially sarcastic.

I watched him. I could not believe he had once been so small. We had fed chickens together. After Mother died, he had cried, sitting on the dirt floor at Auntie's, and I had held his hands, both in my one, they were moist and grubby, his eyes red, looking at me, waiting for me to tell him what to do. He had been as small as my own son now, tufts of hair growing straight up from his head like rice seedlings, nose constantly running, feet too big for his ankles. After Father died, I had kept him from throwing Father's ashes out the window onto the heads of our neighbors gathered to sleep on the sidewalks during the hot, muggy summer nights. He needed me.

"When are you going?" I asked.

"Can't tell you." He grinned broadly, exposing a piece of tobacco stuck between his front teeth. He hugged me. "I've got some stuff to do now. I'll see you later," he waved.

He ran inside his dormitory, a blur of skinny legs and blue jeans. His silly long hair spilling over his neck like a splash of ink as my brother slipped away from me.

I couldn't help but feel I had done something wrong.

A week passed, and I thought I'd hear from him. He'd laugh and tell me it was all a joke. Or he'd laugh and tell me he'd been crazy and now he was on to some new scheme. I went by his dormitory after school one day. Knocked on his door. His roommates were there as usual, but

he was gone. "He's out," said a young man with a long thin face and a nose that curved at the tip.

"Out?" I glanced inside at the messy bunk beds, the papers piled on the long table in the middle of the room. "I'll leave a note for him. Which bunk is his?"

The men looked at each other.

"I'm his sister. We've met before," I prodded them.

One of them nodded at the others and stood up. A short man with a wide chest and hair that stood on end. He gestured for me to follow him. We went outside, stood in the dark just outside the light of the lamp illuminating the doorway.

"Didn't Yong-li tell you anything?" he said and I felt my stomach fall away.

"But—"

"He's not here anymore. That's all I can tell you. That's all I know."

"I know," I said miserably. "I just thought—"

"Don't worry." He smiled at me. I didn't like the way his teeth caught the light. "It's an adventure. It's a good time to be young."

I wanted to punch him, but instead I only turned away quickly and hurried back to the parking lot to find my Pigeon.

Riding home, my bag of books that I'd slung over my shoulder was bumping against my leg, so annoying, the thump, the tug, but I didn't want to pull over, to tie it on the back of my Pigeon, not in traffic, not when I was so cold. I was riding home like this, annoyed, when all at once I thought of how Yong-li would laugh at me, hunched forward, muscles stiff, tense, struggling with my bookbag, too lazy to do anything about it, just drifting, drifting in the stream of bicycles. How he would laugh. And I remembered then that I'd forgotten to tell him to be sure to bring some food with him, something dried, something easy to eat.

Dates, dried plums. Something to eat on a long trip. Just in case. And I forgot to tell him to be sure to visit all the special parts of Nanjing before he left, so that he'd never forget his home: the city wall, the park at Sorrow Lake, the statues in front of the Ming tombs. The one time Mother had taken me to see the stone elephants I was young. I remembered climbing on their backs, fingering the cold stone trunks. But Yong-li was not there in my memories. He must've been too young. He must've stayed at home that day. Mother must not have taken him with us. Perhaps it was before he was born.

Then something hidden tight inside of me broke open, a loud crack, and I cried like a child, in public, on my Pigeon, surrounded by everyone. We should've taken a family picture. How would Bao-bao remember him? We should've gone out to eat. I should've cooked a special dinner for him, crackling rice, a hot pot, duck. He was so thin, no fat on him, all that cafeteria food, and it was so cold now. And I didn't tell him anything. I didn't tell him that I loved him, or that I'd miss him. Or that I needed him. I hadn't said anything important at all.

What was wrong with me? I wondered. I was like that woman they found in the glacier, near Nepal or Siberia, I remembered reading about it in the paper, perfectly preserved, hair, skin, clothing, everything normal, but frozen to the core.

How on earth had I become this person?

13.

The Fight

A few days later, my life fell apart. Or you could say, a few days later, I woke up from a long sleep and the real me, the one who used to like to laugh, the girl who fought boys on the playground and won, the woman who used to be considered smart, that me finally put her foot down.

It began with the dance lesson.

Cynthia was worrying about the assembly, she was worrying about making Chinese friends, she was worrying about never doing anything "Chinese." I had promised to help her. There would be a dance after the assembly, a combination of Western disco and waltzing music. Cynthia had told me she didn't know how to waltz, and I told her I'd teach her.

"Then you can go to other dances," I said. "You'll make lots of friends."

We met in Cynthia's dormitory, a large six-story building on the university campus nearest the middle school. It was the first time I'd been in a dormitory for foreign visitors. I rode my Pigeon around it several times, circling, gaining confidence, trying to gain a sense of place and the people who could possibly want to live there. Music spilled from each lighted rectangular window, strange thumping sounds and wailing voices, but no laundry flapped from the wires outside the ledges. There were bicycles parked out front, some in rows, some haphazardly chained to trees, to fences, one to the arm of a bench. Forevers, Eagles, Swans by the dozen, rusting, bells fallen in half, brakes loose. Only one or two black Flying Pigeons, to the side, stately. I parked near the Swans, easier to find my Pigeon later.

In addition to the gatekeepers, I found security people were stationed at the main desk on the first floor. A bald man at the desk asked me to sign in. He eyed me suspiciously, as if I were a thief or something equally disreputable. "And show me some ID. Let's see your work card."

I looked at him in such a way that he had to feel my displeasure. "Why?"

"Ha." He took a puff on his cigarette. "If you don't, you can't see your friend."

Why did Chinese people have to be this way? A nation of people who distrusted each other. No wonder the country was still so poor when Japan and Taiwan were wealthy.

The interior of the dorm was not what I'd expected. It wasn't very clean, it was noisy, there were many Chinese people inside, old women pushing thin mops, young girls carrying bundles of laundry, men with cigarettes barking directions; I had seen just two foreigners, a man and a woman talking in a language I didn't recognize.

The hallway to Cynthia's room was dim but I could tell the floors

needed mopping. The wood had been a dark maroon but areas were scuffed nearly white; others had blackened from a buildup of dried mud and dirt. The walls were painted white on top and blue on the bottom. Both halves were smudged with dark finger and palm prints, stains from squashed cockroaches, chips in the plaster. The entire hall smelled faintly of urine. This was not a place where people came to live, it was for parking in between trips. A strange revelation.

Cynthia answered her door on the first knock. She'd been waiting. "I thought for a minute you might not be able to come." Cynthia led me inside. "I know, it's a mess, but, well . . ." She laughed. "I tried to clean up a bit, but then gave up. I'm really not very good at it." She sat on the floor, her legs sprawled out in front of her. "Have a seat."

I looked around but the only chair, by Cynthia's desk, was covered with books and papers. I sat on the edge of her bed. "This is not very good. They should make a better room for our foreign friends," I said, shaking my head. The room was essentially the same as those for Chinese college students; it was not what I had expected for a foreign expert. True, the room was large for one person; my own dormitory had housed eight in a room this size, but foreigners were used to space. China must look very poor if these were the best accommodations the school could arrange for her.

"Oh, do you want something to drink? I've got beer, soda—Coke?" Cynthia scooted backwards on her rear end across the polished wood floor. She opened the door of a small icebox.

"Do you have any tea or just hot water? That would be fine."

Cynthia winced. "Actually, I don't have any hot water. The hot water heater's broken in our dorm. God knows when they'll get around to fixing it."

"How terrible! You should have told me. I could have brought you

some hot water. Really, you don't need to be so polite." I shook my head. How could anyone live without hot water to drink? "How long has it been like this?"

"Oh, I dunno. A week or so. Don't look so alarmed." Cynthia leaned towards me, waving her hands. "It's okay. I can't stand drinking hot water or tea or even coffee. It was really funny when I first got here, it was like ninety degrees outside and I went to the cafeteria and they had these tanks of hot water for everyone to drink. I thought I'd died and gone to hell."

"Really?" I laughed. "What do you drink at your home? Beer and Coca-Cola?"

It was Cynthia's turn to laugh. She shook her head. "Cold water."

"That's bad for your stomach."

Cynthia shrugged, then slid along the floor until she was lying flat on her back, staring at the ceiling. She stretched one hand out into the air, as if grabbing for something. "How am I going to survive here a *year*?" she sighed.

"You'll do fine." I stood up. "Shall I show you how to dance? Do you have a tape player?"

Cynthia jumped to her feet. She took my tape and snapped it into a large box on her desk, digging it out from under more paper and a sweater. The sweet soft music began and I skipped across the floor. It had been so long since I had gone dancing. It felt good to waltz again.

"Oh, you're very good," Cynthia said, leaning against her desk, arms folded across her chest.

"No, no. But it is very easy. Come here. I'll show you." I took Cynthia's hands and pulled her out into the open space between the bed and the closet. "One two three. One two three. Like this." She stumbled a bit and stepped on my right foot.

"Oh, God, I'm sorry." Cynthia pulled her neck down into her shoulders.

"It is all right. I'm not used to dancing like the man." I stepped beside Cynthia. "First this foot back, then the other and step up. Yes. Yes. You learn very fast."

"No, I'm terrible," Cynthia said, staring at her feet, but she smiled.

"Look up. Here we can dance together." I pushed Cynthia gently around the room; the American was a fast learner. "I'll show you how to do a turn." I danced with the music, up down and back, up down and back. I closed my eyes as I twirled.

Cynthia clapped and called out loudly, "Whoo-ieee!" I laughed at her enthusiasm.

"Now you try."

We danced around the room, I hummed along with the music. I had danced on my wedding day, after the banquet. I had danced after our son was born. Then last year, after the school's fall assembly, some seniors had asked for lessons. One boy had been very good. It felt wonderful to move with the music.

The side of the tape clicked off abruptly in midphrase.

"Oh, too bad." Cynthia skipped over to the tape player and flipped the cassette.

"Can you rewind?" I was slightly out of breath. "The other side isn't good for dancing. It's just traditional music."

"Huh. Actually, can we hear some of that? We can take a break." Cynthia's face was flushed and she held her thick hair off her neck with one hand. "So would you like something to drink now?" Cynthia bounded over to her icebox.

"Okay."

"Coke?"

"Mmm, maybe a beer?"

"Sure thing." Cynthia handed me a bottle. "I have an opener here . . . somewhere." Cynthia patted the surface of her bookshelves, looking between volumes. "Here!"

The beer tasted better this time, perhaps because I was warm and slightly winded. I was out of shape, how distressing! I vowed immediately that I would do some exercises every day. I would begin tomorrow.

The *dizi* flute moaned on the tape, and each quivering note rose and fell like the wind. I read the titles of Cynthia's books.

"Feel free to borrow anything you want. I've already read those." Cynthia sighed. "It's so hard to get English books here. I should've brought more."

I nodded. I picked up a paperback book and looked at the cover. It was quite daring—a man and a woman wearing no clothing beneath a hat with wings that floated above them. But it was also beautiful. The paper felt smooth and slick. All the colors were rich and bright. I wished Chinese books were this way.

"That's good but kinda depressing." Cynthia appeared at my side. "Here's one I bet you'd like." She handed me a slim book with a deep blue and scarlet cover. A cat with glowing yellow eyes hovered below the title. I caressed the paper, turned the book over in my hands. A woman's picture was on the back.

"Oh!" I said in surprise. "Is the author a woman?"

"Yes!" said Cynthia, chuckling. "It's very good. Heh heh. This book is all about women who get back at the men who done them wrong!"

"Are there many women writers in America? I've read only Hemingway, Faulkner, Melville."

"Oh, there are tons."

"That's good." I opened the cover and tried to read a few lines.

Sometimes I wondered if there was any hope for my English. The book would be difficult. I looked again at the cover, rubbing my index finger over the paper slowly.

Cynthia had returned to her spot on the floor. She sat with her weight on her hands behind her, her head thrown back, hair cascading to the floor. She looked very unusual, but also very relaxed, as if she was enjoying herself. "I like this music," Cynthia said, her eyes closed. "It reminds me a little of Kitaro. Do you know him? He's this Japanese guy, lives in America. Maybe he's Japanese American. I don't know."

My chest filled with lead. My eyes burned, and I squinted to make them clear. It was wrong of me to feel this way, I knew. Cynthia was so kind. But still I envied her knowledge, to be able to have dozens of beautiful books on her shelves and recommend the authors, to know of women writers, "tons"! To be so young and be able to travel, to talk of so many things so easily, to know of musicians—from Japan, from America, the world. To work so hard all your life and have nothing to show for it. I would die like my mother, like Auntie. Bitterness squeezed my heart. Tight, so tight. I couldn't breathe.

"How's your beer doing? Want some more?" Cynthia called to me.

"No, thank you. I'm fine." The music took my voice. It was slow, reedy, meant to sound like a river. Running to the sea, forever. Never still and never going anywhere. Chinese music was like this, depressing.

The music stayed with me while I rode home in the dark, cold air filling my mouth, my nose, my chest. I pedaled quickly, forcing myself to breathe in the night in gasps that burned my teeth. Winter was coming. The moon was obscured by clouds. I took alleys, shortcuts, clenched my jaw against the bumps that jarred the Pigeon and me to the bone. I pedaled furiously as if I could outdistance the cold. How foolish.

* * *

I was late again. Shao Hong was waiting for me at the table, every muscle in his body tense, his shoulders rigid, his back too straight. I see this moment in my head over and over, like a scene from an opera I saw as a child. I don't recall the name. The hero walks into the villain's trap and although we knew the story, we always shouted out, "No! No! Stop!" as if that would help—they were only actors, not real—as if we could change the story, so old, hundreds of years old, and always the story has been the same. The hero has walked into the trap, Zhuge Liang is taken captive by General Cao, the tiger slayer is poisoned by his jealous sister-in-law, the scholar arrives too late to save his sweetheart. It doesn't matter which story, we know them all, and the hero must always make the one mistake that can't be undone. Only during the Cultural Revolution did the stories always have happy endings. Madame Mao's lover starred in a movie about the Opium War: China won this time. But these stories were not as good. In the real stories, the ones Mother told me, our hero makes a mistake.

I knew Shao Hong was angry, but I was tired and I was angry, too, that he would ruin my mood, my good evening. I sighed as I hung up my coat, perhaps loudly. "Did you find the pork balls I made for you?"

"Where were you?"

"Oh," I said, rushing into the kitchen to heat his dinner. Rushing to be away from him, his foul mood. "I was teaching the foreign teacher to dance. Chinese style. Our school's having an assembly—"

"She won't sponsor you to go to America."

I brought out some cold sausage and set a plate before my husband on the table. "How was your work?"

"I'd go if I had the chance." He took his rice bowl in one hand but did not eat. He sniffed at the sticky rice then turned the bowl upside down onto the table.

"Shao Hong! What's the matter with you?"

"What's the matter with *you!*" He jumped to his feet, knocking his chair over in the process. "You think I work all day so I can support a dance teacher? If I didn't have a family, I could be a translator for a joint-venture company. I could go abroad. At least, I would be in Shenzhen or Guangzhou!"

"You don't have to shout." I scooped up the rice on the table.

"Stop it!" Shao Hong knocked the bowl out of my hands. It fell to the floor and shattered. "All you think about is food! You have no intellectual thoughts."

He slammed his hand against the table. The sound was like a gunshot. He looked at me as though he hated me then kicked the table onto its side. A leg struck me across the knees and I dropped to the floor, landing heavily on one knee, twisting my wrist. I winced, gasping.

My husband fled to his study. I heard a crash, like thunder. He had thrown his typewriter, his foreign typewriter, so expensive. Then silence followed.

I stood up. I thought, he broke his typewriter. How does he think he can buy another one? I didn't pick up the pieces of the broken rice bowl, I didn't right the table. I stepped on the pork and rice now coating the floor and limped into the kitchen. I ran the cold water from the tap over my burning wrist. The water fell in a smooth icy stream.

I looked in the glass of the window and a hideous woman peered back at me, floating in the night sky. Her face was misshapen, swollen with tears, the mouth gaping. She was old. It was the face of Auntie Gao.

I looked away; my heart pinched too tight to beat properly, I couldn't breathe. I hiccupped. I had to do something, so I picked up a cleaning basin and held it beneath the stream of water, which fell with a tinny sharp sound against the bottom. I felt the basin grow heavier, I judged

its pull on my arms, then turned the water off. I stopped crying and found a washrag.

I carried the basin out of the kitchen, careful not to spill a drop. Food stuck to my feet. I didn't care. The poor table looked so forlorn, its underside exposed, legs sticking to one side. It seemed older, more worn. It was not such a nice table after all. I had never noticed before. I set the basin on the floor and knelt down beside it, putting my hand in the cold water. It burned.

But then, I couldn't think clearly. I could only feel the pain. Not my knee, nor my wrist, though they hurt worse, actually, now that the weather was damper. What I felt was the hole that had opened inside of me and I was scared.

I put my face into the basin. I opened my eyes but couldn't see anything, my neck hurt. I panicked and sat up, water running from my nose. I blinked.

I was stupid. A stupid stupid stupid woman.

Another crash in Shao Hong's study. I froze, waiting, unable to get up, do anything. I heard a footstep and realized he must be kicking something. What a mess he must be making.

I forced myself to my feet and hefted the basin to waist level, careful not to spill the water. A wave rocked violently from side to side for a moment then was calm.

I took small childlike steps down the hall. I didn't look at myself, as I usually did, reflected in the glass of the painting there—the phoenix and the dragon, a gift from Shao Hong's parents. I stood outside his door for a second, unable to call out to him; my throat was tight, dry. I imagined my voice back, steady and cheerful.

The door was slightly ajar. I nudged it with the toe of my shoe. Obedient door, it opened. I stepped inside my husband's study.

Shao Hong stood at the far wall in front of a gaping hole where a huge chunk of white plaster had been knocked to the floor. Shao Hong stood facing the wreckage of his typewriter. He didn't say anything.

Pieces of metal lay at my feet. Several large dictionaries had fallen or been flung from their shelf. The papers and files that usually littered his desk had slid together into one shapeless pile beside his overturned chair.

I stared at the framed picture of our son lying on its side.

The bookshelves were in order. They stood three in a row filled with his dictionaries, the bound volumes of his magazines. I remembered when the room had held the red crib, the red quilts, the paper cutouts I'd pasted onto the walls: the characters for "double happiness" in shiny orange, green treasure pots, gold coins.

I looked at the back of my husband's shoulders. They straightened and he turned to face me.

"We can clean this up," I said softly. I meant to say this. But perhaps I only opened my mouth and no sound came out.

"Leave me alone!" His face puckered into a mass of red wrinkles. "Go away."

I felt his voice penetrate my bones. I shook and, without thinking, threw the basin full of water at my husband. His eyes opened wide, so wide, in perfect grape-like circles, round like his mouth. He did not have time to say a word before the water struck his face.

Then I cried.

I rode my Pigeon late into the night, later than I ever had before. It's impossible to cry into a wind, the cold air dries the tears. Such a pleasing discovery.

I watched the streets empty of students, of illicit lovers enjoying the

night sky. I rode with the insomniacs, workers on the late shift, the least powerful members of gangs, still unable to afford anything other than a bicycle. In the middle of the night, bundled in our sweaters, we all looked alike, sexless, lumpy, shadowy.

I rode across the smooth asphalt, tore through intersections—the lights merely flashing red so late at night, not enough traffic to regulate—rode alongside the huge trucks that enter the city at night, bringing large cables, concrete blocks, and steel beams. They moved fast, blinking their headlights only if they saw another truck, stirring up a wind that smelled of exhaust. The elephants had returned to Nanjing. I was like a fly next to them.

Private restaurants were filled with the newly rich, the semi-dangerous, the loud. I heard their voices in my ears as I shot by on two wheels. Laughter and shouts.

I passed fights, men spilling onto the sidewalks, fists raised. A man and a woman shouted while the neighbors pulled them apart.

My city was changing, growing, around me, but the people were always the same. Fighting and shouting and laughing. I was very cold.

I rode to the south, to the remaining section of our city wall. During the war, the Japanese soldiers went through every neighborhood, knocked at every other household, and pulled one member into the street. They brought their captives to the wall's twelve gates and shot three hundred thousand people dead. And still my city was full of life.

The wall was made of bricks, each one signed with the seal of its maker. Hundreds of names, thousands, of people dead for centuries. This was a dangerous section of the city. Outside the wall, the city came to an end. On one road lined with trees, weeds, wildflowers, and thistles, I could ride to a lake that Yong-li and I had learned to swim in more than twenty-five years ago. A quarter century already. I had

thought about taking Bao-bao there one summer, but it was so polluted, completely black, the fish dead.

I could have taken the main road all the way to the sacred path of a dead Ming emperor, and if I kept going, I could have ridden to the Purple Mountains. There were no streetlights, no people. No one rode on these roads at night. I could have disappeared forever.

In the movie version, this is where Gong Li would have gone mad or killed herself in despair. Or both. But I merely rode my Pigeon, circling round and round the streets of my city, until my fingers were numb with cold, my face frozen, until finally the black of night began to seep away and the horizon began to pulse with gold.

That morning, I went back and told Shao Hong I wanted a divorce. He laughed at first, said I was crazy, foolish, that I was not serious. But he was wrong.

14.

Practicalities

Catharsis is good, important, very necessary. You've broken the cycle of codependency, you're on the road to becoming your own person," said Cynthia when I told her about my decision, "but now you need to start thinking about the practical end of things. Can you support yourself and your son? Do you have a lawyer? You told me your husband's work unit assigned you the apartment, right? Where are you going to live? Are you going to need a restraining order for your husband?"

"This is all very American," I said.

"Very *practical*," Cynthia corrected me. We were sitting in her office, huddled around the space heater she had brought back from Shanghai one weekend, but it was still very cold. The windows didn't

fit exactly in their casings, and the wind always managed to find its way inside.

Suddenly Cynthia sprang up from the couch and began to do jumping jacks. "I . . . hate . . . winter," she breathed as she jumped. "I . . . hate . . . winter." She proceeded to jog around the small office. "We need . . . to get . . . your case . . . in order."

I leaned closer to the glowing orange coils within the heater. "So you think this is the right decision?"

"We need—what?" Cynthia paused, jogged in place. "It's your decision."

"That's what I think."

"And you said you were sure?"

"I am."

"Then it's the right decision. Besides, if any man tried to hit me, I'd—I'd do more than divorce him. I'd kill him!"

"You don't think I'm a bad mother, do you?" I ventured at last, now that I was sure what she would say.

"A bad mother? Where did you get that from?"

A tap-tap-tap startled me. Mrs. Mu was standing in the doorway. She knocked on the glass of the window again and waved. She was wrapped in so many layers of wool, she looked like a sheep walking on two legs. Only her eyes peeked out from above the soft piles of her gray scarves and pink and green sweaters.

"Sorry to see you," said Mrs. Mu in English.

"Oh, it's no *bother*," Cynthia said, politely trying to correct her.

"But I come up to see what is all the thump thump noise on the ceiling. I want to see you are okay." The junior-high English teachers' office was below Cynthia's. "A huge chunk of plaster has fallen loose," she told me in Chinese, giggling into her hand.

"Oh, God, I'm sorry." Cynthia had understood her.

"No, no, it's very funny." Mrs. Mu's eyes twinkled mischievously. "Ms. Yu is very upset. Her desk is covered with dust."

"Don't worry," I said to Cynthia, who looked horrified. "Ms. Yu is not a very nice person."

"I'll go apologize. Right now." Cynthia took off in a run.

I didn't want her to go. I wasn't sure how much Mrs. Mu had heard and I didn't feel like providing the mah-jongg gossip circles with any new material at the moment.

"It's so cold. The American has the right idea." Mrs. Mu sat down gingerly by the heater. "My mother-in-law wouldn't like this. She says heat in the winter is bad. 'The inside and the outside of a house should be the same season,' she says. 'This electric heat is not natural.' " She sighed and put her feet in front of the humming orange coils. "You know, Lin Jun, you should be careful what you say to the American." She didn't look at me as she spoke but watched her hands intently, pulling at loose yarn on her fingerless gloves.

"Cynthia is very kind."

"She's very young. And Secretary Wang doesn't like her. 'Our foreigner is not like the blonde they have at the Number Three Middle School. Their foreigner is very *wenjing*, a good girl,' she said. 'Our foreigner is always running around by herself. She's even trying to learn Chinese. She must be up to something.' "

"The Secretary is supposed to be suspicious. That's her job."

"Yes, the Secretary likes everything to be in order. She doesn't like teachers who do anything unusual."

"Naturally," I said, pretending I was dense. I knew the Secretary wouldn't approve of a divorce. I knew she'd try to "persuade" me to

reconsider. I wanted to put off that confrontation as long as possible. I decided I'd be blunt. "You won't say anything, will you?"

"No, no, no. Of course not." Mrs. Mu waved her hand at me. "When do I ever talk to the Secretary?" She leaned back into Cynthia's sofa, half-closing her eyes. "This heater is very nice," she murmured.

"I'll get you some tea."

"You know, Secretary Wang and I were classmates."

"Really?"

"Oh, yes. A long time ago. In junior middle school. I was very bright. I was selected to go to a special school to study foreign languages. Do you know when I was a young woman, I could translate a Russian book this thick!" Mrs. Mu suddenly sat up. "Ha. Now, of course, I can't even read a Russian book. But I was a smart one."

I didn't know what to say. I offered her a mug of tea, but she didn't notice, so I stood there awkwardly, watching as Mrs. Mu squinted out the dust-streaked window. "But the Secretary is very smart too." She laughed suddenly. "She had a very good family background. Peasants on one side, some poor boat people on the other. A very powerful background for her. She denounced my husband as a rightist. My first husband, I mean. It was very hard on him. He had to be reeducated. I followed him all over the country. Oh, we lived in terrible places. You should see how the peasants lived. So terrible. But I followed him while he did some studies of peasant conditions in Heilongjiang Province, near Russia. That's how they put it in those days. 'Comrade Zhou is going to do some studies with the peasants.' " She smiled.

"There were a lot of Russians there, so it was very good for me. I could practice speaking. I had a lot of books. Of course, they were all technical manuals. How to build irrigation canals. Dike construction. That kind of

thing. I really enjoyed myself. My husband hated it, he was just a skinny intellectual, and in Heilongjiang winter lasts ten months. My husband used to tease me, 'How do I know you weren't the one who criticized me, had me sent here, just so that you could show off your Russian!' "

Mrs. Mu suddenly giggled; the sound, like a pigeon's cooing, filled the small office.

I touched her gloved hand. I had heard that this first husband died of pneumonia in a small village. Mrs. Mu had tried to find some way to bring him to a bigger city, where there were real doctors, not just a former medical student who had volunteered to live in the Northern Wilderness to help the Motherland, but it was winter, and a snowstorm made it impossible to travel. I knew that Mrs. Mu would have tried to make the journey under any conditions to get some herbs for her husband, but she was afraid he would die before she returned and so she preferred to stay by his sickbed. I'd heard this part of the story from some of the other older teachers after our disastrous trip to Beijing. They liked to talk about these things, compare their suffering. I didn't like to sit in the office when the older teachers were there.

"That's where I met my second husband. In Heilongjiang. He was a soldier. Later, he became a general. Very good family background. Peasants on both sides of his family. When I came back to Nanjing with him, we never had any trouble. Not even during the Cultural Revolution. And even Secretary Wang had to suffer a little then." Mrs. Mu smiled at me.

"I should go. I have so much work to do." She shook her head. "My students are so stupid. I try to explain the simplest things to them and they can't understand. They're so naughty. Talk talk talk, all the time."

"The students may seem as though they don't pay attention to you," I

said, "but I always know which ones had you for their teacher. They can spell very well."

"I don't know. I think they're stupid." Mrs. Mu rose to her feet slowly. "I don't want to get too used to this heater. It's really convenient, huh?"

"Cynthia bought it in Shanghai—"

"Lin Jun." Mrs. Mu turned and held on to my arm for a moment. "There are worse things than a divorce. Don't worry. You shouldn't worry at your age. You should be happy when you're young." Pulling her sweaters tighter around her body, she waved and was off.

I paced around the office for a while after that. I turned off the heater, I was sweating. I paced some more. Then I was so cold my teeth chattered loud enough for me to hear them. I didn't want to go home, see Shao Hong, talk to him again, fight with him again. But I didn't want to stay at school any longer. I felt afraid.

Pulling my Pigeon free from the tangle of bikes in the teachers' parking lot, I heard a strange voice call my name.

It was Chen Hua. I hadn't recognized her voice at first. It had sounded higher, sharper.

"Xiao Lin!" She ran up to me and grabbed hold of my arm. She was panting and her face was red.

"What's the matter?"

"I just heard."

"What?" Something terrible, I imagined. A death, one of the older teachers? A fight among the students?

"Silly," she said, "your divorce!"

"What?!"

"What do you mean 'What'?"

"I mean, what are you talking about?"

"You are getting a divorce, aren't you?"

"Who told you!"

"Oh, I see. It's like that." She turned to go. "Your foreigner told me."

I ran after her, letting my Pigeon fall with a clatter to the pavement. "Chen Hua! Don't be like that!"

"Don't mind me." She waved me away with one fuchsia-mittened hand.

I grabbed her arm. "Chen Hua, I'm sorry. I've had the worst day. You don't understand. Mrs. Mu knows. I thought she was telling people—"

"You told Mrs. Mu!" Chen Hua pulled herself away from me. She stamped one foot on the ground. "You're too much! You tell that gossip—"

"No, no, I didn't—"

"And you don't want me—"

"No, no, she overheard me."

"So you were telling everyone?"

"Chen Hua, please!" I felt like I was going to burst into tears, that burning sensation right between my eyes. I tried to put pressure on the bridge of my nose, wherever that acupuncture point was that controlled tears, pinching as hard as I could. "Chen Hua!" I called after her desperately.

The tiny figure running towards the school gate turned around slowly.

"What's the matter with your nose?"

"Please!" I waved for her to come back with my free hand.

She approached slowly. I glanced nervously over my shoulder to see if my bike was okay. I didn't want any mischievous students to try to take it.

"What are you doing?" She peered into my face curiously.

I felt despair, fatigue. My nose burned worse than ever. "Ssh!" I hissed.

"I'll tell you, but not here. Please, Chen Hua. You have to believe me—it's been so horrible, so horrible—Mrs. Mu overheard me talking—I wanted to talk to you too but you were in class—it's so terrible now—everyone will know—I don't know what to do—" I was blubbering hysterically.

"Okay, okay, calm down. Let go of your nose—what are you trying to do? You'll get a nosebleed." She pulled a handkerchief from her purse. "Here."

"Thank you," I sniffed.

"Try to look like you have something in your eye, at least. Don't be so obvious!" Chen Hua snatched her handkerchief back and made a show of looking into my eye, then dabbed at the corner with the pink cloth. "The whole school will know you're crying. Really, you could've been a silent movie star, the way you can project your emotions fifty feet in front of you."

We went to one of the noodle alleys far north of the school. I didn't want any of our students to see me in such a state, although of course they shouldn't be wandering around the noodle alleys on a school night in the first place. But nowadays you could never be too sure. For all we knew, some of our students might have been working in the noodle alleys.

The makeshift restaurants were really no more than a few flatbeds with coal barbecues. The patrons sat on knee-high stools at tables nearly as low, made of crates and plywood boards. Someone had strung a line of colored light bulbs from one cart to the next. Although it was very cold to be eating outdoors, each noodle cart was surrounded by customers.

"I'm sure they take in each night what we make in a month," Chen Hua whispered to me, giving me a poke.

We found an empty table. The top was sticky.

The cook was smoking, the ashes on the end of his cigarette dangling perilously over a steaming bowl of rice noodles as he flipped an egg in a greasy iron wok.

Chen Hua ordered two bowls for us.

"I hope we don't get sick," I said.

"I know something that will kill the germs." Chen Hua waved to the cook. "Two beers."

I explained to Chen Hua about everything that had happened—my talk with my husband, my talk with Cynthia, my talk with Mrs. Mu. She listened, nodding, sipping her warm beer.

"You shouldn't worry. Don't allow yourself to get depressed. It'll only make things worse."

"Too late."

"You'll have a problem finding a new husband," Chen Hua said suddenly.

"I don't want a new husband."

"Hmph," she said.

We sat in silence for a while, slurping our noodles.

"You're so lucky," she said finally. "Things have always come to you so easily. Your English is so good, you're beautiful, your students like you. Don't worry. Everything will work out. It always does."

I was so infuriated, I couldn't think of anything to say. Where was this all coming from? Lucky? Not that again! And from Chen Hua. It really was too much. In my anger, I ended up spilling soup on myself. I stood up quickly, annoyed.

"Excuse me," a husky voice addressed me, "is this seat taken?"

I looked up and found a heavy blond woman standing across from me. Her eyes were pale, startled looking. I blinked and glanced over my shoulder to see whom she was talking to.

She sat down at our table.

The woman's Chinese was heavily accented but not impossible to understand. "Thanks," she said. "Girls' night out, eh?" She was wearing a lot of makeup, her lips enormous and a greasy red, her ghostly eyes ringed with black, another layer of color coating the lids.

The noodleman set a bowl in front of the foreign woman with a clunk. Some of the soup spilled onto the table. "Bastard," the woman growled. She blew on her noodles, her huge mouth hovering above the surface of the bowl.

She was wearing a large leather jacket with a red silk scarf tied around her neck. Her hair was pulled back tightly on her head and was smooth and very slick, reflecting the red and blue colored lights. It seemed as though that would hurt. She had enormous breasts.

"You're staring." The woman looked me directly in the eyes.

"Sorry," I said. I glanced at Chen Hua, who rolled her eyes at me.

I felt I should say something. "You speak Chinese," I said stupidly.

The woman smiled, so many teeth for one mouth. "Maybe I am Chinese." She picked up a clump of noodles between her chopsticks and blew on them, then stuffed them into her round mouth.

Then a man appeared, short and very wide, like a square table himself. He had Chinese features, black hair, black eyes. He grabbed the woman's arm from behind. He was very fast. I had barely seen the man's face emerge from the crowd when suddenly he was there, pushing against the table, spilling my soup again. The man shouted in a strange

language at the woman. The woman answered him in Mandarin. "Fuck," she said. "I'm eating." She pulled her arm free.

The man slammed his hand on the table. Both Chen Hua and I stood up.

"Oh, sorry," the man said in Chinese, his voice like a backfire, explosive. He eyed me quickly. The man did not move from the woman's side.

"Hey," I said. "Um. Are you okay?" I asked the woman.

Chen Hua nudged me. Hard.

The woman drew one more strand of noodles out with her chopsticks, bit into the side so that half fell back into the bowl. She chewed noisily, gulping air. Then she stood up and faced the man. She was taller. He moved closer to her now, moving slightly into the light. I could see now that they wore the same style jacket. The woman also wore a very short leather skirt—some of her thigh showed above the top of the table. The man took hold of her elbow. His fingers were short and thick. The man said something to her again in the foreign language. Something ugly, as though he were clearing his throat. The woman tossed her head.

"Thanks for keeping me company, sisters." The woman nodded at us. She turned away before I could say a thing. If I could have thought of something to say. She walked quickly past the other noodle stands, weaving through the scattered tables and squat benches. The man followed, having to hurry to keep up. A large shiny snake decorated the back of his jacket, in red and blue. I could not see where they went once they had stepped out of range of the noodle stands' lights.

I looked at Chen Hua and she looked at me and then we both burst out laughing. We couldn't stop. It was terrible. The cook looked at us funny, and I could see some of the other customers nodding in our

direction, but I couldn't stop myself. I was laughing as I had when I was a child, my mouth wide open, no sound coming out. I could barely breathe. I leaned against the table, trying to brace myself, and promptly knocked my bowl to the ground. It broke into twenty pieces.

"That's bad luck," barked the cook. "That's my bowl. Who's going to pay for my bowl?"

"Sorry, sorry, I'm so sorry," I said, laughing. I dug into my purse for a few bills.

"That's too much money," said Chen Hua. "His bowls are all cracked anyway."

"You're trying to cause trouble, are you?" growled the cook.

"Me? What about the Amazon and her pimp!"

"Ssh! Ssh!" I said, still laughing horribly. I tried to pull Chen Hua away.

The cook followed us down the alley, shaking his ladle at us. "Who needs troublemakers like you here?"

Chen Hua stopped in her tracks. She turned slowly, hands on her hips, and then raised one hand slowly above her head. Then all at once, she began to sing. She sang the battle song from the opera about the White Snake Demon, the story of a woman who is enchanted, who can turn into a snake, who can fight better than any man, and who gives it all up for her lover. The way Chen Hua sang, you would have thought the White Snake Demon was unconquerable.

The cook's eyes bugged out and his mouth fell open. He dropped his ladle.

Chen Hua's performance was a huge success. The other customers cheered and clapped. One table of drunken men jumped to their feet as they tapped their chopsticks against the sides of their soup bowls. Some of them whistled.

We took off running. "Hurry, hurry!" I pulled Chen Hua behind me. Chen Hua was so tipsy, she could barely get on her bicycle. "Oh, hurry!"

We rode off into the night, pedaling fast, the alley so bumpy, it was hard to ride straight. But soon we were on the main boulevard, streetlights casting wide nets of bright light for us to ride through, traffic swirling around us, and I could feel safe, calm at last.

"Slow down," Chen Hua called to me. "It's freezing!"

I smiled into the wind. I felt inexplicably free.

I did not allow myself to ruin the moment by thinking of anything practical.

15.

Woman of Steel

The euphoria wore off soon enough.

It was all right so long as I was asleep. But waking every morning, that was something else. Lying next to Shao Hong, waiting for the pale light of dawn, hoping he was still asleep, listening to him breathe, neither of us touching. Thinking. He hates me, he hates me now. Finally, when the sun had risen just enough to lighten the charcoal color of the air to a foggy gray, I could rise, slide out from under the quilt. I tiptoed to the bathroom, shut the door softly. I didn't bother to turn on the light. I didn't want to see my face. I didn't want to see the confusion of my features, the half-wakened blurriness in the eyes, the slackness in the mouth, my face trying to pull itself into shape.

If I was lucky, he would still be asleep, and I could leave for work early, huddling in my office, grading papers. Some of my students

discovered I was coming early, and they would come with their home-work, the English diaries I had assigned them to write. One girl, a thin-faced solemn child who was as smart as the boys, as the other teachers liked to say, often brought me copies of the Shakespeare play she was retranslating from Chinese back into English, so that she and her class-mates could perform it for Cynthia at the upcoming assembly. At work, it was easy to forget.

But if I was too slow, or dropped something that made a loud noise, if Shao Hong woke early for some reason, I would return from the bath-room to find him sitting up on the edge of the bed, listlessly staring at the door, waiting for me, his eyes dark and hollow.

Like the first morning, when I returned, frozen, my face bleached white from riding until dawn, and I found him awake, waiting for me. He'd cleaned the apartment, righted the table, straightened up the mess of his study. His hands were covered with chalky white dust, except for a long dark smear where he'd cut himself and bled.

He laughed at first when I told him.

"I'm serious," I said. "I can't stay married to you. I don't love you anymore."

"'Anymore'?"

I wouldn't let him continue. "I've thought about it for a long time now. And I think it'll be better in the long run. For both of us." I told him that morning, standing still, calm, while he sat staring at me in shock, his face as pale as the moon.

"What about our son?"

"I've been thinking all night. How I should tell you. How." He still did not move. I could see that he knew I was serious. He looked surprised. I was surprised. I thought he would feel as I did, that it had been inevitable, this decision. We had been moving toward it for five years. It

felt familiar to me, like a friend I hadn't seen for years and who suddenly appeared at my door. The recognition felt so complete. "This is probably not the best way to tell you, but I didn't think I could pretend anymore."

"Pretend?" He didn't move. He stared at the floor now.

"We can arrange the details later. But I don't want to wait too much longer . . . Shao Hong, do you understand what I'm saying to you?"

"You want to deprive your son of a father? You can't get a divorce. We can't, it's not right." He stood up. Holding himself stiffly, he walked towards me.

I shook my head, turned to go. He ran towards me now, grabbed hold of my arm. "Are you going to hit me again?" My calm felt natural.

He let go.

I fled our apartment, the atmosphere of sorrow, the heaviness. I went to the market, where peasants were cheerfully setting up their displays of cabbage and peppers, eggs and parsnips. Bin after bin, baskets, blankets filled with vegetables. Steam rising from the basins they used to wash their faces, whole families setting up their stands. It didn't seem real.

When I came back, the cold morning air slipping in the door beside me, my husband was pacing in the living room. He turned, a startled look on his face.

"I'm sorry," he said.

I hung up my coat on the nail by the door, took off my shoes. I brought my purchases into the kitchen, the mesh bag of green pears—too hard to eat—and twelve dried mushrooms. Who knew what I had been thinking.

"I'm sorry," said a voice behind me, louder this time, in case I hadn't heard the first time.

I dropped the pears into the metal sink, one by one. "Well, what do

you want me to do about it?" I answered quickly before he could say any-thing more. "It's too late." Then I locked myself in the bathroom for three hours.

I continued this way, avoiding him, avoiding any talk, day after day, morning after night. It was not the proper way to behave. It would have to break sometime, I knew it. And it wasn't that I was afraid of an argu-ment; I wasn't afraid anymore. But it was the sad broken way he spoke.

"Did you ever love me?" he asked me one morning, a week after I had told him.

"Of course," I said. "But surely this doesn't surprise you. You had to know. You had to feel it. You have to understand."

But he still looked like a child who had had his candy stolen by the class bully, confused and angry, a little afraid.

Once, in the disoriented first moments between my dreams and my life, when I had no memory, I reached out in my sleep to my husband at my side, touched his shoulder, and then when he touched my hand, I snapped back awake, in the present, my heart swollen, and I pulled away quickly, pushed away my sheets and scrambled to my feet.

"I'll quit my job," he said the next week.

"You're crazy."

"What's the point of working, wasting all my life for these idiots? What's the point? Every night I go out with my senior editors, the assis-tant editors, the assistant to the assistant editors. We smoke, they drink, we talk about how clever our senior editors are, they talk about how clever they are, for what? Do I ever get an assignment? Will I ever write my own articles? I'm a translator. I translate their editorials. I translate foreign writers' articles. Do you think I enjoy this life?"

"Why are you telling me this?"

"I don't want a divorce. They'll laugh at me."

"That's too much. Really too much."

"No, you don't understand. I'll be a fool. Let's just be separated. No divorce. I'll never let you divorce me."

He was panicked and hysterical.

The next week, he slunk around the apartment like the chickens tethered by a string around their legs in the alleys around the school. Meek and worn, he cried when he looked at me. I was worried when Bao-bao came home and Shao Hong would only glance at him and his eyes would fill with viscous tears.

At supper Saturday night Bao-bao looked at me, grains of rice dotting his cheeks. "I want to go back to school."

"No, no, that's not necessary," I said.

"But I want to."

I gathered up our bowls. My temples pulsed. I felt very close to a nervous breakdown. I wanted Shao Hong to snap out of it. "Shao Hong, I have a lot of schoolwork tonight. Can you look after Bao-bao?"

They both looked at me, identical expressions of surprise and horror. I had never realized how much they resembled each other until this moment.

"Why don't you grade your papers tomorrow?"

"We're going to see your parents tomorrow. And I'm not grading papers."

"So what are you doing then?"

"I need to prepare for Cynthia's class. Remember? Our American teacher."

"*Your* American is causing a lot of trouble. You should be more careful. Full of poisonous ideas. American women are wild."

"And you know all about American women."

Bao-bao sniffled, and his mouth fell open. He put his two hands, balled into fists, to his temples. I wiped the rice off his face quickly with the dishtowel to distract him. Shao Hong sat with his head in his hands. He mumbled something incoherent. They were both absolutely pathetic looking.

"All right, Bao-bao, go play with Daddy." I nearly sang, my voice oozing cheer. I swung him up from his seat and brought him to Shao Hong. "Mommy needs to use the table." I prodded Shao Hong with a finger.

He sat up, blinking. "Come on, Bao-bao. Daddy'll read you a story." When Bao-bao was a toddler, long before he started school, he'd sit on the edge of his bed, his eyes round, as Shao Hong read to him about the Monkey King. Shao Hong couldn't make up his own stories, but Bao-bao clapped away and begged him to read the same story again, over and over and over.

"It's too early for a story," Bao-bao said. He looked at Shao Hong then looked at his feet.

It was a disaster, but I forced myself to spread my books and dictionaries across the kitchen table while I watched them from the corners of my eyes.

"What do you like to play at school?" Shao Hong asked him awkwardly.

"We watch TV." He sighed, loudly and dramatically. "But Mommy said ours is still broken."

"TV is bad for your eyes." Shao Hong spoke a little too quickly. Bao-bao took a step or two backwards. He glanced towards me. "So, do you have homework?" Shao Hong tried again.

"No."

"What kind of school is this? When I was your age, I could recite classical poetry. What do they teach you?"

"He's only five." There was no hope for this, I realized. Secretly, I felt a little pleased. I grabbed Bao-bao under the arms and swung him around and around. He giggled happily. "Come on, show Daddy your new song."

Bao-bao smiled at last. He faced Shao Hong, took a step away from me, and began to sing in a surprisingly clear, loud voice: "We love China, she is our Motherland . . ." To accompany the words, he had been taught a few stylized dance steps, in which he moved his arms and legs just slightly out of sync. The whole effect was slightly alarming.

The song and dance routine ended abruptly with my son standing frozen, smiling, head cocked to one side, arms flung out to the left, one foot up in the air, toe pointed. It took us a few seconds to realize this was the end.

Shao Hong's face was turning red, from his ears to his cheeks. He sniffed loudly.

I clapped frantically.

I knew it would be hard—what isn't hard?—but I never realized how hard this would be.

Cynthia was right. There were a lot of details that needed to be sorted out. How to tell Bao-bao. How to live together in the meantime. How to live after. How to arrange for space in the unmarried teachers' dormitory. How to endure. Without absolutely going mad.

16.

Reality Like Cold Soup

It is very hard for a woman to get a divorce, especially now," said Secretary Wang. "After the counterrevolutionary activities at Tiananmen, our society needs to reexamine itself. Our young people have become too selfish, too individualistic. This is what causes tragedies."

I had been sitting in the hard plastic chair in the Secretary's office for nearly two hours and there was no sign of her energy flagging. I, on the other hand, felt wilted.

"Naturally, if your husband beat you regularly, that would be something else. Or if you couldn't have a child—"

"The Marriage Law says 'absence of love,'" I quoted to her. "'Absence of love is enough for a divorce.'"

"But you were in love when you got married. I remember. I attended the wedding banquet the school threw for you. I saw you and your

handsome husband, the two of you were smiling. The two of you were happy. Nobody forced you to get married, did they?"

I stretched my toes within my shoes. I pressed my hands together.

"You see? I think you can undergo some counseling—"

"I've made up my mind. This is a private affair—"

"A divorce is never a private affair!" The Secretary stood up angrily. I imagined how she must have looked during the Cultural Revolution, leading struggle sessions, denouncing the poor intellectuals, the teachers, the odd worker with an unfortunate family background, flames from a bonfire reaching high above her head, banners waving against the blackened sky. Such unhappiness.

I was standing on the platform for the assemblies in the playground, all the teachers from our school seated on folding chairs in neat columns before me. Secretary Wang was shouting into a microphone, her voice distorted into a screech: "Lin Jun has caught the red-eyed disease. She is envious of foreign ways. She is cultivating the germ of advanced-nation's disease, infecting our school."

"This is ridiculous," I shouted at her, straining to make my thin voice stretch above the sound of the P.A. I smiled and shook my head in disbelief. I shrugged to the teacher forced to watch this bizarre spectacle, but no one was smiling at me. Everyone looked very serious, the corners of their mouths turned down, a sea of unhappy faces. I searched the crowd for Chen Hua, spotted her in a back row, but she wouldn't look at me though I waved at her frantically. Purposefully, she turned her head away.

"Listen to me!" I shouted. "It's not fair!"

But the Secretary's voice drowned mine. She shouted, "Down with Lin Jun, the counterrevolutionary! Down with Teacher Lin, the antisocialist spirit!"

I sat up with my eyes still closed, panting. I was sweating profusely, my hair damp against my neck. I forced my eyes open and looked around my bedroom, dazed.

My husband was in the bathroom. I could hear him gargling.

Cynthia was right. I was unprepared.

In order to get a divorce, Shao Hong and I would have to apply at the marriage registration bureau. If we were in agreement, and we told them how we had decided to share our time with Bao-bao, if we explained there was not much property to divide, even then, they would insist on mediation. But if Shao Hong did not agree, if he refused to agree . . .

I lay back in my bed and kicked my twisted blankets off. Awake or asleep, it was all a nightmare.

"The mediation can last for years," Chen Hua said, slurping her noodles, as calm as if she were talking about the weather. We had agreed to meet for lunch Sunday while Shao Hong took Bao-bao to visit his grandparents. I couldn't bear another nightmare lunch with my in-laws. My nerves were frayed enough, and I was afraid I'd break down in front of them.

We sat in Sorrow Lake Park. It was not a beautiful park, the lake dark from pollution, the trees sparse, the stone benches cold. There was a poured concrete statue of a woman who had supposedly thrown herself into the lake after she found out her husband had been unfaithful to her. Because she had been a selfless and therefore virtuous woman, known for her good deeds, her care of the sick, alms to the poor, someone in the city government had decided to erect this statue. The statue was as white as bone. It was not a beautiful

park, as I said, but it was also nearly always deserted. A good place for us to talk.

"They'll want to bring it to your work units," Chen Hua continued, her mouth full. "They could insist on talking to everybody, not just Secretary Wang, and that would be a disaster and a half right there. They'll talk to the neighbors—did anyone ever see you two fight? Hear anything unusual? They'll talk to your in-laws. You know what they'll say. They're being deprived of their grandson, they're being deprived of peace in their old age, after all they've suffered, blah blah blah. They'll talk to Bao-bao's teachers."

"This is very feudal."

"Ha!" Chen Hua snorted and pointed her chopsticks at me. "Even if both of you agree, it could take years."

"Years!"

"Believe me, my parents' divorce was a nightmare." She shook her head fiercely. "And if anyone had reason to get a divorce . . . Just a nightmare."

"Yes, but that was just after the Cultural Revolution, before the new law. It was harder then."

"Mm-hmm, and now after Tiananmen, after all the criticism: China has let in too many flies when she opened the door. Too much Western influence. Now there's AIDS. Now there's all this corruption talk. Prostitution. Drug abuse. Some gang was just broken up for smuggling heroin in Mercedes cars from Hong Kong, did you read about that?"

"So what? That has nothing to do with me. I'm a shrimp. These are all big fish."

"How many overseas students come back?" she asked abruptly, almost hostile.

"What? I don't know."

"I read it in a Hong Kong paper. The American president let them all stay; anyone in America before June fourth, instant green cards. Bad public relations, Xiao Lin. Bad for you. Nobody likes divorce. And they like it even less when things are looking bad for China."

"But people get divorced all the time."

"How do you know?"

"I read it in the *People's Daily*."

"Exactly!" Chen Hua clapped. "That's what you're supposed to think. Society in a downward spiral. You know what I read just the other day? Our government is now insuring marriages. Stay married for fifty years, and they'll give you more than three thousand yuan."

"That's not very much for fifty years."

"It's the principle, Lin Jun. Don't you see? Someone's panicking. Someone high up. Do you remember when they discovered that entire village in Yunnan infected with AIDS? All two hundred forty some people. Because the health clinic only had one needle and inoculated the whole village with it. Remember the big anti-AIDS campaign after that? 'We will test ten thousand hotel workers in Tianjin to stop AIDS in the Motherland!' What were they testing hotel workers for? Because they have the most contact with foreigners, right?"

"What on earth does this have to do with anything? You're babbling."

"No, no, no, it's all very important. You have to read the political climate. I'm telling you, everyone's paranoid right now. It'll be hard for you."

"What about that man, the math teacher? No, chemistry. For seniors. He was divorced last year!"

Chen Hua was not ready to let up, however. "What about that couple in Beijing?"

"What couple?"

"Lin Jun! You know. The couple who blew themselves up."

"Oh, what are you bringing that up for?"

"And how long had they been trying to get a divorce?"

"They were crazy. Besides . . ."

"Besides what?"

I swallowed and stared at the trash blowing across the cold waves of the lake. "I thought you were going to help me. I don't have the energy to argue with you, too, Chen Hua."

She put her hand on my arm and gave me a shake. "Don't get maudlin! Don't you see, I am trying to help you. You have to be prepared for the fight, the Long March. Okay?"

I didn't answer. I felt so very tired.

"And whatever you do, don't tell Secretary Wang!"

I jumped to my feet. It was really too much. "Do you think I'm stupid?" I snapped the lid back on my lunch tin, capped my thermos, packed them both in my green mesh shopping bag. I pulled my Pigeon away from the tree where I'd leaned it since the kickstand was acting up again. "I'm sorry, Chen Hua. I'm a little tired today. I should be going back. I've got the laundry to do."

She cocked her head to one side. "You can't be so emotional. It's going to get a lot rougher than this."

"I know." I hopped on my Pigeon.

"Hey," she called to me, "maybe we should get that book by Zhang Yimou's ex. You know, about their divorce."

"Why would I want to read that? She's the one who opposed the divorce!"

"Yeah, for what? Five, six years? Even though it was pretty obvious her husband was both unfaithful to her and no longer had any love for her.

Not to mention he was living with Gong Li. Should've been an open-and-shut case. We could read it for her strategies for stalling. Just in case your husband tries to pull something like that, we'll be prepared." Chen Hua threw back her head then and laughed loudly enough to scare away a flock of seagulls circling the garbage cans.

"Just great." I gave her the thumbs-up sign and rode away.

Cynthia, too, had been worrying about my apparent lack of initiative.

"Guess what?" she sang when I went to visit in her office before our teachers' class. Then suddenly she covered her mouth and whispered, "Whoops, almost forgot. Sorry."

"Forgot what?"

"That I have to be quiet!" She pulled her hair away from her face so that she could bug her eyes out at me, as if I were the one who was acting dense. "Here, here, here." She flapped a scrap of newspaper at me.

It was a portion of an article in English about increased soybean production in Jiangsu Province. I looked at her. "Is this a new assignment for us?"

"Other side." She reached out impatiently and flipped the article over.

It was an advertisement. "The Double Money Happiness Joint Venture Co. announces openings for interpreters, guides, hotel service personnel. Must be fluent in English. Interview and examination on site." There was an address in Shanghai and a date, a month away.

"It's perfect, don't you think?" Cynthia was beaming, smiling so that all her teeth showed, even the bottom ones.

"You're going to quit?" I felt terrible, loneliness sitting bitterly in my stomach like cold soup. I tried to smile. "This would be a good position for you. I'm sure it pays much better than a middle-school teacher."

"Not me. You!" She laughed, rubbing her hands together.

"Me?"

"Yes! How are you going to support yourself without your husband? You don't want to live in that dormitory, do you? This would be great! You'd be perfect. And it's in Shanghai! I love Shanghai! It's like New York! It's like Hong Kong!"

"I've never been to Shanghai." She was a silly girl. She meant well, but she was silly and didn't understand anything about me and my situation.

"I'm sure you could get this job. They like pretty faces in these hotels. And your English is great. You have a friendly personality—"

"I couldn't. It's impossible."

Cynthia stopped dancing around the room to look at me, shocked.

"I mean, I can't leave Nanjing. It would be so much harder. I would have to leave Bao-bao. Or else, take Bao-bao with me—"

"Of course, you could take him—"

"It would make the divorce more complicated, more difficult—"

"Everything worth fighting for is complicated and difficult. This is a perfect opportunity for you. Think about it. You would meet all kinds of people. It's a joint venture, so no work unit. More pay. You could live well in Shanghai. It's such an exciting city. Nightclubs, jazz clubs, shopping, so many kinds of people—"

"I don't know," I said firmly, harshly. I sat down on the sofa, in my usual place for class. "We shouldn't talk about this now."

"But—"

"Sssh!" I folded the ad up quickly and tucked it into my pants pocket.

We sat in silence while I held our English text open on my knees, pretending to read over the lesson for our class. We sat like this for a long time until the other teachers began to arrive and Cynthia greeted them

cheerfully, asking them about their other classes, listening to their gossip about mischievous students. I sat silent, smiling and nodding, fingering my text. But even when Cynthia began her lecture, I could not concentrate, I did not hear her voice. My heart racing, my stomach turning over and over, I thought of myself in Shanghai, in a new job, a new life.

17.

High Society

Cynthia said she would help me prepare for the interview. Actually, what she said was, "We're going to get you in top shape, girl. You're gonna blow them away." What she meant was we would practice the interview, all the questions they might ask, all the ways I should answer, so that my English would sound even better than it was and I wouldn't humiliate myself too much by doing this stupid crazy silly thing. But once infected with the idea, I couldn't stop thinking about it. What if, what if, what if.

It's strange, too, because I always wanted to be a teacher. Even though, when I was growing up, many of our teachers were supposed to be criminals, wearing dunce caps in the street, on their knees in front of their students. But I always thought the teachers were noble, somehow purer than other people, because they would suffer for their work. And I

think I was always drawn to martyrs, like the Martyrs of '27, the young university students who were killed by Chiang Kai-shek. Even though they were imprisoned for many weeks, alone, and never allowed to see their families, their comrades, they continued to scratch revolutionary poems into the bricks of their prison cells. I remember their pictures at the Martyrs' Memorial at Rain-Flower Terrace Park, the blurry black-and-white images, these photos like a reflection in a pond. And there was one young girl who looked a little like me, I thought, when I was eight and our teachers took us to see the exhibit. I remember staring at the placard. Very little was known about her—her name and the date she died—but behind a sheet of thick glass was the tiny blue handkerchief she embroidered in her dark cell.

Of course, our teachers took us to see these exhibits because these dead people were students and we were students, and young people in those days were taught to admire anyone who had died fighting for the Communist Revolution. But because they were university students, and the only former university students I knew were my teachers (besides my parents, who were also teachers), I assumed, when I was eight, I would be just like them. A student—a good student whom all the teachers praised—then a university student, then a teacher. An intellectual heroine all the way.

I guess I really was a snob at heart.

After I became pregnant, Shao Hong used to give me a ride to school on the back of his bicycle every morning for months until I could take my maternity leave. One morning I insisted he come in, just to see. It was the only time he ever visited my school. I remember smiling at him as he protested—he didn't have the time, he'd be late to work—as I walked backwards, nearly skipping, past the large iron gate painted red and blue, the wall of blackboards lining the entrance emblazoned with

our students' tentative colored-chalk calligraphy, the children's voices shouting in the playground, music blaring over the P.A., while Shao Hong rushed after me, calling, "Careful, you'll fall."

"This is my school," I said, sweeping my arms around me as if I were showing off a museum full of famous paintings, a seven-story pagoda inlaid with gold.

And even though I could see with his eyes the walls of the classroom buildings crumbling, some of the more mischievous boys tossing darts and paper off the balconies outside the second-floor classrooms, the broken windows patched with cardboard, I was filled with pride. *My* school.

"We have to get you started thinking like a capitalist," said Cynthia. "Like a member of the global service economy. Like someone who wants a tip."

In an effort to achieve this overhaul of my psyche, Cynthia decided we should visit the infamous Jinling Hotel, thirty-six stories, the tallest building in Nanjing, our most celebrated tourist attraction. Peasants came from three provinces to get their pictures taken in front of our sky-scraper. Sometimes the hotel allowed tour groups from the elementary schools to come, let the students see the infamous shopping arcade. I'd never been there.

"It's not my favorite place," Cynthia assured me, a little sheepishly. "But it'll give you an idea of what this Shanghai hotel is looking for."

We agreed to meet one night after classes. I rode my bike slowly up and down the street in front of the hotel. It was illegal to park anywhere in front or on the side of the hotel. Too many bicycles were an eyesore? There were rows of pedicabs, rusting taxis, and even shiny Mercedes with unmarked plates lined up on the street. I parked one and a half

blocks away and walked back. Peddlers had set up stands, some no more than a tarp thrown on the sidewalk, in front of the Jinling's concrete wall, where they sold ashtrays emblazoned with the hotel's likeness, Chairman Mao keychains, Nanjing brand soap. At one roped-off area in front of the circle drive, a lone photographer waited to take pictures of tourists. The end of his cigarette glowed orange. He ignored me as I walked past the gates, wrought-iron with enormous spikes, which could be locked from the inside.

I tried to walk with confidence, as if I always went into four-star hotels, where it cost three, four months' salary just to stay the night.

An old man with the face of a spider monkey hobbled out in front of me. "Hey, where are you going?"

"I have an appointment."

"Oh, yeah? Let's see your ID."

I followed him to the tiny guardhouse next to the gate, almost invisible behind a concrete pillar. The man had a red thermos of hot water, a small radio playing Beijing opera, and a calendar with a picture of a roast pig on a plate. Real cozy. I looked over my shoulder at the brightly lit facade of the Jinling, the Chinese flag flapping under a hidden spotlight.

"Is there a problem?" I asked, smiling politely. The man was holding my work card up to his desk lamp while he squinted at it. He sighed and laboriously copied my name, school's address, home address, and ID number into a filthy ledger.

I watched a group of very young men in blue jeans, shiny jackets, permed hair that floated four inches off their foreheads, and their dates, or what I assumed must be their dates, in wobbly high heels and shiny tight dresses, waltz right past the guardhouse towards the hotel.

"Excuse me, what about them?" I pointed.

"This is a hotel for foreigners." He tossed my ID back to me. "No Chinese."

"They were Chinese!" I protested.

"Don't cause trouble," he barked.

"I have an appointment with a foreign friend. I'm going to be late. It's very important."

"You shoulda asked them to write you a letter of introduction."

"But—" I tried to turn and walk towards the entrance but, moving faster than I would've thought possible for him, he ran and blocked my path. He put a rough hand on my shoulder and tried to turn me around.

"I will report you to my business associates," I said, trying to sound important. "This is really out of bounds."

"Hmph," he grunted. He crossed his arms across his chest.

Why did Chinese have to hate other Chinese so much? There were enough of these bitter old men in this country to supply guards for the gates of every foreign hotel, every joint venture, every government office, every university, every wall in China.

Fortunately, Cynthia appeared behind us. "Oh, there you are, Lin Jun. I was getting worried." She turned to the old man and said in her funny, slow Chinese, *"Bie zhaoji. Ta shi wo pengyou."*

"It's so good to see you," I said to Cynthia loudly, deliberately, in English, just to show off in front of the guard, but he merely grunted and waved me away, imperiously.

"I'm so sorry," said Cynthia when we were out of earshot.

"No, I'm the one who should feel sorry. It's my country."

We walked in silence the rest of the way up the long paved driveway to the glittering doors of the hotel. Two men in red uniforms complete with hard-billed red caps and white gloves opened the full-length glass doors for us. I blinked.

Everything was bright light and shiny metal. There was heat! It was difficult to breathe, the air was thick and swampy. A crystal chandelier hung in the absolute center of the high, high ceiling above the center of the lobby, where a single marble stand held a single black vase with an enormous bouquet of silk roses, yellow and red. A tall foreigner with light brown hair and sunglasses—although he was indoors and it was night—signed something at the long glossy counter, where a row of the tallest Chinese women I had ever seen smiled in matching red and yellow uniforms and neckties. The tall man was accepting money, palm upwards, while one of the smiling women counted out bill after bill, pinks reds blues. Several hundreds of yuan. The man didn't bother to recount but folded the bills into his wallet and slipped it casually into the pocket of his suit jacket. Chinese men in suits, black and white (like Panda bears? I thought, trying to understand the theme), carried small trays with slender crystal goblets, beer bottles, and short thick glasses to a circle of sofas, where couples sat waiting as piano music from somewhere floated around us on the air. I watched an old foreign man hand the Chinese waiter three days' salary as a tip.

"Well, where should we go first?" Cynthia advanced, hands on her hips, ready to get down to business.

"Please," I whispered, "let's sit down, rest a minute."

I couldn't breathe, I couldn't breathe. It was warm, but no one else was sweating, shedding their jackets, wiping their faces. The air was still, it smelled odd, like candy.

We sat on the soft maroon sofa in the center of the lobby opposite the group of foreigners with all the drinks. They didn't look at us.

"Well, you could get any one of these jobs." Cynthia made a sweeping gesture with one hand towards the women at the counter, the men carrying trays. "There's also a business center, you know, faxes, long-distance

calls, electric typewriter rental. The ad didn't say. Maybe they're hiring for everything. So what do you think?"

Her words were a blur of sounds. I felt myself sinking into the cushions.

"Don't worry," her voice said in my ear. "It's pretentious, it's ugly, it's the new world order: a service economy. But, hey, if it pays well . . ." She laughed.

"Yes," I said, trying not to sound weak.

"You okay?" She sounded genuinely concerned.

I tried to laugh. "I'm fine." But I realized how stupid that sounded, as I was sweating so much I could feel the water pouring down my sides. I unbuttoned my sweater, as Cynthia fanned me with the sleeve of her puffy coat.

"Let's get you something to drink—"

"No, no, I'm fine. It's just . . . a little hot."

We sat in the lobby like that for a while. I noticed when the doors opened, a slight wave of cool air followed and if I leaned forward, I could catch a draft on my face. I began to feel a little better.

"Hey, want to go to the top? See the view? We can talk there. It's a little more private?" Cynthia still looked so worried, I felt terrible and embarrassed.

"Yes, that would be great," I said, trying to sound enthusiastic.

"It's not that I really go all that often. I've only been there once. It's kind of cheesy, really. But you gotta do the tourist thing at least once in your life, you know what I mean?"

I nodded, although really I had no idea what she was talking about.

As we made our way across the enormous endless expanse of the lobby, I noticed out of the corner of my eye that some of the tall women looked bored and leaned against the counter wearily, and some of the

foreigners, one young couple, appeared lost: the woman pointed to one of the English signs while the man walked away in the opposite direction. Somehow that made me feel a little better. By the time we reached the elevators, I felt almost normal.

The doors, shiny like mirrors, opened with a *Ding!* A man in a bright green suit rushed in after us. When he turned to push a button for his floor, I noticed that he had a long gray ponytail. I glanced at his shoes, trying to keep from laughing. He had shiny black leather shoes. But no, they weren't shoes, I realized. They were like tiny boots, the sides coming up to his ankles.

A bell, and we were at his floor. He was gone. Another couple, a Chinese man and a foreign woman, ran in before the doors slid silently closed. This man was wearing a black suit, and the woman, very beautiful, with pale white blond hair and black roots, was wearing a very tight pink dress and too much perfume.

I stared at Cynthia and my reflection on the polished walls. I wondered if we looked as strange to the couple as they did to me. Cynthia was dressed as she always was, in her jeans with holes at the knees. (One of the older teachers had offered to patch them for her but she had refused.) She wore a thick gray sweatshirt, turned inside out, and she now carried her puffy blue jacket over one arm. I had tried to dress nicely, but in my thick patterned sweater and worn black pants, I realized I looked like a bumpkin.

"Don't say anything unless I say so," the man addressed the woman in Chinese.

"Of course not." An accent, but she spoke Mandarin as well.

The bell again. Our floor. The doors opened to the faint sound of music. The man and woman walked out first, the woman clinging tightly to the man but dragging her heels slightly.

"Do you remember? It's very important." The man's voice was a little loud.

"Right, right, of course. I say I met you in Komsomolsk last spring. Your brother owns a factory there. Very successful. He offered me a job, told me to come—"

"My brother-in-law!"

"That's right." The woman laughed. "Your brother-in-law."

The man suddenly turned and stared at us.

Cynthia and I quickly started walking in the opposite direction, towards the glass doors at the end of the hall. A pink neon sign hung above them: Sky Palace, it read. Cynthia pinched my arm. "Hmm, pretty spooky," she whispered.

I laughed. I was beginning to feel excited again, caught up in the novelty of our adventure.

Cynthia grabbed hold of one of the doors and opened it dramatically. "After you, Madame."

I skipped inside.

It was the most expensive bar I have ever seen, imagined. The room was round and the walls were all glass. As we stepped inside, I realized the outer room was revolving while the dance floor and the bar in the center, where we stood, remained fixed.

"Weird, huh?" Cynthia smiled at me.

I nodded.

Most of the tables were empty, so we had our pick. I let Cynthia choose. I fought the impulse to run to the glass walls and press my nose to the window.

"I'm buying," said Cynthia, throwing her jacket over an empty chair.

"Oh, no."

"Oh, yes. I invited you." Before I could protest, Cynthia was waving to

one of the waitresses, another foreigner. "Two orange juices." She turned to me. "Orange juice is good for you, especially if you feel faint."

"A lot of foreigners work here. All the waitresses."

"The barmaids?" Cynthia nodded. "Hmm. Well, shall we practice?"

"Practice?"

"Interview questions."

"Oh, right."

Cynthia sat back in her chair, folded her arms across her chest. "So, Miss Lin, tel me, why do you want this job?" She lowered her voice, as if she were a man. She looked very serious.

I smiled. "Because I like foreigners and I want to meet with them. It's very exciting."

"Hmm," said Cynthia, wagging a finger at me, breaking character. "That's a good answer."

"Thank you."

"Okay, why should I hire you?"

"I don't know."

"No, no, you have to brag about yourself. Try again," she commanded.

I tried to think of something. "Well, I am an English teacher so I have studied English many years. My English is still not very good but I will work very diligently if you hire me."

"No, you can't say that." Cynthia laughed hilariously.

"Why not?" I felt a little hurt.

"It's too modest. You should say, 'I'm the best candidate you're going to find. I've studied English for years, I have good people skills because I'm a teacher, and I like people.' And then something funny like, 'And, believe me, after teaching high school all these years, I've seen it all. I don't lose my temper anymore, it's not worth the effort. So I'd be perfect for your hotel.' Then laugh so they know you're joking."

"That's horrible. They'll think I'm so conceited. No one would hire me."

"If it's an American company they would. You can't go in there and say, 'I'm really terrible and stupid but I'll work hard.'"

"But how do you know an American will be hiring me? Maybe it's a Chinese?"

"Oh, you're right. Well, if a Chinese is doing the interview, use your method, and if it's an American, use mine."

The waitress—no, barmaid—brought us our orange juice. She was also very tall, like the Chinese women in the lobby, and very beautiful although she wore a lot of makeup, swirls of color all over her face. She had long reddish hair. She was dressed in a red Chinese-style *qipao* dress. A funny combination, I thought.

"Excuse me," said Cynthia in English, "can I ask you a few questions? About your job?"

"My job?" The woman looked surprised. She had a slight accent. I couldn't tell from where, but it wasn't American like Cynthia's.

"Yeah, my friend here is thinking of going to work for a hotel and so we just wanted to know a few things." Cynthia nodded at me. I felt a little embarrassed but I didn't say anything.

The woman glanced at me and then looked at Cynthia expectantly.

"Well, for example, what kind of test did you have to take?"

"Test?"

"Examination?"

"Examination?"

"Did you have to take an English test, you know, show your language skills?"

The woman smiled. "No."

"Oh. How about the interview?"

"There is no interview."

"Oh." Cynthia was at a loss, but fortunately the woman spoke up.

"My cousin worked here. When she quit, she shows the manager my picture. He likes what he sees and so I get the job."

"Oh."

I slid down in my seat.

"It's not like you think," she said quickly. "I'm a Christian." She turned to me and spoke in a slow deliberate English. "Do you know about the Lord, Jesus?"

"Oh, God." Cynthia put her hands to her head and pulled her hair on both sides.

"Yes," I said. I wanted to say something more, just to show her that I could speak English better than she, with her thick funny accent, but I couldn't think of anything. "Uh," I stammered. "So. Where are you from?"

"Russia."

"Where in Russia?"

"A small town outside Moscow. Murom."

I nodded politely.

"Oh? Have you been there?"

"Oh, no. No."

"Not yet," said Cynthia quickly with a wink at me.

"Mmm. Don't bother," she said with a wave of her hand. "Believe me."

"Why did you come here?" I asked.

"Why do you think?" She smiled.

I didn't like this conversation at all but now the woman didn't seem to want to go away. She stood at the table, laughing. I took a sip of my drink. It was very sweet. I swallowed.

"So why do you want to work in a hotel?" she asked me.

"Why do you?" I don't know how I managed to think of that so quickly.

"I was called to China."

Cynthia rolled her eyes. "To work in a bar?"

The woman leaned towards us. "Do you know the Lord loves you?"

"Pardon me?" I said, though Cynthia made a face at me and shook her head.

"The Lord, Jesus. He loves you."

"Oh," I said.

The woman sat down in the empty chair next to me.

"They don't mind you talking with the customers?" Cynthia asked. "I wouldn't want you to get in trouble with your boss or anything."

"It's okay," she assured Cynthia. She turned to me. I could see the lights of the city behind her head glowing against the velvet black of the sky. I felt a little dizzy. "I am a Christian for one year and nine months," said the woman. "I am saved on February seventeenth. Around three in the morning. I will never forget. The Lord comes to me when I am washing the glasses in my parents' bar. It is very late, all the drunks are gone home, the place is smelling very bad, you know. Like vomit and sweat and the cigarette smoke, and I am thinking how much more money we make if we put water in the drinks, the drunks they never will know. I am thinking about my boyfriend—I hate him so much. He is like a husband really. And I feel like crying, I am just despair, like I take my own life maybe. When Jesus comes to me. He is dressed like a Chinese—a new suit and a Mao cap, you know? Some Bible scholars say Jesus is a Chinese, you know? And he smiles at me and says, 'Anya, I love you.' That is all. And I start to cry, suddenly, I really cry, like baby. I am so happy, this joy I feel, so pure. And then my father comes in. He is cursing. He says, 'What's the matter with you?' He says some more

terrible things. Blaspheme things. Then I know right away that I am saved and I say, 'You should respect the Lord and do not speak the name of the devil's lair in vain.' He is very angry and he breaks some bottles on the ground and calls me stupid and says I am drunk and all kinds of things. Then I know that Jesus calls me and I should leave my hometown and to go China, too, and spread the word of God's love. Jesus is risen and we are saved." She smiled at me.

"You have heard of Jesus?" she asked, frowning suddenly.

"I'm Jewish," said Cynthia suddenly.

The woman looked startled. "You don't look—"

"We're both Jewish," she said.

The woman turned away from Cynthia. She touched my wrist. Her hand was cold. "I will pray for you," she said. "You look so sad."

"Oh," I said. "Thank you."

The Russian woman stood up at last. "Time for work." We had revolved back to the bar.

"Look, it's the bridge," said Cynthia. "Over the Yangtze."

I turned and looked out the window into the black night and saw a tiny string of yellow lights, delicately suspended like stars. It was impossible to imagine the Yangtze rushing beneath.

"You know, the Russians teach the Chinese how to build that," said the Russian woman, and Cynthia and I turned around, surprised she was still standing there watching us. The woman pointed out the window and smiled, nodding, then spun on her heel and walked back to the bar.

"Man, oh man." Cynthia whistled softly. "And I thought the Mormons had the market cornered in China."

"Who are the Mormons?" I asked.

"If you get the hotel job, you'll find out."

Before we left the Sky Palace, we pressed our faces to the glass,

shielding them with our hands so that we could see better. I could see bursts of light from the streetlights so far below they looked like candle flames, a few flashing signs, the glowing red lights on top of the telephone poles, headlights rushing in circles, a night construction crew shooting sparks into the sky. And finally, as we revolved slowly, slowly, like the earth, the Yangtze River Bridge. I had seen the bridge several times on field trips with my students, its sturdy steel cables, massive concrete beams, strong enough to carry cars and trucks and trains across the roaring Yangtze, which killed my mother.

The Russian woman was wrong, I thought. I should have told her. The Soviets did not teach us how to build the bridge. They left, took the designs with them, abandoned the project after agreeing to help, when China was so poor. Everyone knew this, all children in Nanjing were taught this story. In 1960, the Soviets abandoned us, no more aid, and we Chinese had to do everything ourselves.

That night, riding home in the dark, the cold air freezing my face, my hands turning to ice as I'd forgotten to bring my gloves, I thought about the view from the Sky Palace, revolving thirty-six stories up in the air. I had looked down on this street, all the streetlights, the traffic lights, the headlights like so many New Year's decorations strung against the sky, just as right then someone might have been looking down on me as I rode fast fast through the streets on my faithful Pigeon, absolutely invisible to their eyes.

18.

Nai-nai and Ye-ye

I knew they would criticize me in the divorce mediation committee for "disrupting three generations." But if I stayed with Shao Hong, it would be three generations of despair.

Still, I wanted Bao-bao to have grandparents. Know them. They could still love him after the divorce, even if they hated me. They wouldn't hold a divorce against him. They wouldn't, they wouldn't, they wouldn't. I hoped.

But it was hard to predict people's emotions. How many of us could say we'd done the right thing when it was a question of love? Especially within a family.

When Shao Hong said it was time to tell his parents, my first reaction was NO! I wanted to put it off as long as possible. I wanted more time, to build my case, fortify myself against the barrage. I was afraid. But on the

other hand it was a good sign that he wanted to tell them, I thought. He was coming to terms with the idea, accepting it.

We agreed to see his parents on a weekday, when Bao-bao was not home. On Wednesday of the second week of December, the P.E. coaches were holding a big track and field event and our regular classes were canceled so I could take a long lunch. Shao Hong arranged to take the afternoon off from work.

"They won't miss me," he laughed bitterly. "They'd probably be happier if I never came back."

I used to try to help him out of these morose moods, to keep him from hating his job so much. I didn't bother anymore.

We rode over to the university grounds where my in-laws still lived in the apartments for the retired professors, the retired deans, widows and widowers. I tried not to think of all the old people inside, all of whom were born in a time when a woman did not demand a divorce for something so trivial as lost love. It was midday and everyone seemed to be boiling their lunches at the same time. The hall was dark and moist with steam, smelling of noodles. Shao Hong knocked on the door, the sound muted and spongy. At first there was no answer. We hadn't told them we were coming, just took our chances that they would be home. Perhaps secretly we were hoping they wouldn't be.

But the door opened.

"Shao Hong! What's the matter?" Nai-nai peered anxiously past me down the hall, as if she were expecting someone else behind him.

"We just came by to see you. How you're doing. We had some time off."

My mother-in-law frowned.

"Ma, can we come in?"

"Of course, what do you think? You didn't bring our grandson, did you? Is he sick again?"

"He's in school." I walked inside holding my breath.

"Well, I thought you said it was a holiday for everyone." Nai-nai shut the door behind me with a thud.

The apartment was even worse than the hall—the close moist air, the smell like wet dust, the faded paintings, the scrolling hissing television. I saw the tip of my father-in-law's bald head above the back of his gray worn chair. A lumpy-shaped skull. The kitchen table was bare. My husband paced. I stood to the side, watching, wishing I could turn quickly and flee back out the door.

"Don't tell me you're sick, Xiao Hu!" My mother-in-law's voice was too loud in my ears.

"Ma!" Shao Hong shouted. I braced myself. "Ma, can we turn off the TV for once, it's driving me crazy. You know, it's just annoying as hell."

"No, no, the weather's coming up," my father-in-law shouted from his armchair.

"What do you care about the weather for?" Nai-nai said. "Your son's here."

"For my arthritis! I want to know how bad I can expect to feel. You didn't get beaten, like I did. The Red Guards beat me, in the liver, in the back, in the legs. All these places have arthritis, Mother!"

"You can't have arthritis in your liver!" Nai-nai shouted back.

Shao Hong sat at the bare table and put his head in his hands.

"Look, you're upsetting your son!" Nai-nai shouted.

"I have something important to tell you." Shao Hong tried to keep his voice even. "About Lin Jun and me. Very important."

"It can't wait till after we've eaten?" Nai-nai nodded in my direction as if I'd tried to contradict her. She turned back to her son quickly. "Have

you eaten yet? You shouldn't put off meals, it's bad for your stomach." Her voice trailed off as she hurried into the kitchen. A splash and a cloud of steam floated back. She called, "Young people today are always on diets, it's unhealthy!" I assumed that comment was directed at me.

My father-in-law had abandoned his armchair and was now sitting in front of me at the table, holding a pair of chopsticks. He stared at me, big bulgy eyes like a fish. I imagined he had already guessed why we had come. He hated me now. I expected him to say something, attack me, say I was ruining his son's life, but he didn't say anything. Nai-nai brought him a large bowl of noodles, which he dove into even before she had set the bowl on the table, his chopsticks clicking. My mother-in-law set another bowl in front of Shao Hong.

"I'm not hungry, Ma."

"You should eat, it's good," Nai-nai said, on her way back to the kitchen.

"Eat, eat," my father-in-law said, his mouth full. "While it's hot."

I watched my father-in-law gumming his noodles, his cheeks puffed wide as he chewed. He looked just like Bao-bao. I wanted to cry. This was excruciating, torturous. I clenched my fists, dug my nails into my palms. I couldn't break down, not now.

"I'm sorry, but I have to tell you—" My husband sobbed suddenly, burying his head in his arms.

My father-in-law looked at me with his glassy fish eyes and continued eating.

What a nightmare. I wished I could wake up.

Nai-nai set another two bowls on the table, but she didn't look at me. I made no move to sit down. I knew I should say something.

"I'm sorry—," I began.

"Eat while your noodles are hot. This is ridiculous. You'll get a stomach-

ache if you eat cold soup." Nai-nai slurped her broth noisily. "Sit down. It makes me nervous, people watching me eat."

"You don't understand, can't you listen to me for once?" Shao Hong sighed. He grasped the edge of the table dramatically. He hiccuped. "I'm trying to tell you something very important. We're—for fuck's sake, would you stop eating for a minute!" Shao Hong slapped his palm on the tabletop.

"Don't yell at your father! He's hungry!" Nai-nai stood up.

"I'm sorry, I'm sorry," Shao Hong said quickly, but it was too late. My father-in-law was already hunched over his bowl again, like a small boy, hiding his face.

"Baba." Shao Hong stood behind him, put a hand on his shoulder, swallowed. "Look, I don't expect you to forgive me. But I have to tell you something. Listen to me, okay? I just want you to know that I know how hard it's been for you. I understand that now. For the first time in my life."

"What's the matter with him?" Ye-ye looked up out of the corner of his eyes.

Shao Hong hugged his father's thin frail shoulders from behind.

"I can't eat now." The old man put down his chopsticks. "Shao Hong, stop."

"I was arrogant. I always wanted to be the best. And I made everyone suffer. I've always been this way, even when I was a child. Do you know, I even wanted Baba to be sent away?"

His father snorted loudly.

"You don't know anything." Nai-nai set her chopsticks on the table with a snap. "You want to know what real suffering is?" She glanced at me quickly, then turned back to Shao Hong. She poked at her short

steel-colored hair with one hand. "All my life I did what I had to. I did the best I could. Even what happened to your father."

"Your mother denounced me. She had to."

"That's right, I had to," said Nai-nai. "That's the way it was back then. But do I complain about my hard life? Do I go on and on—'*Aiya*, what a terrible thing, what a terrible life, I'm so unhappy'?"

I felt the walls of the room coming closer, the yellowed scrolls, the flapping green curtains, the hissing television, everything sliding towards me. I tried to close my eyes but the vertigo continued. I backed away from the table, leaned against the wall. It felt sticky. How long could this last? I tried to convince myself that if I could stand this, I could stand anything. No meditation committee, no group of nosy bureaucrats could be worse than this.

"Your mother's right. Don't cry over nothing."

"I'm not crying."

"Don't cry," Nai-nai said.

"I'm not crying!"

"Don't shout!" Ye-ye shouted.

"You never cared about me," Shao Hong said. "Ever since you came back from the countryside, you couldn't care less what I did. If I'm married, if I'm divorced, it doesn't make any difference to you. We know how you've suffered. Oh, you've suffered so much. Nobody else counts, do they?"

Ye-ye stood up and walked slowly towards his chair. "What am I supposed to do? Jump up and down with joy every time you come over? I can barely walk. With my arthritis!" He lowered himself gingerly into his chair.

"Ssh. Quit complaining—your weather's on, Father—I've heard this

same complaint for twenty years." My mother-in-law picked up her chopsticks. "Now look, my noodles are cold."

"I'm thinking of quitting my job," Shao Hong said stubbornly, staring at the cold bowl of noodles.

"What are you talking about? You're making absolutely no sense at all." Nai-nai waved a chopstick at his nose.

"I've been trying to tell you! Lin Jun and I are getting a divorce!" Shao Hong shouted at the top of his lungs.

Great, I thought, just great.

"What do you mean, divorce?" Ye-ye's voice floated above the tinny music of the midday weather report.

"Nobody's getting a divorce," Nai-nai snapped back.

I wanted to run away now while I could. I eyed the door.

"My wife says she doesn't want to be married to me anymore." Shao Hong laughed bitterly. He pushed the bowl of noodles away.

"Doesn't want to be married anymore?" Nai-nai laughed shrilly. "Who wants to be married anymore? As if any of us has a choice. Young people today . . ." She eyed me for a moment, the way you look at a chicken in the market, judging the weight beneath the feathers.

"What divorce?" Ye-ye shouted from his chair.

"Your father and I never divorced. And if anyone should have . . ." Nai-nai laughed again.

"We never divorced!" my father-in-law called. "We never thought of divorce!"

"It's not up to me," Shao Hong sighed melodramatically.

"Oh, this is too much!" Something inside me snapped. I was angry, furious, and when I was angry, I cried. I could feel my eyes burning, my sinuses on fire. I tried to control myself. "Shao Hong, this is ridiculous.

And you know it. You're doing this on purpose, and—and—it's not fair!" I stopped. I was crying now. Damn.

Nai-nai turned to Shao Hong. "Don't worry. That wife of yours has always been trouble. She's got no sense. Don't worry. I'll talk to her. Everything will be all right."

"No, it won't!" I hissed. My voice was hollow, trapped in my throat, but their heads all shot up. They stared at me as if I had just fired a gun.

"I've got to get back to work." I turned away and left.

I nearly tripped, running down the stairs, out of the dark halls, back into the cold sunlight. I couldn't run fast enough.

19.

Family History

Shao Hong told me once that what he remembered when his father came back from the countryside was the horrible smell of him. Shao Hong came home one afternoon and knew immediately his father was there although everything looked the same. The wobbly wood table in the middle of the kitchen, the walls bare except for the color picture of Chairman Mao, the crack in the ceiling that ran from one wall to the other like an artery, ready to burst plaster down on them at any moment if the neighbors fought again, throwing things. The apartment was silent. The late-afternoon sunlight came in the west window in the kitchen, the only window, dousing the grayish walls with a mildewed light, the same as always. Shao Hong's mother wasn't home, but he never expected her to be. There were too many meetings to

attend, too much work, she was very active, she was very good. She was never there.

He came in with his books after school and he knew immediately that his father was home. The whole place smelled sour and sweet, like urine and dried sweat, like spoiled rice, like someone who'd been on a train for four days and nights without washing, sweating, packed in with other sweating men, four to a bench, five, standing maybe, pressed against each other, no room to fall over, all the ex-counterrevolutionary dogs coming home.

He stepped into the kitchen. He didn't want to see, he pretended he didn't notice anything, couldn't feel anything different. He poured himself a cup of hot water from the red metal thermos. He sensed that his father was standing behind him. He hadn't heard him come up; maybe he'd been there all along and Shao Hong merely hadn't seen him at first. Shao Hong nearly choked on the water; it tasted like dirt. He faced the wall, deliberately not turning, examined the patterns of dust adhering to the grease there, a giant monkey face, a wall of half-formed words. He could have stood there all afternoon, all evening if he needed to. Finally, Shao Hong heard him shuffle away, very, very slowly, like an old, old man, not like his father. Shao Hong almost turned then, to look at him, to see what he had become, but instead he brought the cup to his lips again and bit down on the warm glass, ground his teeth against the edge. When Shao Hong finally turned, his father was gone. Shao Hong then sat at the kitchen table with his math books and worked on calculus homework until his mother came home.

Ye-ye had brought nothing back with him, no clothes except the dull green Mao suit he wore, his cloth shoes, the black worn into a dusty yellow-brown, and the bicycle, an enormous black Flying Pigeon. Ye-ye

was very proud of this bicycle, he held on to the handlebars, showing it to Nai-nai, even after he could have let go—it would stand by itself with the kickstand down—but he held tight. Like a child, Shao Hong thought. It was funny to see his father that way, clutching the bicycle with a child's concentration, possessiveness, and his old man's face, his bent thin body.

"I've been rehabilitated," Ye-ye said to his wife excitedly, over and over. "So they put me first on the list." He laughed. "A Flying Pigeon. The best."

Nai-nai nodded, circling the bicycle. "We'll give it to Shao Hong," she said. "He can use it when he goes to university next year." She was being optimistic. Shao Hong hadn't taken his exams yet.

Ye-ye nodded, his face impassive. He looked at Shao Hong, this tall adolescent with a hairy lip, so different and not so different from the child he'd left behind. Shao Hong could not read his father's expression. But he thought if he were his father, he would hate a son like him.

"I don't need it," Shao Hong said.

"Take my bike!" Ye-ye shouted suddenly. "Take my bike! Take it!" He was standing in place but he was shaking. The whole bicycle shook, up and down; he bounced the front wheel against the floor of the apartment. It made the rice bowls stacked in the basin by the stove clink together dangerously. But still Ye-ye bounced the bicycle more violently. He pushed it back and forth.

"Calm down. He'll take it. He likes it," Nai-nai said, settling everything, but her face puckered into wrinkles, like a pinched dumpling top. She had had this face ever since.

Shao Hong's father relaxed then. He let go of the handlebars and limped over to the kitchen table and sat down and waited, staring at

Shao Hong with his new old tired waiting face. He stayed that way until Nai-nai made dinner and gave him his rice bowl. Then he put his face down over his bowl and stuffed his mouth full, seeming never to close it as he ate.

Shao Hong sold the bike before we were married. With the money, he bought a new one, shiny, strong, a Forever.

Trying to understand my in-laws never made me feel any better.

20.

Mrs. Mu's Mother-in-Law

Everyone at school was in a bad mood, preparing for the big assembly in honor of our foreign teacher. I overheard some of the older teachers complaining in the lunchroom, "Always something special for the foreigner. Always extra work for us. We Chinese are second-class citizens in our own country." I felt like shaking them or shouting at them, You are exactly the same as those people during the Cultural Revolution who would denounce their colleagues for having cut in line once at the canteen, for having knocked over their bicycles accidentally one day in a rush to get to class, for having expressed an opinion that differed from theirs. Petty, petty, petty. I immediately got up from the table, dumped the rest of my rice in the trash, and left.

I was in a bad mood, too. But for other reasons.

Sensing that her vision for the assembly to end all assemblies was

being jeopardized by the sloth of her teachers, Secretary Wang called an extra series of meetings for the staff. We met after our classes every day to discuss the "Triumphant School Spirit" and "Special Chinese Character" that we would need to tap into during the next two weeks if we were going to pull off her extravaganza.

"Diligence, perseverance, and determination," Secretary Wang recited as we sat in our hard wooden chairs culled from the surrounding classrooms. School Head Hu diligently wrote the characters on the blackboard behind the Secretary. "Work, work, and more work," she said, pounding the board with one hand. "Spirit, initiative, and—" The Secretary paused; she riffled through a few sheets of paper, looking through her notes. "And a correct understanding of things!" she finished triumphantly.

"Hmm, that last one sounded a little off," Chen Hua whispered to me.

"Now, Teacher Chen, please tell us what the art department has planned for the assembly." Mr. Hu pointed a chalky finger in our direction.

Chen Hua rose to her feet without hesitation. "Yes. Of course. We have planned something wonderful."

"Yes?" Mr. Hu nodded.

"Yes. Uh, an advertising campaign. Yes! To celebrate the Chinese spirit of our school and the American capitalist character of our foreign teacher. All my students will diligently design advertisements that will showcase our school's perseverance and work ethic. They will then show their initiative by hanging up their posters all over the school as decorations, including several billboard-size banners that they will determinedly hang from the school's walls. It will take a lot of work, work, work, but my correct understanding of things is that it will be worth the effort, effort, and more effort." Chen Hua sat down.

The other teachers applauded. One of the other art teachers laughed openly. I bit the inside of my cheeks, trying to keep my expression neutral.

"And what will the English department be planning?" One of the bitter physical education teachers looked my way.

"Yes." I stood up hesitantly. "I am helping my students rehearse a play. By the famous English writer—"

"Actually," said Secretary Wang, interrupting me, "we need you to help us in another matter. A special field trip for the foreigner."

I looked at Chen Hua anxiously. She shrugged.

Mr. Hu continued. "The Secretary felt that we should have a day to prepare when the foreigner is not here. We don't want to ruin the surprise, after all. And so, we would like Teacher Lin, as the special assistant in charge of the foreign teacher, to take the foreigner on a field trip. Teacher Mu has volunteered to accompany Teacher Lin and the foreigner to visit her in-laws in the countryside."

Mrs. Mu stood up and waved at me happily.

"This way, our foreigner can see the special character of our peasants and will have a deep impression of their spirit when she leaves China," Secretary Wang added, quite sincerely.

I was a little confused. I sat back down. Mr. Hu continued, "Let's thank Teacher Lin for once again taking care of our foreign teacher."

There was polite applause. I knew what everyone was thinking. Who was getting the special privilege again? Who didn't have to stay at school and rehearse all day with Secretary Wang? Everyone would think I had planned this all along. They would hate me.

Chen Hua nudged me in the side. "You and Mrs. Mu again? Uh-oh. Let's hope you have better luck than last time."

I told her that wasn't funny.

After the meeting, Mrs. Mu came running up to me, trailing her scarf. "Isn't it a good idea?" she beamed. "I just thought of it the other day. Of course, the foreigner should visit the countryside. So I mentioned it to the Secretary. My in-laws will be very excited. I don't think they've ever seen a foreigner up close."

I just hoped they wouldn't do something horrible, like stare at Cynthia and make her feel terrible.

"How far away do they live from the city?"

"Not far, not far." Mrs. Mu waved one hand dismissively. "But you know how the peasants are. It might as well be another world." She laughed.

"Oh, yes," I said. What a nightmare, what a nightmare.

However, when I told Cynthia the next morning, she was delighted.

"I've always wanted to see a farm! When do we go?"

"Whenever the Secretary can arrange for a car to take us."

"Oooh, fancy schmancy." Cynthia smiled.

"Well, you are the special guest. And I think Mrs. Mu wants to show off in front of her relatives."

Cynthia did a little dance around her office. "Won't this be fun? And it'll give you something to take your mind off all your—you know— D-I-V-O-R-C-E problems."

I tried to look happy for Cynthia's sake.

I don't know why I felt so apprehensive. From all the other teachers' point of view, this outing was yet another unearned privilege: Lucky Lin Jun. So unfair for the rest of us. We have to work, she gets to play.

But I couldn't feel excited.

Maybe it was because the countryside made me think of Auntie Gao,

and I felt guilty, and then I thought about Yong-li, and Mother, and Father. And then all I wanted to do was cry.

Pathetic, isn't it?

We met at the school early Friday morning. I did not feel in the mood to chat. I left Cynthia and Mrs. Mu to communicate in their fragmented Chinglish while I paced in front of the gate, ostensibly on the lookout for our ride. All too soon a big black car pulled up and School Head Hu popped his head out of the front and waved to us.

"Ooh," squealed Mrs. Mu like a young girl. "Such a big car."

The driver stepped out and opened the door for Mrs. Mu. He was a large rough-looking man but he wore delicate white gloves. Mrs. Mu beamed at him as she slid into the back seat.

I gestured for Cynthia to get in next but she had run around to the other side of the car, opened the door herself, and popped in.

I turned to Mr. Hu. "So you're going with us too?"

"Oh, sure," he said. Then he lowered his voice. "It's my brother-in-law's company's car. I have to go to make sure nothing happens to it."

"That's very good of you," I said. "So much extra work for you."

He shook his head modestly and ducked back inside the front seat.

"There's only you left." The driver smiled.

"Oh, yes." I swallowed and slid in next to Mrs. Mu.

Mrs. Mu chattered happily the whole trip. "Do you have a car?" she asked Cynthia. Then, suddenly unsure of her English, she said to me, "Ask the foreigner if she has a car."

"No," said Cynthia, "but I know how to drive."

"Oh," said Mrs. Mu, impressed. She pointed at the buildings as we drove by. "There's the Jinling. Look how tall." She patted the vinyl seat, drummed her feet on the hump in the floor. "There's even a footrest for

me." She sighed. "So fast. So convenient." She tapped the driver on the shoulder. "You're a good driver, young man. Very smooth. Very good with the brakes."

"Thank you, Auntie." He smiled at me in the rearview mirror, then he winked. I looked out the window to my left.

It took us only an hour to arrive at Mrs. Mu's in-laws' village, and most of that time was driving through the morning traffic in the city. Mrs. Mu was telling the truth when she said it was not very far outside Nanjing. It was more of a suburb than a village and yet, as soon as we left the last asphalt street and bumped along on the deeply rutted gravel road, everything had changed.

The buildings decreased in size from multistory department stores to single-floor family shops and finally to tiny stands. The number of cars we passed eventually dwindled until there were only our car and an ox drawing a flatbed on the road. Our driver honked furiously but the man with the ox refused to pull his cart over to let us pass. We drove like that, at the slow gait of a tired water buffalo, for several miles until the man turned off finally into a flat brown field, its remaining stubble of cornstalks like so many dried weeds.

"It's so ugly now," tsked Mrs. Mu. "I should have thought of this sooner." She pinched Cynthia's arm. "In autumn, it is more beautiful,' she said carefully. "Green. Water. Not like now."

"Oh, no, it's wonderful," said Cynthia, her nose pressed to the glass. "So interesting."

"Well, it's not wonderful now," Mrs. Mu continued, "but at least you will see how the peasants live." She poked me. "Translate that, okay?"

"I understood," said Cynthia in Chinese.

Mr. Hu and the driver laughed. "Hey, that foreigner is pretty good," said the driver.

"Sure," said Mr. Hu proudly. "She teaches at my middle school."

Suddenly, after miles of nothing, there was a tiny line of three shops selling dried goods, sundries, and cloth things that could have been either kites or men's pants.

"Turn here," Mrs. Mu commanded.

As we rounded the corner, I saw a large yellow dog that had been hit by something and lay dead by the side of the road, its legs splayed apart.

"Oh!" said Cynthia.

"*Aiya!*" said Mrs. Mu. "They have dogs here now!"

We drove till the road ended at a cul-de-sac. Three rows of identical white concrete condominiums faced a courtyard where brightly colored laundry hung on lines. Flowers in pots dotted the cement sidewalks that led to the entrance of each house.

"We're here!" chirped Mrs. Mu.

The driver pulled over to where the cement walk ended abruptly at the dirt road and stopped the car.

"Hmm," said Cynthia.

"Hmm," said Mrs. Mu. She leaned forward against the back of the front seat, peering out the windshield. "Where are they?"

Mr. Hu started to open his door.

"No, wait!" she said.

Mr. Hu turned around, surprised. Mrs. Mu grinned sheepishly. "Excuse me, go ahead. I was just a little confused. . . ." I could tell she was disappointed her relatives were not there to witness her arrival in the car.

Cynthia looked around her with a puzzled expression on her face. She'd brought her camera, and she tugged at the black strap around her neck absentmindedly.

I walked over to her and touched her arm. "Is something the matter? Do you feel carsick?"

"Lin Jun," she whispered, "is this normal?"

"What do you mean?"

"I mean, is this the *countryside* countryside?"

Mr. Hu walked up behind us, beaming. "This is a model village." He spread his arms apart proudly. "The countryside is undergoing modernization at a rapid rate." He nodded at me to translate.

"No," I told Cynthia. "Mrs. Mu's husband is a Wise Commander of the People's Liberation Army. His parents' village was chosen to be modernized."

Mrs. Mu, stepping gingerly over the ruts in the road, gestured for us to follow her to the sidewalk. "We should hurry. There might be dogs."

The driver offered a hand to me, but I ignored him.

Mrs. Mu went ahead to find her mother-in-law. After a few moments she reappeared in the doorway of one of the condos, standing next to a tiny woman, not even as tall as Mrs. Mu's shoulder. Next to Cynthia, Mrs. Mu's mother-in-law looked like a child. She made me think of a stalk of bamboo, slender and delicate looking but really as tough as steel. She stared at Cynthia unabashedly, as I had feared, but Cynthia only smiled.

While Mrs. Mu and her mother-in-law went inside to make lunch, Mr. Hu led us on a tour of the "village." He read from notes about the modern quality of the housing, the cooperative nature of the village, the new farm equipment, the square feet allotted to each family, the quality of the concrete, and the symbolism of a large white statue in the middle of the courtyard of a muscular peasant holding a soybean plant in one hand while his kerchiefed wife brandished a scythe. Cynthia had Mr. Hu and the driver pose beneath the giant stone peasants so that she

could take their picture, but I could see that Cynthia was disappointed. I, on the other hand, felt more and more relieved, the knot in my stomach gradually unraveling.

Nothing here reminded me of my village. It didn't even smell like the countryside, like earth and pigs and chickens, but more like the lime they poured into the lavatories at the far end of the courtyard. The only evidence that we were visiting farmers was the individual garden plots behind the condos—which looked like miniature forests, so dense were the green plants carefully tied to stakes. Paper bags made from pages ripped from magazines and colorful cotton quilts were wrapped around some enormous orange pumpkins to insulate them from the early frosts. Cynthia took a picture of them as well.

It was cold and my nose was running by the end of our tour.

Finally Mrs. Mu called to us. "Come eat, come eat now!"

The inside of the condo was very clean, the walls recently white-washed. It was very empty. Mrs. Mu's mother-in-law stood while Mrs. Mu directed us to squeeze around a small round table. The stools were very low; the driver's knees practically touched his chin.

"It's like the Seven Dwarves' house," said Cynthia cryptically.

Mrs. Mu's father-in-law appeared suddenly. I hadn't heard him until he was standing right behind me, staring transfixed at the tall foreigner squatting in his living room. He was a few inches taller than his wife but twice as broad. His eyes were lined and his face was burnt a deep red-brown.

"This is too much food," I said, after we were all seated.

"Yes, you've wasted too much money," said Mr. Hu.

Mrs. Mu's father-in-law merely began to eat.

It was a meat banquet. Platters and platters of meat—roast duck, fried pig ears and steamed pork balls, chicken legs and duck feet, sliced eel

and sauteed chicken—and one bowl of peanuts. "The soup's in the kitchen," said Mrs. Mu apologetically. "There wasn't enough room on the table." There was chocolate-flavored champagne for the women and little bottles of *baijiu* for the men. I watched the driver's face turn a deep red as he downed his rice wine in one gulp.

Mrs. Mu's father-in-law disappeared shortly after slurping down his soup.

"Where did he go?" Cynthia looked around her.

"Back to work," said Mrs. Mu. She shielded her mouth daintily with one hand as she picked at her teeth with a toothpick.

"In the fields?"

"With the animals. The pigs."

"Pigs!" cried Cynthia loudly, startling everyone. "I'd love to see the pigs."

I translated her request.

"Oh no," said Mr. Hu quickly. "It's too dirty."

"I don't mind," said Cynthia.

Mr. Hu looked annoyed but I pretended I didn't notice as I translated for him.

"It's far away," he said.

"It's not too far," said Mrs. Mu.

Mr. Hu looked very annoyed.

"You can stay here. Just point me in the right direction. I don't mind. I'll walk. You can stay here." Cynthia said this in Chinese.

Mrs. Mu's mother-in-law laughed delightedly. I saw that most of her teeth were gone. "The foreigner speaks Chinese!" she chortled. She had a gruff voice, like a bullfrog—it surprised me, coming from such a small woman—and a very strong Nanjing accent. Cynthia could not understand her.

"Nanjing dialect," Mrs. Mu explained.

Mr. Hu chewed his lips unhappily. "All right," he sighed. "Wait here." He tapped the driver on the shoulder and they left.

Cynthia stood up.

"Don't worry. You can wait here now," said Mrs. Mu.

"I can't just go with them?"

"They have to arrange things first," I explained. "They have to warn the men you're coming. They'll want them to make sure everything looks nice for you."

"Oh, I don't want to see another showplace," Cynthia said, disappointed.

"Don't fret," I said. "Pigs are pigs."

Mrs. Mu's mother-in-law brought out a corncob pipe from the pocket of her puffy nylon jacket. She lit the end and puffed furiously while Mrs. Mu told her in Nanjing dialect that I was getting a divorce, that I didn't love my husband anymore, even though he was handsome and an intellectual and we had a son.

I was so surprised I didn't know what to say.

Mrs. Mu's mother-in-law nodded at me. "I killed my first husband," she said.

At first I thought I had misunderstood her.

"He was a reactionary. A bourgeois landlord. I was betrothed to him when I was a little girl. I was very beautiful," she said, calmly without emotion. "Even more beautiful than you. Those were feudal times. My husband did not treat me very well. Then the revolution came and the Chairman liberated us peasants. We killed the landlord's whole family, set the house on fire. We set my husband's old man on fire, too. He was unrepentant to the end." She laughed heartily, sucking on the end of her pipe.

Mrs. Mu eyed me pointedly, nodding.

"What did she say?" Cynthia whispered.

Mrs. Mu's mother-in-law laughed again, hearing Cynthia's English.

"Uh, she's talking about the revolution. How she, uh, followed Chairman Mao's path," I said.

"Oh, the Cultural Revolution?" asked Cynthia in Chinese.

"Oh, no," said Mrs. Mu, laughing. "After the war for Liberation. Nineteen forty-nine."

"Nineteen forty-nine! How old is she?" asked Cynthia, her eyes widening.

Mrs. Mu nudged her mother-in-law. "The foreigner wants to know how old you are."

"Eighty-seven," said the old woman. "I was born in the Year of the Snake."

"Eighty seven!" I cried. "Nai-nai," I said politely, "you look much younger. Only sixty."

The old woman nodded as she calmly blew a smoke ring.

"She'll live forever," said Mrs. Mu matter-of-factly.

21.

Helen of Shanghai

lthough I had been practicing for the interview every week with Cynthia, it had seemed unreal, like a game, certainly not something I would really do. Even after our last "practice session" in Cynthia's office during which I made change in English with her American money, I still felt as though I were merely practicing new vocabulary, another classroom exercise, like word problems in math: if train A is going 350 kilometers per hour and train B is going 455 kilometers per hour and they are both headed towards each other on the same track, from points 721 kilometers apart, when do they collide if they leave their stations at a quarter past two? Just as I never worried about the impact of such a collision when I figured the math, I blithely played along with Cynthia's interview games as if they too were without consequence.

So when Cynthia appeared in our English teachers' office after classes on Friday and handed me a train ticket to Shanghai, I stared at the thin slip of paper blankly, waiting for her to tell me what I was supposed to do with this now.

"Feel ready?" she asked brightly, clearing a space on the corner of my desk to sit on.

"Ready for what?" And then it occurred to me that she really expected me to go through with it. "You shouldn't have!" I fingered the ticket unhappily.

"You still have to buy the return ticket."

"But—but—I'm not going."

"What do you mean you're not going?!"

"I mean—I mean—I'm not going. I can't. It's impossible. I have my work here—"

"The interview's Sunday—"

"My son is home on Sundays—"

"Your husband can look after him for once. Show him how much work it is. Might help in your custody fight." Cynthia laughed, then stopped. "I shouldn't joke about that. Sorry. But, seriously, your husband can look after the kid. Say that you have to take me on another field trip. Your school made you. You had no choice. You'll be back in the evening. It's not that far away, Lin Jun."

I bit my lower lip. "I think I'm coming down with something. I shouldn't travel."

"It's only Shanghai! It's only two and a half hours away! Come on!" Cynthia flew around the office, pulling her hair. "I came all the way to China for this job."

Two of the junior-high teachers passed by the window. They tapped on the glass and smiled at me. I smiled back tightly.

"Look." Cynthia crouched in front of my chair. She grabbed both of my arms. "You don't have to take the job if you get it. But why are you so afraid to try?" She gave me a shake.

"I'm not going to force you," she sighed. She walked to the door, her hair bouncing about her head with each step. She slipped outside then pressed her face to the window. "But you better do it!" she mouthed, shaking a finger at me.

I smiled, but inwardly I quaked.

It was easier than I expected. I told Shao Hong I needed him to look after Bao-bao, that I had to take the foreigner to visit some historic sites of Nanjing. He nodded meekly. Everything about him these days was meek. He looked afraid when I came home. He spoke only when I spoke first. He sat in his study with the door open, quiet. I'd look up from my textbooks, from my students' papers, and he'd be standing in the doorway, watching me. And if our eyes met, he looked away quickly. He seemed to be losing weight.

I packed a small satchel for my trip, Bao-bao helping me. Nothing was suspicious. My paperback English dictionary. A notebook, with the maps of Shanghai that Cynthia had lent me hidden inside. A small lunch tin filled with rice crackers, a couple buns, and a pear. (I would try to get something hot to eat in the city.) A tin mug. Bao-bao played with each item before he would let me put it in the red cloth bag. It broke my heart. I felt as though I were planning to run away, to abandon him.

That night when I made up his bed, I held Bao-bao close to me. He squirmed away.

"I'm not a baby," he said, rubbing his eyes.

"Do you want Mama to tell you a story tonight?"

"Tell me about Mickey Mouse."

"Mickey Mouse?"

"At school we watch Mickey Mouse and Old Comrade Duck and the dog. What's his name? You know, the dog. What's his name?"

"I'm sorry, I don't know this story."

Bao-bao frowned. "They're the best. I like Mickey Mouse. He's funny. He has a car and a big house and a dog."

"Why don't you tell me a story tonight, okay?"

Bao-bao yawned. "I only like Mickey Mouse stories. Can you get the Mickey Mouse book? I want—I want that one. Like at school. We have lots of them."

I tucked the red quilt with the dragon and tiger pictures all over it around his shoulders, close to his neck.

He rubbed his nose.

I took hold of his hand.

He opened his eyes. "I want the Mickey Mouse doll, okay? Not the other people, okay? Just Mickey. The big one. Can I have one?"

"Of course," I said, and then I realized I had no idea what Mickey Mouse doll he was talking about or where they were sold or how much they cost. "Try to sleep now."

But he was already asleep.

I couldn't sleep at all. The hours passed so slowly, each minute like a drop of water from a leaky faucet. Drip drip drip. When it was finally time to get up, I felt exhausted. My stomach hurt. I couldn't eat.

I waited for the bus to the train station in the dark, alone. Not many people were out at all. Two trucks—one loaded with steel pipes and the other, cardboard refrigerator boxes—rumbled by. A lone bicyclist whizzed past the corner.

The bus lumbered up, wheezing and shooting sparks from its electric cable. The doors opened to a black empty hole.

I wandered through the train station in a daze, looking for my queue. It was dimly lit, smoky and crowded. Entire families of peasants slept on the concrete floor, crumpled into heaps. There was no place to sit on the long wooden benches. I had never traveled anywhere alone before. I pretended I did not notice the men staring at me. I pretended I was a tough independent businesswoman and that I traveled like this all the time, a cell phone in my bag, a book of appointments to be kept in Shanghai, big business, a tough tough tough woman.

I was so stupid. I should have asked Cynthia to go with me. I'd never find the hotel. I'd never find my way back to Nanjing. But I never really believed I'd do this. A stupid stupid stupid woman.

Cynthia had bought me a ticket on the double-decker *tekuai*, the express to Shanghai. Expensive. But a very nice train, I discovered. On the upper deck where I found my seat, the floor was carpeted. It was clean. Trash and spit and cigarette butts did not litter the floor. Two other women were apparently traveling alone this morning. One looked out the window, bored. Another wrote in a small notebook. Neither looked particularly apprehensive. Both were well dressed—a leather coat, a fur coat, nice shoes, leather, heels, I noticed. I was the only bumpkin on board, I realized. I leaned back in my seat as I waited for the rest of the passengers to board. I tried to remember to breathe.

I must have watched the scenery roll by as gradually the sun rose and the sky lightened and I lost the sensation that I was traveling at high speed into a big black ocean, but I couldn't absorb a thing I saw. Empty fields of dirt. Small houses next to the railroad tracks. At our stop in Wuxi, women in brightly colored kerchiefs rushed towards the windows and thrust up baskets of steaming *baozi*, greasy *youtiao* stick donuts,

boxes of fruit juice. Many passengers slid open the windows and leaned out, handed over money and took the food inside. Then more flat brown empty fields. A distant ox. Where were all the people? I wondered.

Then as the sky turned white with the noon sunlight, the fields diminished rapidly, replaced by a line of shanties, then warehouses, then taller buildings that blocked the sky. Trash grew along the tracks. Everywhere I looked—wandering between the buildings, floating by on bicycles, poking through trash barrels, pulling wooden carts piled high with coal briquettes, stranded in their cars cars and more cars as the traffic backed up to a standstill—were people.

We were approaching Shanghai.

I tried not to lose my head. Keep your bag close to your body, I commanded. Get your return ticket first. You don't want to have to buy a boarding ticket only and stand all the way back. You'll be tired at the end of the day.

The station was huge. Everyone moved very fast. Everyone was shouting. I could hear horns honking from outside, peddlers shouting inside. The sound of train whistles, of engines, of bicycle bells, of beggars, of children, of a baby shrieking at the top if its lungs. I walked fast like everyone around me. "Always pretend you know where you're going," Cynthia's warning echoed in my ears.

It took an hour to get my return ticket. The only seat available was on the latest train, arriving in Nanjing after midnight. I was exhausted, ready to go home, and my day was only just beginning. I tried not to think about it.

Keep focused. One thing at a time, I told myself.

The bus to downtown was one of the most crowded I had ever ridden

on in my life. After transferring twice, I ended up on a tree-lined street that was nearly deserted. Construction was going on everywhere, scaffolding and exposed beams like skeletons against the sky. The wind carried the sound of bells from a small temple set back from the street on my right. A strip of clothing stalls advertised Big Sale, Huge Savings on the left. None of the buildings had numbers on them. I'd never find the hotel, I panicked. It was a terrible mistake. I had to go to the bathroom. I was thirsty. I was lost.

And then just ahead, snaking around the corner, I saw an odd line of people filling the sidewalk. Hundreds and hundreds. Most sat or squatted, reading papers or books or playing cards, but everyone was dressed as if they were models from the pages of a Hong Kong magazine. As I walked closer, I saw the line stretched down the block. I could not see the end.

"Excuse me," I asked a very young woman wearing three-inch heels and about three pounds of makeup. "Do you know where the Double Money Happiness Hotel is?"

She smirked at me and pointed vaguely toward the front of the line.

"Is this the line for the job interviews?" I asked, not sure whether I hoped she'd say yes or no.

But she only turned her back to me.

"Better take a seat," said a voice beneath me. I looked down and saw a tiny woman with wire-rim glasses and short spiky hair sitting on a newspaper by my feet. "It's going to be a long day," she said.

The woman turned out to be nice. We took turns holding each other's place in line so that we could travel to the toilet a block and a half away. She was a returned student back from England. Earned her Ph.D. in British literature from Oxford. Her undergraduate university had promised her a position when she returned but had hired someone else

instead. She'd taught in night schools and TV universities for the past two years while applying for other jobs. "I'm not pretty," she said, "but this one has an exam, so I thought I'd try again." She accepted half of a pear.

"You have a Ph.D. I don't have a chance. I'm just a middle-school teacher."

"They'll snap you right up," she said without bitterness. "But this is what I figure—they have to hire someone to work the night shift, right? Who's going to answer the phones when the foreign guests call the lobby? They won't care what I look like then. I'm just a voice on the phone. And I can speak four languages."

Another man a few yards up from us said he was a medical doctor. A couple behind us were engineers. The beautiful girl who had been rude to me actually was a model.

I shouldn't have come, I thought.

Three hours later we finally could see the lobby doors. Once inside, men in shirtsleeves carrying clipboards and walkie-talkies separated us into groups. One of the men ushered my friend with the Ph.D. towards a young hunchbacked boy standing to the left. I was told to follow the model to the right.

"See what I mean," my friend called to me.

"Good luck," I called back.

The lobby was still in the process of being built. Several electricians on tall spindly ladders struggled with a chandelier. Carpenters drilled and hammered at the lobby counter. More men crawled across the floor laying tile. Everywhere, the floors were covered with drop cloths and plastic sheets, and everywhere, everyone was rushed, shouting, anxious.

A group of six of us were ushered down a hall to what would be the restaurant when the plastic and the ladders and the men screwing light

fixtures shaped like shells were gone. Men with notepads were seated at the tables.

For this exercise, said a man with a small bullhorn, we would pretend to be waitresses. We were to speak only in English. We were to stay "in character," whatever that meant. "Remember," the man with the bullhorn shouted, "be pleasant. Remember you are representatives of the company."

We were each handed a tray piled with plates and glasses and told to carry it over to one of the tables. Each table had little red flags and little green flags. If someone made a mistake, the interviewer put up the red flag. One woman in front of me tripped on the carpet and her tray went flying, the dishes clattering against the floor. A little red flag went up. The man with the clipboard gestured for her to follow him. "Please," she cried, "one more chance."

I walked very carefully.

"What's your name?" said the man at my table as I set his plates down.

"Helen," I said.

"That's an unusual name for a Chinese girl."

"My American friend gave me this name."

"It suits you," he smiled. "Do you know the story of fair Helen of Troy? 'The face that launched a thousand ships.' She caused a war, which lasted for ten years. Thousands died in battle, just because two princes wished to possess Helen."

I did not like this man. I did not like this kind of interview. "Well," I said quickly, "that was Troy. This is Shanghai. Please let me know if you want any more food."

I walked away. I had had enough.

They stopped me in the hall.

"Wait." The man with the clipboard handed me a form to fill out: name, address, experience.

"What about the English exam?" I asked.

"You just passed," he said. He turned to go.

"When do we find out—"

"After Spring Festival, we'll let you know if you're hired," he said brusquely.

"I have some questions—"

"You'll have plenty of time to ask them if you get a job," he said, hurrying back to the new crowd of applicants in the lobby.

It was half past six. I had waited in line for nearly four hours and my "examination" had lasted less than fifteen minutes. I wandered wearily past the new crowd in the lobby. I did not see the woman with the Ph.D. I pushed my way out the doors. The cold air took my breath away. It had been too hot and stuffy in the hotel and now it was dark outside and freezing. My first time in Shanghai and I had seen nothing.

"Hey," a shrill voice called to me. "It's me." The model ran towards me.

I waited for her to catch up. "How'd you do?"

"Oh, I'm sure I'll get a job here. I'm hungry. Would you like to get something to eat with me? I don't like going alone and I don't know anyone here."

Well, she wasn't exactly nice, but I was hungry.

"Do you know a good place?"

"Oh, sure." She took off down the street quickly. I had to jog to keep up with her.

We stopped at another foreign-owned hotel. It was enormous. It made the Jinling look like a stalk of dwarf bamboo. But no one stopped us at the gate here. The lobby was too bright, everything glittered. Classical

music mingled with the sound of a waterfall, which I could not see any-where, although an artificial stream had been built into the floor.

The model hopped over the stream and gestured for me to follow. I was so tired, I nearly tripped and fell into the water.

She stopped at a small kiosk with glass cases showcasing three kinds of sandwiches. She ordered two, both for herself. More than a day's wages each. I couldn't believe it. But I was starving, and the slices of cake were even more expensive. I ordered a sandwich. It was very dry and thin and tasted like canned meat.

"Do you eat like this often?"

"Oh, all the time," she said, her mouth full.

"Why?"

"You don't like sandwiches? They're very popular in the U.S."

"Have you been to the U.S.?" I asked, knowing she hadn't.

She tossed her head. "I'll go someday," she said with confidence. "You know, you could be really cute if you spruced yourself up a little." She said this matter-of-factly without any sense of her own rudeness. "You should cut your hair. And you should dress better. There's no point trying to make yourself look less attractive. Not at your age."

"Thanks," I said tightly. I tried to think how funny this would be, looking back from some distant point in the future.

A Chinese woman in a tight *qipao* clinging to the arm of a very old white man walked up to the sandwich kiosk. She put her finger in her mouth and stared at the case as if bewildered. The man laughed at her and selected a sandwich for her. He paid with a hundred-yuan note. She giggled as he broke the sandwich into little pieces and fed them to her piece by piece. She licked his fingers.

"Ugh," I said.

"What's the matter?"

"No self-respect."

"But I bet he's got money," the model said with a shrug.

"She'll give foreigners a bad impression. They'll think Chinese women are complete idiots because of her."

"Ha! I think she's very clever. If she wants a lot of rich boyfriends, that's the way to act. Really, you shouldn't be so judgmental."

"I like being judgmental," I snapped.

I threw away the rest of my sandwich, then searched the lobby for a women's toilet. I found one hidden in an alcove behind a huge plant with white flowers and a bronze statue of a water nymph. The bathroom was magnificent, larger than my bedroom at home, brightly lighted, each toilet in its own little room. It smelled of perfume. I locked myself in a stall and threw up repeatedly.

It was a very long train ride back to Nanjing.

22.

The Middle Part

When I took Bao-bao back to school on Monday, he was restless, tugging at my legs all morning as I made our breakfast porridge. He kissed Shao Hong good-bye as we left, but then also poked him in the ear. And when I said, "That's not nice, Bao-bao. Don't poke people," he laughed and ran down the hall away from me.

He seemed eager to return to school. As I adjusted his child seat on the front bar of my bicycle, he suggested that he ride on the back. "When you're older," I said.

"I am older," he insisted.

And when I let him down by his school's gate and knelt to kiss him good-bye as I always did, he pulled away from me quickly, waving to his friends. I was about to follow him inside, say hello to his teachers, when he stopped running and turned around. "Go back home," he called,

looking at me as he walked backwards into the playground. "Bye-bye!" He waved me away.

I didn't want to be a clingy mother, the kind I saw on the streets every day, carrying their children way past the age when they could walk by themselves, cradling them in their arms, dressing them like babies far too long in colored quilts and tiger hats. I didn't want to treat my child like a pet.

Riding back to the apartment, I realized how ugly winter was. Months of clouds, low and gray across the sky, like another layer of concrete. The cold, the rain, the sleet, everyone in layers of wool and puffy down jackets, the sleeve protectors, the coal dust. And yet technically the first day of winter was still four days away.

But I didn't go home. I circled round, back to the alley behind Bao-bao's school. The street was pitted, the stones in the road uneven, some missing. I had to walk beside my Pigeon, pushing the bike between me and the wall around the school. The wall was gray cinderblocks, precisely built, the mortar scraped off evenly and not spilling out in gray bulges. A solid wall. Strong. I could hear the children playing in the courtyard. I imagined I could see them through the concrete blocks, their cheeks flushed as they ran. They were playing a game based on an American television show. I could hear the strange shouts—"Hands up, cowboy!" They fired imaginary guns. Then someone screeched like a monkey, and I couldn't make out what they were playing anymore.

The gate was approaching, and I found myself slowing down, taking smaller steps, furtive like a spy. A mother has the right to check on her son, I told myself. A woman must follow her instincts.

I peered through the metal bars of the gate into the schoolyard. It was time for them to go in. The pretty young teachers were rounding them up, lining them up. All the children looked alike in their thick sweaters,

the boys and the girls wrapped in layers and layers against the cold. They were all short and round, waddlers. Then I saw Bao-bao, standing a little bit apart from the others, facing my direction. The other children called to him but he ignored them. How could he have seen me? I wondered.

I couldn't read his expression. Then he crouched down slowly, still staring at me, and ran one hand against the ground. He stood up quickly and hurled a rock in my direction. Then he turned around and ran back to his playmates lined up in front of the door.

The rock fell against the wall, bounced on the dirt yard. It was a strong throw for such a young boy.

I had never felt so tired.

My mother-in-law came to visit that afternoon after my classes. There was a sharp, determined knock on the door, and at first I thought it was Shao Hong, that he had forgotten his key. But it was my mother-in-law, dressed in navy blue, looking determined. "Oh, Nai-nai, come in," I said, against my better judgment.

Nai-nai sat down in my chair and looked at the sticky table. The clock was ticking loudly in the kitchen. I saw the mess of the living room, the dust on the bookshelves, the soot on the once-blue curtains, the squalor of my life, of her daughter-in-law, the one who would divorce her son, revealed before her.

"Can I get you some tea?"

"Don't worry about the tea." She stared at me, her eyes as wide and round as a tiger's behind her glasses. "I've got some things to tell you. I've arranged for a place for Shao Hong to stay temporarily while you two sort out this problem. It's an apartment on our campus. The wife got a research appointment at an American university. Her husband's visa finally came through so he went to join her. He had to leave their

kid with his parents for the time being. They don't know if they're going to try to emigrate or not so they're still keeping the apartment. Her mother's a good friend of mine so Shao Hong can stay there for a while. Just a few weeks, mind you, maybe a couple months. My friend's going to try to rent out the place after the new year. I can't expect her to lose money just because my son and daughter-in-law are having a few problems. But that should be long enough."

"That's very considerate of you but—"

"No, don't interrupt me. I'm not finished yet. Just let me speak. I'm an old woman and I've seen quite a lot in my day. Quite a lot."

I sat back and fixed my gaze safely on the back of my hands, looking at the tangle of blue veins pulsing beneath the surface of my skin while the clock ticked in the kitchen, the footsteps of my neighbors drummed across the ceiling, bicycle bells rang out on the street below. I would need to conserve my energy.

My mother-in-law was tough, knew how to do everything right. The first woman in her neighborhood to organize a Mao Zedong study group, the first woman to give up all the iron skillets, the ladles, the keys, during the Great Leap Forward. The other women looked up to her. As did my husband. I'd heard all the stories. His mother, the true heroine of the revolution, never home. He'd come home from school and his mother would be gone, organizing another block meeting, a committee to collect trash from the banks of the Yangtze on weekends, a committee to study the trash for signs of counterrevolutionary leanings.

I remembered one story in particular. Shao Hong told me shortly after we were married, before Bao-bao was born, when we sat together in the dark in the kitchen, candles burning on the table, a blackout in the neighborhood. We loved the blackouts then. An excuse not to do our

work, to put away our papers, and sit close on the couch, in the silence, in the flickering light, wondering what kind of parents we would be.

My husband was a little boy, younger than my students, his hair cut straight across his forehead, his cheeks full and soft like two rice-flour buns. He was sitting at the kitchen table, memorizing his multiplication tables, when his mother stormed in the front door, kicking it open, it seemed, from the loud bang of its hitting the wall. "Where are my glasses? We've found the adulterer's diary and I didn't bring my glasses!"

His father sighed, looking up from the onionskin pages of his book. "What's it matter? Leave it to someone else. It's none of our business. Bad luck."

"You don't understand ANYTHING!" my mother-in-law shouted as she ran through the apartment, rifling through piles of paper, old newspapers, books, looking under sacks of MSG and salt in the kitchen, running to the bedroom to look through the pile of laundry on the floor.

"It's immoral," my father-in-law shouted after her, sitting at his desk, his own glasses sliding down his thin flat nose.

"Exactly!" my mother-in-law shouted back. She returned triumphantly with the black heavy frames resting on her nose. Her glasses made her eyes look very large—round five-inch circles. They were scary eyes that could see anything. She was powerful although she looked like everyone else: short black hair, green and blue Mao suit. But she walked with determination, stomped through the apartment and out the front door. Bang!

Other women were scared of her. They looked at their feet when she passed, on the sidewalks, in the hallways, in the neighborhood meetings. Older women with gray steely hair, young pretty women who giggled normally. Students nodded when she spoke on campus and the other teachers looked at the floor. Afraid. Even the neighbors avoided

her eyes. Especially the neighbors: the elderly man and his senile wife. They had once been very wealthy, then they had to write self-criticisms six hundred and forty-seven pages long.

I thought of my husband's telling me this story in the dark, holding my hand, my baby—our son—kicking ever so insistently, as I laid my head against his shoulder, as my mother-in-law sat at my kitchen table, ignoring the mug of tea cooling at her elbow, and said: "Let me tell you something about my son.

"He was born in the Year of the Monkey, the fire monkey. He was clever, I taught him to recite Tang Dynasty poetry."

(I did not interrupt my mother-in-law but all intellectuals teach their children to recite Tang Dynasty poetry, and there is nothing worse than monkey children for their conceitedness, except perhaps the pride of the mothers of these monkey children.)

"He was a beautiful baby, such a smart child. He was destined for great things. Naturally I thought this way. He was my only child. I'm as vain as the next mother. But now you see what he has become. He is thirty-five years old, a failure—no, don't interrupt. An assistant editor at a third-rate business monthly. He is a translator. He will never be a famous writer. He knows it, I know it. You don't know how it hurts me to see my only child have to give up his dream. But if you live long enough, you see many hard things.

"I have no intention of being overdramatic. Don't worry. I'll tell this story straight.

"Shao Hong joined a gang when he was thirteen. Older boys. They were ruthless. What was there to fear? Death meant nothing, it meant becoming a 'martyr for the people,' brave, immortal. You remember these times as well as I. The other boys were bigger, stronger, but they let Shao Hong in. He was smart, not just bookish smart, but useful

smart. They needed him. I should have intervened. Looking back, I have my regrets, but I envied him. I admit it. I would have liked to have been a boy too.

"He denounced his father. It was a Thursday. I was out, hanging posters against spiritual pollution on the wall outside our campus. My husband was Dean of Social Sciences, you know. Another woman came running up to me. She was flushed, excited. She could barely contain her joy. 'Comrade Xu, you must come quickly. It's your husband.' She smiled, not bothering to cover her teeth. I wanted to spit on her. But I finished pasting up my poster—'Down With Bourgeois Influences! Study the Proletariat!' It showed a picture of a ruddy-faced peasant woman and a woman worker holding a wrench in her hand as if it were a rose as they stood side by side in front of a beautiful red sunrise. I remember, because I stared at this poster and not at the woman as I answered, 'After I have finished my work, Comrade.'

"By the time I reached the alley in front of the middle school, my son was burning my husband's books, and my son's math teacher had pissed his pants. They were clinging to his legs. My husband was shaking. There was a placard around his neck listing his crimes. His nose was bleeding and his forehead was scraped raw. The boys had made him kowtow on the cobblestones.

"After that, I knew things would be very difficult. To be the wife of a counterrevolutionary could be as bad as being one yourself. And to be the son of one was even worse. I knew I had to act quickly.

"I wrote my self-criticism very carefully. I wrote all night long. The history of my family, the history of my husband's family, a history of failure, of missed opportunities, of idiots who did not understand the correct interpretation of the class struggle and my valiant attempts as a mere woman to correct the wrongs of the past, to continue the revolution, to

do the Chairman's will. I created a history that night that would save my son.

"The next morning he was running through the apartment. Excited. He wanted to be with his friends. I grabbed his arm. I made him stay with me and read what I had written. I made him memorize every word so that he could recite my account of his father's failure from memory, no matter where he started in the narrative. No matter how anyone tried to confuse him, his story would stay the same.

"That night I denounced my husband. Hundreds of us, thousands of us gathered in the courtyard of the university. They led my husband in a line of men wearing dunce caps and placards. His sins were written in thick uneven strokes; one word was misspelled. But when he knelt on the stage before us as the man with the bullhorn shouted, 'Counterrevolutionary!' I shouted too, louder than the others, 'Counterrevolutionary!' I made Shao Hong shout as well. And when it came time to list my husband's crimes, I led the others in the attack.

"No one would be able to say that I was not a model citizen.

"My husband was sent away to be reeducated three weeks before Shao Hong's fourteenth birthday. The other boys were cruel. You know how it was. I found him one afternoon in the hallway outside our door, lying on his side. They'd beaten him. They'd taken off his pants and kicked him and then they made him sit on broken glass. I'd been washing the laundry when I found him. My hands were raw, red from the cold water, the harsh soap, but I remember how warm his blood felt on my hands when I helped him up, eased him back into our apartment.

"It wasn't easy for me, those years alone, a single mother, raising Shao Hong. I had to work all the time, every committee, just to protect him so that he would not be branded a black element's son.

"My husband wasn't an easy man to get along with. Before he was sent

away, he was very, very difficult. He was a smart man, but very proud. Arrogant. He would shout at us. When Shao Hong was a baby, he cried through the night; nothing I could do would make him stop. My husband would shout at me, 'You spoiled him!' On occasion he slapped me. It was very hard.

"He was very critical of Shao Hong when he was a boy. Nothing he could do was good enough. If Shao Hong received a ninety-eight on an exam, my husband would ask, 'Why not a hundred?' You know how it is with a child at home. If the apartment was messy when he came back from his meetings, he would shout at me, 'How did I get this lazy wife?' He was high-strung. Everything would set him off. And when he was angry, he would shout at us. When the neighborhood committees formed to beat pots on the roof to scare the birds away or when the committee formed to keep the street swept in front of the apartment and the clouds of dust rose up and blew into our windows, when the school assigned him an extra class on politics to teach or when the deans were required to check on the political backgrounds of their professors, he took it out on me.

"I'm not complaining. This is the way it is with ambitious men. When they feel frustrated, they take it out on their families. Don't think I don't know what you've been through. What your marriage's been like. I know. It's always the same.

"I have no delusions about your intentions. Even if I wished you were a monster, an opportunist, ready to use that face of yours to get out of your dreary school, out of this dreary city—don't interrupt—I don't believe it anyway. I know we women act to protect our sons from bad influences. To protect them from their fathers. To keep them from becoming their fathers. To keep them to ourselves.

"It doesn't work.

"Men go through stages. There comes a point when they realize they aren't going to accomplish everything they dreamed they would, that they think they deserve. They're frustrated and they're mean. My husband was the same. But when my husband came back from the countryside, he was calmer. He had matured. I'm not saying it was good that he had to go away, but it shook him up and he appreciated us more when he got back. Not that he's easy to live with now. You've seen what I have to put up with. Complaining about this, about that, nothing's ever right, but he doesn't blame me.

"Marriage is good when you're old. You don't want to be alone when you're old. You want someone to talk to. Someone who knows what you've been through. Someone who'll stay with you even when you look like I do. Marriage is good at the end and it's good in the beginning. If you can just survive the middle part.

"That's all I had to tell you. Please, don't see me out. I want you to think about things. Don't think that I don't understand. I do. But I don't want to see you make a big mistake. Your generation has to learn to eat a little bitterness. You can't have everything you want."

She got up quickly, an energetic woman, even at her age, while I sat exhausted, staring at her cold tea still on the table, untouched. She paused at the door.

"You know what Shao Hong told me? He said, 'Ma, I love Lin Jun. Why does she want to do this? I don't understand. I have always loved her. There's never been anyone else.' He's not an evil man. He's a good man. But he's like any other man. They're difficult. Remember, they're all like this. Most are worse. You won't do better."

23.

Happy Family

I helped Shao Hong move after work on Tuesday. The apartment looked as though the former occupants had left in a rush, afraid the U.S. Embassy would change its mind and revoke their visas. There were stuffed animals on the floor in the living room, a big pink dog and a yellow-haired blue-faced cat. When I picked them up, the cloth felt a little sticky, matted. A baby's slobber, a spilled Coca-Cola? It felt strange, cleaning up after someone else's child.

It was musty smelling so I opened the windows, despite the cold, let the December wind blow through every room, blow the books in the bookshelves, the dust, the happy-colored flowered curtains. I mopped and cleaned the surfaces while Shao Hong brought boxes of his most important books up the stairs. My fingers swelled with the cold, my nose ran, eyes stung, so much coal dust in the air, but I was so pleased to be

moving Shao Hong out that I didn't care. If only there were some way to bring his desk over without involving our neighbors, I thought evilly.

It was close to midnight by the time we had exorcised the happy family who had lived there before; nothing left but cold, cold air, blue-and-white walls, ugly furniture, a mismatched green sofa and plaid armchair, a metal kitchen table and three slightly wobbly chairs.

We had managed to go the whole evening of working together without speaking more than the occasional "Move your foot," "Hand me the dishrag, please," and "Look out for the box." But then just as I was ready to go home, Shao Hong stopped me in my tracks.

"How do you propose we explain this to our son?" he said.

"We'll tell him the truth."

"That his mother wants me to move out while she thinks over our marriage?"

No, I thought, that his mother wants you to move out until we get the details of our divorce in order. But I held my tongue. I did not want an explosion at this moment. I hadn't the energy to cope with it.

"It's a separation," I said. "After he gets used to that idea, we can tell him—"

"Shit, I forgot to bring clean sheets."

"Check in the closet. Maybe they left some."

"No," he called.

"I'll go bring you some." Anything to keep him from coming home for one more night.

"Don't bother," he said wearily. He shuffled in from the bedroom. "I'll sleep on the couch tonight."

"It's no bother—"

"You can bring them by tomorrow," he said, with a sigh. He stretched out on the sofa, his arm draped over his head. "At least they have a TV

that works." He pointed the remote and turned the huge color set on, but there was nothing on but static and a blurry station identification symbol.

I put my shoes back on, buttoned my coat. "I brought some food. Something for breakfast and lunch since you haven't had time to go to the market. I figured they wouldn't have anything left in their—"

"You needn't have bothered. I'll just eat out."

"Right. Well, then, I'm going." I turned to go.

"Lin Jun," he called. "Thank you . . . It's been a lot of work for you tonight."

I wanted to ask him if his mother had told him to say that. I wanted to tell him it was too late for that kind of talk now. "Good night," I said. Riding home in the dark, I wondered why I felt so much angrier at him when he pretended to be polite than when he was outright rude.

It was strange coming home to the apartment alone, knowing that he would not be coming back in the middle of the night, waking me up when he flushed the toilet. I walked through the three rooms slowly, peered into the corners, seeing everything new again. I hadn't kept house very well lately. The paint on the ceiling had cracked in spots. The floor was scuffed. I should've made some throw rugs. The curtains were six years old and limp. They would have to go definitely. I could turn the study into Bao-bao's room again. I could work out an accommodation with his school—he would have to live at home, he was too spoiled. He needed more intellectual activities—what was all this talk of TV programs? I could repaint. I could invite Chen Hua over to help me redecorate. Something interesting, out of a magazine. More color. Cloth draped from the ceiling. Shao Hong never wanted me to change things much. "Why bother?" he'd say. "Why waste money?"

And then I remembered, it was not my work unit that owned the apartment, and I would be the one moving out, forever.

I brought the sheets over to Shao Hong's apartment the next afternoon. I had left school immediately after my last class and had not lingered in my office to talk to the other teachers or grade papers. I had not even waited to talk to Cynthia. I wanted to drop the sheets by when he was sure to be gone, and then leave.

He had eaten the food I'd brought despite what he'd said the night before. He hadn't bothered to wash the dishes from his breakfast—and also from lunch, it seemed, from the pile in the kitchen sink. I almost started to wash them before I remembered that I didn't have to clean up after him anymore.

I tossed the sheets across the room so that they landed on the sagging green sofa. I put the quilt, folded neatly, on a chair. I left the key on the table. And then I quickly fled, ran down the hall, the three flights of stairs. I did not want to be trapped inside the building. It felt so sad and damp.

I stopped to do some grocery shopping on my way home at one of the private markets set up in an alley. As I made my way down the street, inspecting the carts of fresh cabbages, pickled peppers and cucumbers, baskets of fresh eggs, fresh slippery *doufu* and charred dried *doufu*, stinky *doufu*, firm *doufu*, and soft *doufu*, I didn't know what to buy. What would I want to eat after all? Just me. I didn't have to cook to please anyone else. Just me. I didn't have to worry that Shao Hong hated *doufu* or that too many peppers made his stomach burn. I could cook anything for dinner that I wanted. Looking at all the food, I couldn't think of a thing to make. Finally I bought four kinds of bean curd and three kinds of spicy peppers.

Riding down the street, my purchases hanging from my handlebars, I felt positively giddy. I passed a small park, just a few trees and stone benches, and I thought, Why not? I didn't have to go home. I didn't have to start someone's supper. I didn't have to try to keep things neat. The late-afternoon sun was a deep orange and warm against my face. I turned around and rode to the park.

A group of old men in Mao caps and bright nylon parkas were playing chess, another group stood gossiping while their bird cages hung in the trees, their parakeets singing happily. There were no women in sight. Their wives were probably at the market or looking after the grandchild or cleaning or playing mah-jongg or any of the other hundred activities that old men and old women did not do together.

I parked my Pigeon in front of me so that I could keep an eye on my bags while I sat on a stone bench, the thick honeylike sunlight lapping at my feet, my face. Maybe I'll go ahead and redecorate anyway, I thought. When's the last time I did something just for fun?

I thought I heard someone call my name. I looked around me, alarmed. It was a strange, raspy voice. Unfamiliar. And then I saw an old man staring directly at me.

My father-in-law. I had forgotten I was so close to my in-laws' home.

I considered pretending I hadn't seen him or didn't recognize him, but it was too late. He waved at me to come over. "Lin Jun!" he called.

For a moment, I thought about jumping on my Pigeon and pedaling away as fast as I could. But I couldn't run forever. This was the kind of problem I had to deal with. Better now alone than with the members of the mediation committee. I walked with dread, pulling my Pigeon along like a security blanket. Was he going to denounce me in front of his old men friends? This is the shameless hussy who wants to divorce my son! Would he try to pressure me into a reconciliation? Or would he pretend

that everything was okay? My feet grew heavier with each step. It had been such a beautiful afternoon.

"This is my daughter-in-law," he told several of the old men.

They nodded at me politely. I couldn't tell if they knew anything about the divorce or not.

"We're going home now," Ye-ye said, waving to them.

I looked at him with surprise.

"You can walk with me. I can't stand still too long. My joints. I can't walk too much either, though. Really doing too much of either is bad. Winter is terrible, very hard for me."

I nodded. We walked out of the park, turned onto the sidewalk that ran parallel to the boulevard. Sunlight fell through the sycamores and scattered like raindrops at our feet, sliced by the thick branches.

"I used to like winter. It was my favorite time of the year. I thought the cold air was invigorating. Sunlight reflecting off the snow, the clean wind." He laughed. "I never would've guessed I'd become like this. It's not good to be old."

"You've really had to suffer," I said.

"I remember during the war, I would take long walks outside the camp. We were in a beautiful valley. The mountains all around. Capped with snow. Blue sky. Bright sun. If it hadn't been for the war, it would have been perfect. But the war was not so bad for me at first, you know?"

I had no idea what he was talking about.

He stopped walking abruptly. "Did you know I was a translator for the army?"

I shook my head.

"In Korea. I interviewed all the American prisoners. Psychological profiles." He laughed suddenly. "You didn't know my English was so good, did you?"

I thought I could see where this was going now. Shao Hong had evidently told his parents about Cynthia. Now Ye-ye was going to denounce Western influences, advanced nation's disease, the breakdown of the family. Do you know they have a fifty percent divorce rate? No wonder they have AIDS. No wonder they have street gangs. I braced myself for the barrage.

"The Americans were very lively. Always playing tricks. Some of them caught a rat and dressed it up in military clothes. A little parachute. A little pilot's cap. I don't know how they did it. Probably cut up their own clothes when we weren't looking. Sewed the scraps together somehow. They hung this rat from the tree and tried to scare the Korean soldiers. 'Look, the fighter planes are throwing rat paratroopers to give you the plague.' Little games like that.

"I really liked them. It's a shame we're enemies, I thought. But of course we were, and I was very patriotic. I believed I was doing a good thing. I observed how they ate, how they lived together, things they fought about. I remember one group of the soldiers were from the southern part of the United States. They did not get along with the black Americans. We had to keep them separated or they would try to fight all the time.

"We had guards watching them continuously. Not because we thought they could escape. They were very weak and we had taken them very far north. They would die before they ever reached their bases again. But it was important to observe anything that would help us fight them, win the war. I remember one of the guards came to me, very nervous, very worried abut something. 'At night, when the prisoners pretend to sleep, they are really whispering to each other. I've seen them,' he said. 'They don't even look at each other. But they lie on their backs, on their sides, or crouch on their knees, whispering.'

"Naturally I went to investigate. I stayed up all night and watched the prisoners in their tiny cells all night long. And sure enough, it was as their guard had told me. Many times they would whisper like this, sometimes making no sound at all, just moving their lips. They were praying to their gods.

"I, of course, did not believe in any god. I was a Communist. I was not superstitious. But I knew that when the peasants prayed, they wanted a good harvest, or their ancestors to help them or something like that. I wanted to know what the Americans prayed for.

"We put one of the men in solitary confinement. To see what would happen. He was one of the bigger men, very hairy, red hair all over his face, his body. We called him the Tiger Prisoner in Chinese. We left him alone in a cell for several weeks. And after a while, he would say his prayers aloud. He would cry and chant and beg. 'Help me, Jesus.' That kind of thing. But most of the time, he was calm and he would pray for long periods of time, hours and hours, just repeating the same kind of thing. 'Please, God, help me to see my family again.' He'd pray to see his parents, his wife, his little child. Over and over. And he would tell his thoughts to the god, tell him all his memories of his family, and he would ask the god to tell his family he was okay—'Let them know that I'm thinking of them, that I love them more than anything.' That kind of thing.

"I was very surprised. If I believed in a powerful god who could do anything, I would pray for liberation. I would pray for revenge. For the god to save me, strike down my enemies. And here was this American praying about his family." Ye-ye fell into silence, thinking about the American prisoner.

"So after you found out what they prayed for, what did you do?"

"Oh, naturally I told my superiors. And that helped them when they

made the propaganda messages. You know, 'Your God has abandoned you. Your government is going to keep you here until you are dead. You'll never see your families again.' "

"How terrible," I said.

"Yes," Ye-ye agreed. "It was too bad. But it was wartime. We all did what we thought was right."

The sun had fallen so low on the horizon that the tall department stores and offices blocked most of its light. It was cold walking with Ye-ye down the street towards his university. The traffic had increased, everyone going home after work, and we had to weave our way down the crowded sidewalks. Many people gave me a dirty look for walking my bicycle on the sidewalk, taking up too much room.

We reached the alley that led to the back gate of the university grounds. Ye-ye stopped.

"I'm nearly home now. You can go on."

"It's no trouble," I said, although I dreaded the thought of running into my mother-in-law.

"No, really. It's better if you don't come. My wife is home now, you know. She'd want to know what we were talking about. I don't have the energy to argue with her."

"Take care, Ye-ye. Don't try to walk too fast." I was about to leave him when he touched my handlebars.

"When I was in the countryside, at first I was very bitter. I never wanted to see my family again. But as time passed, I became very sick— all we did was work. The peasants hated us and it was always cold in the winter, hot in the summer, never enough to eat. All I could think of was coming home someday. I wanted to see my wife, I knew she would take care of me. Even if we fought, she wasn't like those peasants who wished I were dead so they could have my rice. I wanted to see my son.

"Look at all the people here." He gestured to the crowds inching their way slowly down the street on their bicycles, the crowds waiting at the medians for the buses, packed with bodies pressed against the windows. "So many people. Like an endless river that will never run dry. But the only people who care about you are your family. To everyone else, you're just a stranger. Even with friends, you will never mean as much as their own family. Even if you hate your parents, even if your child hates you, you are always connected."

Ye-ye left me then. I watched him shuffled down the darkening alley. He did not turn around again. Eventually, too many other people, bicycles, carts passed between him and me, and I could no longer see his slight figure walking home.

24.

Happy Holidays

It was the day before Christmas, the big American holiday, and two days before our big assembly, when I discovered Cynthia was sick. I went to her dormitory that evening after school. I wanted to apologize about our argument and invite her over for a little dinner, to enjoy the apartment while it was mine.

The day before, she'd asked me how the interview had gone, and I'd told her how terrible it had been, how degrading, how despicable.

"Well, don't give up so easily," she said. "This was a good first step. By the time you're ready for a new job, you'll be a pro."

We were sitting in her office, her space heater turned up to high, but still it was cold. She sat on the edge of her desk, drumming her feet against the side. The thump thump thump was driving me crazy.

"I don't want a new job," I said.

"Oh, come on. Don't let one bad experience put you off."

"I'm serious," I said. "Besides I have too many other things to worry about." I was thinking about the divorce, my in-laws, the sad stories they would tell. And what could I say in my defense? I'm not happy? As if that would count.

But Cynthia could not read my mood. She flew around the room describing all the exciting career opportunities I could have in Shanghai, opportunities to travel, to meet people from all over the world, to make more money.

"I don't want to," I said firmly. "I like my job."

"You're kidding? Lin Jun, you have the potential to do so much more than teach grammar to fifteen-year-olds. You're intelligent, you're witty, you have a great sense of humor. You should go into advertising!"

"Why would I want to do that?"

"Excitement. It's the field of the future. Look at how China's changing. Every foreign company needs someone who understands China, how people think. You have the language skills—"

I hadn't the patience to explain things anymore. I stood up. "And what's wrong with being a teacher?"

"Well, for one, the money sucks. There's no respect. The hours are bad—it's a never-ending job. I mean, sure, if the facilities were better, maybe you could make an impact. But a forty-five-to-one student-teacher ratio just doesn't cut it. How many of the school's seniors actually make it to college? Mrs. Mu told me three last year. Three. That's pathetic. Doesn't it depress you that we're leading these kids on? I mean, what's waiting for them after they graduate? If they graduate. We don't have a language lab. The electricity comes and goes. The textbooks are ancient.

There's no science labs. There's no library. There's no gym equipment even. Are they going to be like those peddlers selling plastic handbags and cheap luggage at the train station? If their parents had good enough connections to find jobs for them after they graduate, they would've had good enough connections to get them into a better school."

I was seething inside. I tried to remain calm. "I didn't realize you hated teaching here so much."

"I don't hate it. It's just depressing. I don't mind hard work, but I want to know I'm getting results." Cynthia jumped off her desk and paced, pulling at her hair. "I mean, I only have to be here a year. It's okay for a year. But if I were you—"

"Well, you're not me. If you were me, you'd stop lecturing people about things you don't understand. Quit trying to change me. I can't become you. And I don't want to become you. You're a rich American who can do anything she wants as long as she has the money!"

I didn't realized I had shouted until I saw Cynthia's face turn red. I hadn't even made sense, but it was too late to take my words back. Cynthia sat down abruptly on a folding chair by the door.

"I'm just trying to be helpful. I didn't mean to try to remake you in my image. Sorry."

"No, I'm sorry," I said quickly. "I'm just so tired. I've been helping my husband move his things. It's been very hard. I'm not angry at you. I'm very grateful to you."

"Ugh," said Cynthia.

"I'm sorry."

"Don't worry about it," she said, but I could feel that things were not the same between us.

I tried to visit her at her dormitory that evening but she was not in when I came by. When I went again the next night, she was sick.

She looked whiter than I had ever seen her when she answered the door. "Oh, hi," she whispered. She left the door open for me as she turned slowly and walked back to her bed. She lay down.

"What's the matter?"

"I'm sorry for being so rude," she said.

"No, I'm the one who is sorry. It's my fault."

"Please, let's not argue again." She lay still, then curled up into a ball.

"Cynthia, what happened?"

"Bad wontons," she groaned. "I should've known they weren't done."

"We should take you to the hospital."

"No, I don't want to go. I just want to rest."

"I'm sorry. I shouldn't bother you. Can I bring you something?"

"Food makes me sick. The thought of eating." She shook her head slowly. "I just hope I'm better by Monday. I already bought my tickets." She sighed. "Sick, just in time for vacation."

I got up early the next morning to go to the market before classes and bought Cynthia some Coca-Colas and Fantas, some soft buns, and a bunch of bananas. She was still very pale and weak when I brought them to her.

"Happy Christmas," I said, holding up the sacks.

She smiled. "Oh, you remembered it was Christmas."

"Don't worry about classes today," I told her. "I'll tell them you're sick. You should rest."

"It's lucky for me you like being a teacher," she said. "I think I would've gone mad this semester if it hadn't been for you."

"You better lie down quickly," I told her with fake urgency, "you sound very, very ill."

It felt good to laugh with her again.

*   *   *

Secretary Wang turned even whiter than Cynthia when I explained to her that Cynthia was ill. "But she'll be fine tomorrow, won't she? The assembly!"

"I don't know," I said slowly, thinking about her pale face, the uncustomary slowness to her movements. "Maybe not."

"This is terrible!" Secretary Wang dismissed me then and I didn't find out until much later, from Mrs. Mu, that the Secretary and School Head Hu had gone to see Cynthia for themselves. She wasn't in her dorm room when they knocked and they had waited in the hallway for half an hour and still Cynthia had not returned. The Secretary began to suspect that Cynthia was playing some kind of trick on them, when Mr. Hu suggested she check the bathroom at the end of the hall. There, the Secretary found Cynthia hunched over, vomiting into a concrete sink.

The assembly would have to be postponed indefinitely. Cynthia's vacation began the next week, and she wouldn't be back until mid-January. The Secretary had agreed to this vacation when she'd first hired Cynthia, based on the recommendations of other middle schools who had hired foreigners in the past. Keep their work schedules like those of their American universities and you get better candidates. The Americans didn't like the Chinese schedule, which allowed for only three days off for Spring Festival. The older teachers shook their heads. There was talk that the assembly might be postponed until after Spring Festival, when the students would be more refreshed, but the lunar new year didn't begin until February this year, and it was a long time for the students to have to remember their skits. It seemed, from the clamor in the lunchroom as news spread from teacher to teacher, that everyone had found something to complain about. Was it any wonder Cynthia hated teaching at my school?

As I left school that afternoon, Chen Hua's students' banners proclaiming the virtues of our middle school flapping in the breeze, I realized how lonely I would feel until Cynthia was back.

I invited Chen Hua to come over for New Year's Eve. I had agreed that Bao-bao would spend the holiday with Shao Hong and his parents. Holidays were for families anyway, he had pointed out. And I had had Bao-bao to myself since Shao Hong had moved out. I didn't want the committee to accuse me of wanting the divorce just so that I could have the child to myself, I wanted to show that I could work out a compromise, I was reasonable. So I agreed. But that meant I would be alone all week and all weekend.

I hadn't realize how dependent I had become on Bao-bao's visits. I didn't bother to clean the apartment anymore until Friday night. I didn't bother to cook anything but instant noodles until he was home—what's the point of cooking for one, I figured. I spent the week planning what fun things we would do together.

Chen Hua agreed my lifestyle didn't sound too healthy. "Better watch out," she warned. "You're going to turn him into a Little Emperor. And you don't want to be the chief eunuch."

We were walking together from the main classroom building to the bicycle parking lot. It was nearly dark. A gust of wind blew a fistful of dried leaves and trash in our direction. I batted at the air as Chen Hua pulled the back of her fuchsia jacket up over her head.

"So can you come?" I asked. "I'll just make a little something for the new year if you can bring some fruit for dessert."

"Mmm," she said cryptically, glancing around at the milling students, the boys throwing basketballs, the girls carrying their books in front of them like armor. "Let's talk about this in a minute."

"What's wrong?"

"Ssh." She put her finger to her lips. I followed her to the parking lot.

The lots were covered with strong plastic sheets along the back and on top that supposedly kept the rain and the snow off our bicycles. Not much protection against the elements but at least a small windbreak. We waited for one of the junior-high music teachers to pull her bicycle free and ride off before we could talk.

"What's the matter, Chen Hua? You're worrying me."

"Don't worry." Chen Hua put her hand on my arm and suddenly burst into giggles. "You'll never believe it."

Chen Hua told me then that for the last month she had been going to all the major companies in town, offering her services as a graphic artist/public relations specialist. "I offered to redesign their logos, their letterheads, print ads, billboards, anything really. I was even hand lettering signs for them. I didn't charge much. In fact, sometimes I lost money—if I had to furnish my own supplies. But I wanted to make as many connections as I could. Anyway, while I was making my rounds one day, I met . . . this man." She paused again to giggle. "He's amazing. A private businessman. A widower. He's in his fifties, but"—she shrugged—"who cares? Very, very sweet. And he loves my artwork. He thinks I'm great. I'm going to design all the ads for his new product line, as soon as he works out the details. His second cousin lives on Taiwan and the family wants to invest in a mainland business. So they're going to start shipping over something, we don't know what yet, and he'll see about marketing it here."

"That sounds very unusual."

"That's how things work. You have to be very adventurous in business. Always taking risks. Always ready to try something new."

I nodded.

"Anyway, he's very wealthy already. He's been working in resales up till now. You know, traveling south to Guangzhou, buying up merchandise that we can't get here, and then bringing it back and selling it for a profit. He's made a fortune off CDs and laser discs, he says. And oh— look at this." Chen Hua unzipped her coat for me. She displayed her sweater, a bright fuzzy pink affair with leg-of-mutton sleeves. "What do you think? *He* bought it for me."

"Didn't you already have this sweater? I remember last year—"

"Yes, that's just it! I did already have a sweater just like this one. But he didn't know that. He went out and bought me this sweater and it was just like one I had. Don't you see what that means?"

"Well, I guess you couldn't very well tell him after he'd bought it for you."

"No, don't you see? It shows he likes me the way I am! He doesn't want me to change! We have the same taste! And he likes that!" Chen Hua shouted.

I glanced around us nervously to see if anyone had overheard.

"Whoops." She put her hand to her mouth sheepishly. "Anyway," she continued in a whisper, "he's going to be in town for the new year. And so naturally . . . well, he already asked me to spend New Year's Eve with him."

"Oh, of course." I nodded quickly. "You should spend the holidays with—with your . . . boyfriend."

Chen Hua giggled. "Yeah, with my boyfriend. It's crazy, Lin Jun, who would've thought? He's had a hard life. He really knows how it is to suffer. I think that's what makes him so—"

"Be careful," I said, suddenly, interrupting her. "If he travels all the

time, he may—you know, see other women. He may not be serious in his intentions."

Chen Hua burst into loud laughter. "Don't be silly. It's not like I'm going to marry him."

"Oh? He's already told you he doesn't—"

"It's me. I've decided what's the point of being married? I mean, look at you. No, I'm sorry. What I mean is, the only reason people get married is so that they can have their one kid, you know? And I don't want a child."

"You don't? Are you sure?"

"Ha! I've been teaching for more than ten years now, and if there's one thing I've learned, it's that I hate kids."

"Hmm. Well, be careful."

"And you know what, Lin Jun?" Chun Hua shook my arm. "He's a wonderful lover!"

"What! Are you joking?"

"Lin Jun! It's not like this is my first affair."

"It's not?"

"Didn't I tell you? You remember why I left the opera in the first place? I got involved with that stupid man, wouldn't leave his wife all those years. . . . Of course, I was really young and confused then."

I felt like telling her she still sounded pretty confused to me, but I held my tongue.

"Anyway, anyway, anyway." She danced with her bicycle, rolling it in circles. "I'm afraid I'll have to miss your New Year's party. I'm sorry."

"It's okay. I have a lot of work to do anyway. I need to get my ideas in order, I need to think about things—"

"I just wanted to thank you."

"Thank me?"

"Yes, you've really inspired me. I've always thought you were like the 'foolish old man who dug the mountain,' a real stick-in-the-mud, afraid to try anything new. But you've really shown me. Going all the way to Shanghai to look for a job. The divorce. I realized I shouldn't be so complacent. If even you could shake up your life, why couldn't I!"

I didn't know what to say to that. After six years of marriage, I couldn't imagine inspiring anything so carnal. "Well, have fun," I said, unlocking my Pigeon.

"Oh, I will," she laughed as she hopped on her bicycle, a pink Swan, and rode away.

So I prepared to spend New Year's Eve alone. Really, I had a lot of work to do. I was terribly behind in the laundry. Dust was collecting along the bookshelves, under the couch, on top of the radio. The windows needed washing. When was the last time I had cleaned out the refrigerator? Really, there was a lot I needed to do before the new year arrived.

It was late. I had fallen asleep on the sofa. The radio was on, no longer playing the latest pop songs from Hong Kong, but a man's voice monotonously intoning the news. Some foreign dignitary was touring a cigarette factory in Xiamen. I tried to sit up. My back ached, my shoulders burned, my neck was bent at an angle and simply would not straighten. This was why I always put off the laundry. I read in an article once that a Japanese company was selling paper clothes. Wear them once and throw them away. If they ever came to Nanjing, I would buy. I sat up gingerly. At least the apartment smelled clean for once.

There was a sharp rap on the door, more like a kick than a knock. I froze. I couldn't imagine who it could be. I hoped for a moment that perhaps it was a mistake, someone bringing home a new appliance for the new year, a refrigerator or washing machine, and they had accidentally bumped the box against my door. Then someone banged on the door again.

"Someone at the door," I called. "Don't get up, I'll get it!" I shouted. "No, no, everybody don't bother, I'll get it!" It was ridiculous, pretending this way, but I suddenly felt very much alone.

I crept on tiptoe towards the door. Then quickly I rushed back to the living room and quietly pulled out the chairs, put some papers on the table, to make it look as though someone could have just gotten up and gone into the other room. I held my breath and opened the door a crack.

A young man dressed in a leather jacket with lots of metal studs on it, long hair, blue jeans, and shiny black shoes. I didn't recognize him. "Yes?"

He squinted at me. "Are you the sister of Lin Yong-li?"

My first thought was, The Public Security Bureau has found out! But then I realized this young man couldn't possibly be with their office.

"Yes?"

"Here." He smiled, then thrust a piece of paper into my hand. He turned and started back down the hall.

"Wait!" I called after him, but he didn't turn around.

I shut the door again, locked it, then looked at the creased note. It was a postcard. On one side there were pictures of beaches. I turned it over quickly but there was no note for me, no note at all. There was only an address scrawled in Yong-li's impatient handwriting, not mine but

Yong-li's old dormitory, and a name, a man's name. I squinted to read the postmark. A foreign city. At first, I thought the name was in English, and my heart jumped, hurt, I nearly cried out, but then I saw that I was mistaken. The letters were blurred, as if it had rained somewhere along the card's journey. I held the card close to our floor lamp. C-O-L-O-N-P-A-N-A-M. I had no idea where that could possibly be.

And then I realized how stupid I'd been. I threw open the front door, looked down the hall, but no one was there anymore. I ran down the stairs, pausing on each landing, but the young man was gone. I ran outside. It was very dark; the light from the street lamps did not extend to the back of our apartment building except in a few thin fingers of light pointing at random across the pavement. I searched the bicycle lots, ran down to the street, but I couldn't see anyone like him walking about or riding by.

Of course, he was gone. Of course.

It was cold and clouds covered the moon. In the distance the pop of firecrackers. Someone's radio wailed against the sound of traffic. The sound of bottles smashing. A New Year's celebration already under way. I stood very still, hunched over from the cold, and listened. Voices rose and fell, singing, cheering. Bicycle bells. A bus hissed and farted.

I stood on the sidewalk and looked up at the windows of my apartment building lit up like jewels. I saw shadows flicker behind pale yellow curtains, back and forth, back and forth, as if the people inside were dancing. The window above was orange with light and the drapes were open. A family sat in front of their television set. I couldn't see the TV, it had to be placed against the same wall as the window, but I could tell they were watching it, the way they all sat on their sofa, staring straight

ahead, not talking to each other, not moving. I saw an old man pacing back and forth, his hands behind his back. Other windows were dark.

I remembered our first New Year with Bao-bao. The explosion of firecrackers at midnight made him awake in terror. He screamed so loudly the neighbors banged on the walls; the neighbor below us beat on his ceiling. We could feel the strange thumps traveling under our feet. It was Shao Hong who suggested dancing, American disco style. We danced like crazy to the firecracker beat. I held Bao-bao against my shoulder. "Break dance!" Shao Hong cried as he hopped on one leg across our neighbor's ceiling. We laughed so hard, we nearly cried.

I did not imagine this. It really happened. We had fun, we enjoyed ourselves, we laughed together.

I was so cold by the time I went back inside, my fingers had swollen so much, I could barely open the door. I shivered, my teeth chattered in my head. I'd left the door unlocked. I looked at the empty apartment and it seemed suddenly strange and unfamiliar to me. I ran to every room, flipping on the lights. I went back again and checked under the bed, under Shao Hong's desk, in the closet. But of course the apartment was empty, everywhere I looked.

When my father taught us how to shoot off firecrackers, I was still a little girl, although I felt that I was quite sophisticated with new red ribbons in my braids, holding on to my mother's hand as we waited side by side on the sidewalk while my father lay the long ribbon of red firecrackers on the concrete like a sleeping dragon. And then he showed Yong-li how to light the very end with a slow-burning stick and within seconds, the line of firecrackers sprang to life, jumping up and back, twisting upon itself, with that noise like a gunshot, each BANG louder than the last, as I covered my ears tight and looked at Yong-li, who covered both his ears and shut his eyes and cried, tears running down his

face, his mouth a big O. But when the string was spent and nothing but the red wrappers was left, which I kicked, over and over, until the slips of paper flew into the air like sparks, it was Yong-li who begged our father to let him light another round. "Let me, let me!" he shouted. "I can do it!" And my father knelt down and held Yong-li's hands in his own while they put the burning stick to the string. And I held my ears again while my mother stood next to me, clapping and laughing. And at that moment, with the new year just beginning, all those noisy firecrackers to scare away the evil spirits, I had no reason to believe that we would not be happy like this forever.

25.

Dreams

I was dreaming when I heard something in the living room and I woke up, sat up in the dark, and recognized my son's voice, crying for me. I ran out to him.

"Bao-bao, it's okay, I'm here."

Shao Hong was standing over Bao-bao, trying to ease off his coat. Bao-bao was crying. His face was red. He looked tired and cranky. He sucked on his fingers. He ran towards me.

I knelt next to him, took his hands in mine. "Don't cry, Mama's here." He clung to my neck.

"He didn't like the other apartment," Shao Hong explained. He pulled out a chair and sat at the table. He slouched forward, elbows on his knees. "I didn't want to wake you up. I tried to tell him it was okay. But finally—"

"You don't ever have to worry about waking Mama up," I told Bao-bao, kissing his head.

"The university students are really wild these days. Parties all night long. People shouting, breaking things. Loud music." Shao Hong laughed bitterly. "Not like us, that's for sure. We were glad to be able to go to school. We were grateful for the opportunity."

"Do you want something to eat?" I asked Bao-bao.

"We ate at my parents'—"

"Yes," said Bao-bao. He whispered, pressing his wet mouth against my ear, "I don't like Nai-nai's food. She can't cook. I like your cooking."

I set Bao-bao on the couch, let him lie there in his coat. I slipped his shoes off, let them fall to the ground, clunk clunk. It was a happy sound. "Just rest here. I'll make you a little snack." I glanced at the clock on the wall. It was nearly three in the morning.

"Has he been up all night?" I asked Shao Hong, my voice low.

"I tried to put him to bed several times. But all that noise." He clicked his tongue against the roof of his mouth. "Living on campus is bad. You don't know how these students are."

I quickly scrambled some eggs, added some rice. Too bad I hadn't bought any tomatoes. Luckily, there was one bottle of Fanta left. I brought Bao-bao's snack to the table, but he was sound asleep, his mouth partially open, his cheeks still flushed.

"So are you hungry?" I asked Shao Hong. I set the food in front of him. "Go ahead. It's okay. He's sleeping," I whispered.

Shao Hong nodded at me. "My mother can't cook," he said. He picked up the chopsticks. "I'm sorry, Lin Jun."

"You don't need to apologize for bringing him back."

"I mean for everything."

Not that again. "Yes, I know," I said. "Let's not talk about it now. Let's not wake him."

We left Bao-bao on the couch, I didn't want to disturb him. As Shao Hong unzipped his coat, slipped him free from the dusty jacket, I covered him with his quilt. His cheeks were warm, but he wasn't feverish. Poor kid.

Shao Hong yawned. It was nearly three-thirty. "I should be getting back now." He looked tired and downcast, watching Bao-bao sleep.

It was strange, having him back in the apartment. But it was even more odd to feel awkward after all the years we had been together. Was this how love left you? Feeling like a stranger; the past, your memories, erased, with nothing to fill the gaps, the holes inside you.

"You can go home in the morning," I said, feeling awkward and melancholy.

He nodded.

We slept on opposite sides of the bed. Fortunately we were both very tired. I remembered listening to Shao Hong's even breathing, slow and deep, finally drifting into a faint snore, before I too fell into sleep.

I had so many dreams so quickly that before one could end another began, the images like raindrops in a pond, each one sending out another band of ripples that overlapped and fought until the surface was never smooth but always in motion. The stories were incoherent, frightening. A dog nibbled at a pile of bones. I looked closer and saw they were pig bones, boiled dry. Auntie Gao was crying. "What's the matter, Auntie? Tell me, tell me," I begged, but she seemed not to hear my voice. She leaned over her knees, holding her head, the tears running out between her thick fingers. A boulder rolled down the side of a mountain, a giant Buddha's head, pinning me to the ground. I called out

to Auntie Gao, but she couldn't hear me above her own sobs, loud, like a pig snorting.

I awoke to find Shao Hong holding my arm. He was crying.

I touched his head. His hair was stiff under my hands. He pressed closer to me. It was too dark to see him, but I could smell the familiar scent of his sweat, a faint trace of garlic, the detergent in his shirt. His tears tasted like iron. When he entered me, I held his head, felt his nubby ears in my palms, and thought of eating onions, the sharp bitter taste, a little sweet.

I waited until he fell back into sleep, exhausted. I was glad we didn't have to talk. I slid out of bed, careful not to let the cold air slip under the blankets and wake him. I tiptoed on the cold floor, my toes stinging, to check on Bao-bao, but he was still sound asleep, wrapped in his quilt like a red cocoon.

I could not sleep. Everyone would hate me, I thought. Ye-ye would hate me. I was not family, not child or wife or parent, no blood between us. I was the outsider who would hurt his son. My mother-in-law would despise me. For being weak, for being unable to bear as much as she, for being so petty, so selfish as to want to be happy. I was making everything more difficult.

It occurred to me suddenly as I stood in the hall, leaning against the cool wall, watching the gray light through the blue curtains, I could be pregnant. I'd had my tubes tied after Bao-bao, but there were mistakes, accidents. I knew a teacher, it had happened to her when she was forty. If I was pregnant, it could be a girl this time. If it was a girl, I would stay married to Shao Hong. If it was a girl, a sister fo Bao-bao, a little sister, a daughter, I'd stay married if I didn't have to have an abortion. I'd tell my in-laws, these are the conditions, this is it. My divorce or my baby. My mother-in-law had good connections, she might know someone,

someone in the registry, someone who could help us keep a second child. We could hide her. I could teach her at home. When she got older, she could hide in the countryside, they'd never think to look there. I'd pay for a tutor, what was money? There were always ways to make more money. I'd pay a tutor for her, teach her English. She could go to America for college.

But I couldn't have a daughter. Even if I was pregnant. I could never have a daughter. My mother-in-law was old, her connections were to other old people. She was no longer powerful. She was so weak that she was afraid of me, the problems I would cause her. And I would never send a girl to the countryside. I could never protect her there. As a second child, my daughter would never be allowed to go to school. We would be fined more money than we could ever earn. I'd have to have an abortion. And even if it was a girl, and I was stubborn, so stubborn, if I fought every day, and I finally gave birth, I would be forced in the end to put my daughter in an orphanage and she would be adopted by some foreign family and she would become another woman's daughter, never mine.

I was crazy, dreaming while I stood, awake.

Everyone would hate me for this divorce. I was making everything more complicated. I felt so tired, leaning against the cold wall. It would be easier, so much easier, to continue as I had, married, with my husband, with my son, with my in-laws, three generations of ambiguous relationships, nothing changed. I didn't love Shao Hong yet many couples who were not in love stayed married.

But I thought of the silences between us and I knew they would grow, and I would not be happy. I would never feel lightness inside of me, I would never feel free. The weight inside me would grow like a tumor in my intestines, a boulder, until I would have no joy left in me, and I

would be like some of the teachers who never smiled but complained about other people all the time, my face so tight, my voice like wet paper, and I would spread my unhappiness to everyone around me, I would infect my students with my resignation, I would infect my son with my despair, and the unhappiness would never go away.

And I knew then that I would find the strength to fight for my divorce no matter what.

When Shao Hong awoke in the morning, I was crying.

He didn't ask me what was wrong. He dressed, and saying good-bye to Bao-bao, said he would be going, he had work to do, translations to prepare before work the next day, and he would see Bao-bao the following Friday. He bent to kiss Bao-bao good-bye, but when Bao-bao pulled away, he tousled his hair instead, and then left us.

26.

The View from the Drum Tower

I had bundled Bao-bao up very warmly so that when I strapped him to the seat on the crossbar of my Pigeon, I almost felt as though I were really strapping on a large watermelon—albeit one with legs—rather than a child. It was very cold this morning, our breath froze the air. "Pretend you're a dragon," I said as I pedaled, my face burning in the wind. I blew a puff of smoke over Bao-bao's head."Grrr!"

"I'm smoking," he said, and drew on an imaginary cigarette.

We rode on this, the first day of the new year to the Drum Tower in the center of the city. In summer they sold potted flowers around the terraced base. There was a café that sold soft drinks and ice cream bars. In January, however, it was deserted although groups of art students were trying to sell their paintings in the vacant lot opposite the tower.

The scrolls flapped like laundry on the clotheslines they'd strung between the trees.

I took Bao-bao's hand and led him inside the tower. It was even colder in the heart of the stone building, but as we climbed the steps up and up again, I felt my circulation return.

Bao-bao pulled free when we reached the top and ran in the fresh air along the flat stones of the walkway. I chased after him. "Don't you want to see over the railing?"

He came back to me.

I picked him up and held him against my hip so that he could see over the guardrails.

"Six hundred years ago, soldiers lived in this tower," I said. "They could see for miles and miles over the city wall, across the countryside, nearly all the way to the Purple Mountains. And when they saw the colored banners of the enemy coming from the north, they beat the drum, DOOM DOOM DOOM, and the people rushed to close the twelve gates of the city. And the soldiers would mount the guard stations. They would load the cannons. They would stand with bows poised. Waiting, waiting until they could hear the horses' hooves pounding across the earth, at first soft like distant thunder, then louder and louder, like a rainstorm, like an earthquake. And while the rest of the people in the city scurried about, nailing boards across their windows, across their doors, hiding their children, burying their money, only the soldiers on top of the tower could see the tips of the enemy's red flags spreading like flames across the countryside. Coming closer and closer. Can you imagine?"

"I would shoot them!" Bao-bao shouted. And he pretended to fire his imaginary cowboy rifle at the advancing Mongol army.

The view was not extraordinary anymore, to be honest. There were

too many billboards, too many high rises. We could not see very far. We could look down on the streets below us, the intersection of honking horns and tinkling bells, and watch the blue-and-white buses, the black Mercedes, the belching motorcycles, the hundreds, the thousands of bicycles, circling the tower.

Riding home, I experienced a strange sensation. I felt that I was still on the Drum Tower, peering through the stone battlements, and yet I could see myself on my Pigeon, my son wrapped like a ball of cotton batting, a small woman and a small child on a big black bicycle, and soon we were lost in the flocks of Pigeons flying across the asphalt, and we were very happy.